UNDER LOCH AND KEY

Kathryn Cockrill

Copyright © 2021 Kathryn Cockrill

The moral rights of the author have been asserted.

The characters and events portrayed in this book are fictitious. Any similarity to real persons, living or dead, is coincidental and not intended by the author.

In order to create a sense of setting, some names of real places have been included in this book. However, the events depicted in this book are imaginary and the real places used fictitiously.

No part of this book may be reproduced, or stored in a retrieval system, or transmitted in any form or by any means, electronic, mechanical, photocopying, recording, or otherwise, without express written permission of the publisher.

A catalogue record for this book is available from the British Library.

ISBN 9798451448199

Cover design by: Rebecacovers

To everyone who believed in me and this book even when I didn't believe in myself.

Disclaimer

This book is not suitable for younger readers due to scenes of violence and torture.

Trigger warning - Torture, manipulation, fantasy genetic engineering on animals and violence.

Prologue

Myths and legends are funny things. For the sake of either one we'll give up our money and our time, spending hours and days fixated on something that might not even exist and then trekking across land and ocean to find out if it does. I guess that's the appeal of it, the draw; it's that possibility of discovering something magical, something that people tell their children in a fairy-tale but don't actually believe. For some people it becomes an obsession, the need to prove one of these mythical beings exists as strong as blood calling to blood. In reality, it was probably made up by a farmer who had drunk too much homemade beer whilst walking his fields and hallucinated a giant, furry man. Most people who chase legends return home empty-handed, with muddled dreams, barren pockets and the commemorative t-shirt. The lucky few will snap a blurry picture and get their fifteen minutes of fame. It's definitely a fool's game.

I look up from my internal monologue to gaze, or squint rather, through the mist and across the Loch. I couldn't really judge legend chasers when I was sat on a freezing cold, moss-covered rock in the Scottish drizzle staring determinedly at a Loch. Like I had been for the last five hours. For the last two days. Really it wasn't important how long I'd been here.

With a sigh, I opened the notebook I'd been shielding on my lap, covering the battered pages with the edges of my sleeves in an attempt to prevent any water damage. As it was, the ink on the pages had faded to a sea-foam grey, years of wear and tear, of fingers running over the same lines, rubbing away all but the faint indent. It didn't matter though, I knew the words on the pages by heart, having re-read them countless times in the last three years. I traced a finger over a drawing that took up half the page, or at least it did once, fluttering over phantom curved lines and razor points. The drawing was annotated, my brother's handwriting sticking out in spiked peaks even on the faded paper suspended, it seemed, in mid-air.

I smiled at the shadows of the doodles sprinkled in the margins, cartoonish animals grinning back at me. He drew them for me, back when I hounded him every second of every day to pay me attention. Instead, he found a way to distract me, drawing tiny landscapes on scrap pieces of paper, punctuated with their animal counterparts. As I turned the page now, a lion bared its teeth in an over-the-top grin. My brother had never been that interested in animals that actually existed, but they provided entertainment for his annoying kid sister, so pretty soon they were cropping up everywhere. Now, most of his drawings in the house had been covered up, an attempt on the part of my parents to forget him and move on but these drawings, the ones in his notebook were mine and mine alone.

A sudden crack of thunder in the distance made me jump, the booming sound ricocheting off the landscape in waves until it broke over my head. I closed the notebook quickly, passing the thin leather cord around the cover once, twice, three times before looping it over the tarnished catch. With a final glance at the Loch in front of me, I pushed myself up from the slimy rock, my knees cracking as I stood, protesting against the movement with a groaning symphony that rivalled even the approaching storm. Grabbing my backpack from the ground next to the rock I hastily shoved the notebook inside, tucking it between a wool hat and my crumpled map. Zipping it up, I threw the pack over my shoulder and began to make my way back up the trail I had all but slipped down earlier. The near constant drizzle, the same drizzle that had been going on for days now, had bogged down the path, watery-brown patches of mud sucking at my boots as I picked my way through the mossy undergrowth. The only good thing about this rain was its ability to get rid of every bug in the vicinity. Much more effective than Deet! Overhead, the thunder clouds continued to roll in, their blackened shadows turning the landscape a grey ombré. With a grimace, I pulled my hood tighter around my face, the toggles dangling at my chin as I stomped through the sludge.

Can your eyes get frostbite? It certainly feels like it.

The drizzle was slowly giving way to rain, fat, heavy droplets interspersed in the mist. You could hear them audibly hit the leaves and branches as their tempo picked up, becoming an overwhelming melody. Another clap of thunder broke the horizon, though this time I felt it before it hit my ears, that low rumble carrying through the soles of my shoes and up my arms in a goosebump wave. There was only time for a few breaths before it rolled again, this time accompanied by blue-white lightning that lit up the trail around me. For a brief moment, tree branches seemed to reach out, arthritic fingers twisted in the eye of the storm. Shadows that had previously crept along the ground, slinking over roots and around rocks now leapt forward, edges sharp against their barked backdrop. I stumbled over an outstretched limb, the paranoia of being alone in the storm shooting up my spine. Taking a breath, I forced my feet to stop, my panicked soles protesting as I leant against the trunk of a tree, closing my eyes against the elements.

Almost as quickly as it had come, the lightning faded and the thunder remained silent coaxing the landscape to settle back into its charming, albeit slightly soggy, façade. The heartbeat that had been hammering in my throat relented, calmly sitting back in my chest. For a few seconds there was a peaceful hum, the kind of sound that comes from nothing but things existing.

Then, with the fanfare of a brass band, the thunder and lightning resumed their schedule, the blazing electric light casting a blanket of white fire over the trail. I pushed off from the tree, my feet squelching in the mud. In the surrounding chaos, the edges of the trail seemed to scurry away. My shoes began to slide, the boggy ground too loose to keep any kind of traction. I felt my left leg go out from beneath me, flying to the side as the path became more and more of a river. Instead of the resounding squelch of more mud, my foot met air, the edges of the narrow trail apparently closer than I had realised. With a cry that was quickly gobbled up by the storm, I slid off into the foliage, my ankle rolling as it dragged along the edge of the rocky ground. The vegetation hid a slope that seemed to drag me down, my balance forfeited way back in the mud and I felt my shoulder hit the ground with a thud as I careened down the hill. Each limb was met by a rock or root; new bruises marked under the surface, ready to flourish in a matter of hours. My hands scrabbled, trying to grab hold of anything I could reach but my cold, wet fingers simply washed off of any solid object.

Slowly the hill levelled out, the slip n' slide of mud making way for a boggy swamp instead. I juddered to a stop, now the same colour as the rest of the landscape. I had no idea how far down I'd fallen, or how far off the trail I'd ended up and the raging storm overhead showed no signs of stopping. Gritting my teeth at the pain in my shoulder and my ankle and, well, almost every part of my body, I scrambled up with all the grace of a very muddy new-born giraffe and tried to see through the torrential rain. Ahead of me, trees curved like giants, their branches knotted together to form a sort of canopy; although it may not have been the safest solution for the lightning, I needed to get out of the rain so I could try to get my bearings. There was no way I could do that with a waterfall running down my face.

With shaking footsteps, I made my way over, arms outstretched in a desperate attempt to keep my balance. Once I was under, the rain eased, the leaves catching most of the droplets; I wiped away the torrent of water that was still running from my scalp, distantly hoping none of it was blood and had a better look around. The trees here seemed to stretch on for a while, their trunks thick and old, lining what appeared to be various pathways. Or, at least, they had once been pathways but were now so overgrown with brambles and nettles that they seemed more like vague suggestions of trails. The largest path took me deeper into the forest, most of the path fading into shadows. Glancing back over my shoulder I tried to decide if I could climb back up the hill, but the incline told me I'd probably break my neck trying. Shuffling my backpack, which had somehow clung on during my rapid descent, higher onto my back I turned back to the path in front of me, hoping no lightning decided to hit.

Although the sodden dirt was still squelching underfoot, the soft covering of grass combined with the fact this clearly wasn't a well-trodden path, meant I could walk quickly, still mostly sheltered from the rain. The thunder still rumbled behind me and every so often the trees would spark with lightning but, as I walked further into the canopy of trees, the sounds from the storm dimmed, buffeted by the foliage.

A glint caught my eye, nestled in between the large leaves of a plant at the edge of the path. Stopping, I crouched down so I could see the mystery object in better detail. A curved piece of metal gleamed at me, almost meeting in a perfect circle. Despite being sat in the undergrowth, there was no tarnishing, no rust, only a couple of bits of debris. Pushing the leaves aside I wrestled the metal out from the soil. It was the size of a dinner plate, with holes notched on one side of and pins on the other. I pulled the two ends of the metal together with more force than necessary since I'd expected at least a little resistance, then pushed the closest pin into the closest hole. It slid in smoothly, fastening with a satisfying *click*. I stared at it for another few seconds, trying to equate the lush forest around me with the cold metal in my hands.

It looks like a collar... But what kind of animal would be wearing a collar this size?

I didn't even want to think about it. As I went to drop it back in the grass, something stopped me; for some unknown reason I found myself unzipping my sodden backpack and dropping it in, the weight pulling down the bottom of the bag.

Keep going, you still need to find shelter.

I walked back into the centre of the path and continued through the trees. It was only another minute or two of walking before the wide mouth of a cave appeared on my left, sprouting out of the surrounding foliage without warning. Ahead, the path continued but I couldn't see where it ended or even if it ended at all. The storm was still raging in the distance and fat droplets still made their way through the canopy every now and then. Without any other option, I stepped up to the mouth of the cave. Cool gusts of air hustled at the entrance, but the cave itself was dark and somewhat muggy; I could make out the vague shape and didn't see any creatures who had lost their giant metal collar waiting in there to eat me, so I stepped off of the spongy grass, feet meeting the dusty cave floor. The furthest wall looked the most inviting (and least damp) so I slumped against it, back sliding down the smooth mounds of stone until I felt my butt hit the ground. The thumping pain from each bruise was making itself known, my shoulder and ankle loudest of all. Tilting my head back, I rested it against a bump in the stone, relaxing as I did.

Click.

My eyes flew open as the wall seemed to disappear from behind my back. I tumbled over, landing hard on another piece of stone that hadn't been there a few seconds ago. In the shadows, a flickering light buzzed to life, pulsing like it hadn't been used in a while. Forcing myself upright, I realised that the wall had, in fact, disappeared. Well, swung to the side. Instead of cave, I was now faced with dark, slightly stale smelling air accompanied by a faint buzzing.

I mean I'm kind of done with adventure for today.

I was already on my feet. My body might have been done with adventure, but clearly my mind wasn't. Hands extended into the darkness, I stepped in, following the flickering and the buzzing. The space got wider, the walls either side of me falling away, opening into a larger cavern. Fumbling, I grabbed a torch and shone it around in front of me.

Maybe I've got a concussion.

Instead of another chamber of the cave, as I had been expecting, I was greeted by what appeared to be a lab. Inside a cave. In the back and beyond of Scotland. Swinging the beam of the torch back across the walls I had just walked past, I noticed a small set of switches embedded in the stone. Hobbling over, I flicked them all on, waiting to hear any kind of reaction. Nothing.

Were you really expecting them to work? I mean this place could be decades…

The faint buzzing suddenly got louder, accompanied by a series of clicks, like machines turning themselves on. The flickering light on the ceiling slowed down, casting a tiny halo of light for a few seconds at a time. Then, with a loud *whirring*, the cave around me was flooded with light, bulbs that had been hidden in crags in the stone coming to life, casting bright LEDS across the room.

What the hell is this place?

I shuffled forwards, towards the centre of the room and the lab equipment abandoned there. Stainless steel tables supported microscopes and monitors, full of machines that I'd never seen before. As I reached the centre of the room I spun, trying to take it all in. At the far side, the room opened up into a cavernous ceiling, grey rock laying perfectly flat.

Weirdly flat.

Spurred by the need to *figure this place out,* I hurried over, placing a hand on the rock, looking for another button hidden somewhere, anywhere. The stone was cool beneath my palm, feeling almost damp but there was no actual water on it. I continued running my fingers along the smooth surface, but it remained unblemished, expanding at least fifty metres across. Eventually, the rock merged back into the craggy cave wall and as I reached it, I saw another switch hidden in the shadows. Stomach fluttering, I flipped it, hoping it opened another door whilst at the same time, really hoping it didn't. Clanging noises filled the air, a rattling sound that groaned and wheezed. Painfully slowly, the flat piece of rock split in the middle, pulling back like a pair of curtains. I stepped backwards, hitting one of the tables, mouth open, as it continued to pull back, somehow disappearing into the cave wall. Behind the flat surface, glints of murky blue and green sparkled. My stomach dropped. Even before the wall had finished moving, I could see tiny schools of fish darting about behind a pane of glass. Kelp danced at the bottom, fronds floating on a watery breeze. There was no obvious end to the water, no outer wall that could be seen through the murky grey-blue depths. Every so often, the water lit up and seemed to vibrate.

The storm. That's the storm.

I stepped up to the glass again, placing my hands on it, still unable to believe what I was seeing.

"It's the Loch." The words slipped out before I could stop them, falling into the stagnant air around me for no one else to hear. As soon as I said it though, I knew it was true. Somehow, this lab, this underground cave lab, had a viewing window into the Loch. Lightheaded, I moved backwards again, arms searching for a chair, a table, somewhere to sit so I didn't fall over. As I found another table, I felt something soft hit my palm. Turning around, I picked it up.

A notebook?

The leather was pliant under my fingers. Unwrapping the cord tied tight around it once, twice, three times, I let the front cover drop away over my wrist. My breath caught in my throat as familiar spiked handwriting, handwriting I hadn't seen for three years, stared back at me. My fingers turned the pages, slowly at first, then faster until the writing became a blur, until I reached the back cover. A small sob worked its way up my throat as I stared at his name, scratched into the leather with a black BIC, the same place as always.

Oh brother, what have you done?

Part One
England

Chapter 1

The day my brother disappeared I woke up to the sound of my mum screaming. I heard it distantly in my dream, like a school bell ringing across a playground or an annoying phone alarm. Grumbling, I flung my hand onto the bedside table, patting around for my phone to turn the alarm off. When it didn't stop, I sat up, blinking tiny pebbles of sleep away from my eyes. It was barely light, the sleepy tendrils of dawn still painting the sky outside and, as I started to fully wake up, I realised it wasn't an alarm, but my mother screeching at the top of her lungs.

Shit. What's happened now?

My mum had a tendency to scream over the smallest thing, like a plate breaking in the kitchen or a stain on a rug. Or any type of insect intruder. Normally, however, she reserved her screams for waking hours. With an irritated sigh, I scrambled out of bed, the carpet still warm under my toes from yesterday's sun. My dressing gown was on the back of the door so I shrugged it on and quickly cinched it at the waist, my still-tired limbs welcoming the soft fabric. The screaming began fading as I opened the door, high pitched wails dissipating into the early morning air. The grating halogen of the hall light forced my tired eyes into a squint as I padded down the hall. By the time I reached my mother, she'd transitioned into making whimpering sobs instead. It was only when I actually stopped, taking in her shaking hands and messy hair, that I realised we were outside Eli's room, just one door down from mine. That length of corridor always felt like an age when I was younger, sneaking down the hallway in the middle of the night, nose snotty and eyes weeping from another nightmare. He never told mum or dad, not even when I would wake him kicking and screaming in the early hours of the morning before school or when I had such a bad dream that I hadn't wanted to go to the toilet and had ended up wetting the bed; he just took care of it, then held me until I stopped crying. Now, as I stood next to my mother, with a sinking feeling in my stomach, I realised I didn't want to look at his room. I placed a hand on Mum's shoulder and she jumped, her pale face turning to stare at me. Her teeth were biting at her lower lip, pulling off tiny slithers of skin, miniscule droplets of blood rushing forward in their place. She continued whimpering, eyes unfocused, flitting around the hallway, barely focusing on my face before she turned away.

"Mum?" My voice stuttered, the vestiges of sleep still clinging to my throat. She didn't look at me again, just blinked. Silence hung in the air between us, crushing the atmosphere. Abruptly, the whimpering cut off, replaced by a rasped whisper. I leant in as she spoke, ears straining to hear.

"He's gone." Her voice broke at the end, lips snapping shut like she didn't want the words out in the world. I'd frozen, those two words confirming what I'd felt in my gut since I'd stood next to her. With jerking movements, I turned my head until I could see inside Eli's room. My stomach clenched. It looked like a bomb site; the bookcase was on its side, paperbacks strewn across the navy carpet with haphazard care. The sheets from his bed sat in a tangled ball in the corner, wilting against the wall, the now-depressing dove grey only adding to the warzone. His desk was bare, its contents scattered on the floor in a graceful arc, paperclips decorating the rug, Post-It notes arranged like a mosaic around them. Even his wardrobe had been pulled open, the finite collection of clothes torn apart, arms of jumpers hanging weakly from the doors, jeans crumpled in a pile. The only thing that had remained pristine was his bedside table, the black paint glowing in the pale light. On it sat his notebook, or one of his many notebooks, a framed photo of us and the mutated DNA model he'd made in Year 11. My gaze caught on the photo, taken a few months ago on his 24th birthday. I'd dragged him out to the beach, the freezing wind biting our faces, turning our cheeks cherry red. You could see it in the picture. Unbidden, tears built in my eyes, but I wiped them away furiously.

You don't get emotional. You're not Mum. Stop it.

Forcing my eyes away from the destruction, I turned back to my mother who had fallen deathly silent now, her eyes glassy, caught in some faraway nightmare. Across the hallway a door opened and shut quietly, and I spun around, catching my dad's eye as he exited the office, a phone pressed to his ear.

"We don't know how long he's been gone. It will be less than 12 hours." His voice was tight, each word clipped. I couldn't tell if they were clipped with anger or with pain. A tinny voice sounded on the other end of the phone and he raised his eyes to the ceiling. "I know it's still early and I know he's not a minor, but his room looks like there's been a fight or something… yes I can write down a description… thank you." He pulled the phone away from his face and tapped his thumb on the screen, ending the call. Then his eyes dropped back down to me.

"They're sending someone over to look for fingerprints or signs of forced entry. But if they don't find anything, they won't do anything else until tomorrow… They think he's run away." He ran a hand through his thinning hair, the barely-contained frustration now evident in his voice. My mother, who had been so still I'd forgotten she was there, suddenly spun around and disappeared across the hallway into my parent's room, slamming the door behind her. From the hallway we could hear her begin sobbing, the thin wood doing little to soften the blow. My dad looked from the door to me, then back again. I gave him a thin smile and a nod. One hand reached out, stroking my hair quickly before he also turned and walked into the room. As the door opened, I could see my mother sat on the bed, tears streaming down flushed cheeks. The door shut again, leaving me alone with the silence of the hallway.

The scene in Eli's room felt even dimmer than before when I turned back to it. My eyes went back to the bedside table again, the tiny piece of him that somehow hadn't been touched. Before I could think about it, I strode into the room, picking my way around the debris on the floor and grabbed the photo frame, hugging it to my dressing gown. I made to leave again, then hesitated, eyes dropping to the notebook. I had a pretty good idea what was in that notebook and I also had a pretty good feeling that it wasn't something that the cops should be reading. I grabbed that too, the pages rough against my palm and darted back across the room and down the hall, not pausing until I had reached my own bed. The sheets were still warm, but I was shivering, the dressing gown doing nothing.

Slowly the golden hue of sun washed across my room, but I ignored it, photo frame and notebook hugged to my chest, trying to ignore the tears that slipped slowly from my eyes, dampening the pillowcase. I heard the police arrive, the front door shutting seeming to shake the whole house, ringing in my ears. Lifting my head from the pillows, I could see the shadows of feet pass by my door, stomping down the hallway towards Eli's room. Guilt gnawed at me as I clutched the photo frame and notebook in my hands, hoping my parents hadn't noticed them in there earlier.

My dad's voice filtered through the thin walls; he was talking low but very fast and even through the wallpaper I could pick out the growing panic. I was sure my mum hadn't been the easiest person to deal with whilst we waited for the forensics team to show up. I almost pushed myself up and went down the hall to join them, the small, childlike part of me wanting to help her dad, but if I left the room and went down there, saw the forensics team, it would all become a lot more real. Instead I gently pushed back the bottom of the duvet that I'd tangled my feet in and slid out of bed, leaving my dressing gown behind. The low murmur of my dad's voice got louder as I pressed my ear to the wall, for once glad that the walls were paper thin. Shortly another voice responded, a gruff muttering that I presumed to be one of the forensics team.

"Looks like…idnap."

I was going to fill in the blanks and guess he meant kidnap. My stomach seized, the tears threatening to come back.

"How can you be sure?" My dad sounded how I felt, like the floor had dropped from under me. I flattened the rest of my body against the wall, straining to hear the response.

"From a preliminary look, it appears there was some kind of disturbance in the room. There is a collection of hairs on the far wall that look as though they were ripped from someone's head and I've found a small blood splatter under the window." I gasped then shut my mouth as the forensics investigator trailed off. There were a couple of seconds of silence as I held my breath then the investigator continued *"There's also this…"* More silence. Years ago, my brother and I had talked about making a hole in this wall and putting in a little window, so we could talk to each other when one or the other was grounded. Right now, I was wishing we had. After a couple of seconds my dad spoke again,

"Why would there be a needle?"

So, they could drug him and get him out of the house.

"*So, they could drug your son and get him out of the house.*" The investigator echoed my line of thought. I slumped against the wall as the room fell silent again and tried to breathe. I could feel the grey creeping in at the edge of my vision that signalled the beginning of a panic attack. I tilted my head back against the wall, focusing on my breathing.

Breathe in, hold, one, breathe out, breathe in, hold, two, breathe out...

There were distant noises in the room behind me, but I forced them out of my head and closed my eyes against the encroaching panic. Eventually, the haze receded, my hammering heartbeat steadying, and my eyelids fluttered open. Even though it hadn't been a full attack, my hands were shaking, cold and clammy, as I clutched them to my chest. As I sat there, the investigator spoke again,

"*I'll take this back to the station and send an officer round to get statements. They'll start the investigation straight away. I'm...I'm sorry.*" There was a shuffling, the heavy clump of boots vibrating across the floorboards and seconds later, a shadow passed under my door again. Only one. Trying to ignore my shaking hands, I pushed myself up and pressed my ear against the wall again.

From the other side I could hear heavy breathing and could imagine my father struggling to keep his composure. I knew he would come to my room in a few minutes and ask if I was okay, pretending he was. I knew he would have to go to my mother and tell her that her son has been kidnapped. There was a small sob, then a long breath in and out as if everything was settling back into place, the mask coming back down. I fought to keep my own composure as his slippered feet padded down the hall and paused outside my room. He knocked softly, then opened the door slightly when I didn't answer. His gaze was directed towards the bed when he poked his head towards the door and concern flitted across his face when he realised I wasn't there. Before he could start freaking out, I moved, drawing his eye over to the wall. His shoulders relaxed and his expression smoothed out as he took me in then realised where I was sat.

"Oh, sweetheart...?" I couldn't respond, my throat dry, so I just nodded my head and watched the understanding settle over his features. He opened the door fully and crossed the room, long strides eating up the beige carpeting before crouching and enveloping my torso in a hug. I leant my head on his shoulder and stopped keeping the tears back. After a few seconds, I heard my door close softly and then a second pair of arms were around my shoulders. My mum leant her head on the top of mine and made small 'shh' noises into my hair. We stayed like that until another knock rang through the house, breaking the tentative bubble we were in. My dad moved first, his hands wiping away silent tears and hurried down the stairs, whilst my mum stayed hugging me. We could hear the muted sounds of conversation and I started wiping away my own tears, ready to be called down. Sure enough, seconds later my dad called back up the stairs and dragged us out of my cocooned room to talk to the police.

It felt surreal. Almost like I was watching myself on a TV screen. I sat on the couch opposite the two officers with a dazed nod. I was still in my pyjamas. The tiny cotton shorts were doing nothing for me now, my dressing gown still abandoned in my room and the early morning chill somehow seeping into every corner of the house. It might have been shock. The first officer, a woman with a severe bun and soft eyes, talked, her mouth pulled into a sympathetic line. I realised when she paused that I hadn't been listening and she was now expecting an answer.

"I'm sorry. Could you repeat that?" My voice came out croaky, harsh against my tongue. The officer, smiled at me and nodded,

"We wanted to ask you a couple of questions. First of all, my name is Officer Dunn, and this is Officer Blake. We've been assigned to your brother's case. Your parents have told me that you and Eli-" I flinched at his name, "-were quite close, is that correct?" I nodded, biting my lip to keep it from shaking. Officer Blake noted something down, his brows pulled together. I kept my gaze on Officer Dunn. "Did he say anything to you about anyone who would want to hurt him?" I shook my head, almost before she had finished asking the question. Eli wasn't enemies with anyone. He always said he hated the idea of hating another person and I always told him he was soft.

"Eli was nice to everyone. I don't think someone would have tried to kidnap him out of malice." I muttered, glancing across to Officer Blake, who had started scribbling more stuff down as soon as I started to talk. I turned my head to look at my parents who were sat at the table behind the sofa. They gave me encouraging smiles, although my mum's was more of a watery grimace. Officer Dunn cleared her throat, bringing my attention back to her.

"Can you remember Eli acting strange at all? Perhaps worried?" Officer Blake's pen paused as he waited for my answer.

What, stranger than normal?

I shook my head again.

"He wasn't out of sorts last night. We'd watched a movie before we went to bed, just the two of us. *Blockers.* He found it pretty funny." I don't know why I felt the need to tell them that. Maybe it was just reassuring myself that he wasn't acting strange. I know he'd made some kind of breakthrough in his notebook; he'd been so excited to tell me over dinner. But I didn't want them asking where the notebook was, not when it was still tangled in my duvet. Tampering with evidence and all that; I also really didn't think Eli would want them to see his research.

Officer Blake made a sound at the back of his throat, like a small scoff, before Officer Dunn turned to glare at him. When she turned back to me, she had once again schooled a perfectly sympathetic expression onto her face.

"If you think of anything that could help, please let us know." I nodded, "Also, if Eli contacts you, you need to tell us right away. We might be able to trace his location." She smiled then her gaze flickered over to my parents and she stood up. "We are going to start the search immediately, using the evidence forensics collected. The best thing for you all to do would be to resume your normal routine. If this is malicious," I opened my mouth to object, but Officer Blake glared at me until I shut it again, "If this is malicious, there is a chance the kidnappers will contact you with demands. They might be monitoring you all so we would also suggest making sure doors and windows are locked at all times. We will keep you up to speed as much as we can and, with any luck, we will have Eli back very soon." My dad got up as she finished, reaching his palm out for a handshake. After the moment in my bedroom both he and my mother had seemed to put on impenetrable masks, neither of them showing any slip of emotion during the police interviews. I couldn't understand how they did it, especially my mother. As the officers got up to leave, Officer Blake shot me a wary glance like he thought I was hiding something. I glared back at him. Yes, I was hiding something, but it wasn't anything they needed to know about.

I waited until my dad had closed and locked the door behind them before getting up from the sofa and padding back up to my room. My parents started a whispered conversation, but I didn't make any attempt to listen. I moved on autopilot, shuffling into the bathroom to clean my teeth, then going back to my bedroom and pulling on a pair of jeans, a t-shirt and a baggy jumper. As I shrugged it over my head, I realised it was Eli's university jumper that I'd stolen last night when we were watching a movie. A sob worked its way up my throat, but I forced it back down and hunted for a pair of socks. Barely ten minutes after I'd gone upstairs, I was back in the hallway, backpack slung over my shoulder. I dumped it by the back door and walked through the living room and dining room into the kitchen. My mother stared at me as I slunk past her, making my way to the fridge.

"Are you...are you going to school?" Her voice was quiet but incredulous as I grabbed a yoghurt from the shelf and shut the door, turning to face her. Both of them were watching me, my mother in shock and my dad with concern. I nodded, ripping off the top of the yoghurt and licking the foil before dropping it in the bin.

"The police told us to resume our normal routine. Normally I would be eating a yoghurt and wishing I didn't have to go to school. So here I am." I checked the clock on the oven. I'd lost track of time over the last few hours and for all I knew I was three hours early for school. Luckily, or unluckily, 07:45 blinked out at me. I had 15 minutes before I needed to leave. Looking back at my parents, neither of whom had responded, I shrugged and grabbed a spoon from the drawer. My mum made a move to grab my arm as I walked past but she was stopped by Dad, his hand accompanied by a subtle shake of the head. I say subtle. I saw it but I appreciated that he had tried to be discreet. Although she clearly wasn't happy, Mum dropped her arm and watched me walk and sit at the table. Spooning yoghurt into my mouth without Eli making comments about how messy I was was strange.

I know to my parents it looked like I had just moved on but inside I wanted to scream and cry.

I just didn't know what I could do to help, other than what the police had told us to do. So that's what I was doing. My parents resumed their whispered conversation, although this time it was more likely to be about me than Eli. The minutes ticked by at an agonising dawdle but as soon as it hit 8:00am I was up from the table and heading towards the door. As I was picking up my backpack my dad appeared behind me. I faced him as I slung my backpack over my shoulder; he attempted a smile and gave me a quick hug.

"If you need us, give us a call. We'll come get you." I nodded and hurried out the door before my lip started wobbling, throwing my bag into the back of my car and starting the ignition forcefully. If I didn't, I would run back to my bed and hide and possibly never come out. The radio started playing and I turned it up louder, drowning out any attempt on behalf of my brain to drag me back into the crying, weeping mess I'd been only a couple of hours before.

By the time I got to school, everyone knew. It's that kind of town. As soon as the forensic van had pulled up outside our house in the early hours of the morning, someone had seen it; then that someone had told someone else and that someone else had told everyone. I felt it as soon as I walked into school; it didn't matter that I slunk through the doors, hood of the jumper tight around my ears, eyes down. I could feel everyone looking at me. A couple of them had siblings who knew my brother and they murmured sympathetically as I drifted past. But most people stared with intent to gossip. I caught a few people's eyes as I walked to my morning tutorial, mostly because I was looking for Jacob and Becca. I hadn't texted them, I hadn't talked to anyone but my parents and the police, but they would know and, with a sudden Eli shaped hole in my life, I really needed to talk to my closest friends. I didn't see them before I got to class so I knew I'd have to wait until 3rd period. More sympathetic glances were thrown my way as I sat down, immediately dropping my gaze to the desk and trying to shut out everything.

"Hey, are you okay?" the girl next to me, Clare, whispered as our tutor walked in. I shrugged and gave her a small smile because it was nice to know someone cared enough to ask. Then I lifted my eyes as Mr Donnalley began to go through the morning announcements and take the register, keeping them firmly fixed on the date written in faded blue whiteboard pen at the top right-hand corner. At least when Donnalley was speaking no one looked at me or tried to talk to me. The police might have told us to stick to our usual routine, but I guessed that they hadn't factored in the effect of gossip in a small town. The school day hadn't even officially begun, and I was already headline news. As soon as the bell rang for

1st period I pretty much ran out of the room, the need to get away almost making me run straight out of school.

No. You have to stay in be normal.

Frantically, I looked around until I spotted the toilets sign and ran towards that instead. Luckily all the cubicles were empty, something that was unusual for just before 1st period when normally most of the girls were in here to fix up their makeup. Finally, it seemed I had caught a break. I was well overdue for one. Locking the cubicle door, I sank onto the closed lid of the toilet and took a few deep breaths. This wasn't going away any time soon, even if Eli turned up safe and well in time for dinner. This was the kind of thing that this town didn't let go, even if it wasn't said to our faces. I'd worked so hard to keep everything of my personal life tucked away, to be perfect and it had crashed down in a matter of hours. If Eli had been here, he would have known what to do.

Oh God. Eli. Where are you?

I felt the tears spill onto my bottom lashes in a waterfall I couldn't hold back any longer. Burying my face in my hands, I let myself cry, for the third time today. It wasn't even lunchtime yet. I was going to be severely dehydrated by 2nd period if I kept this up. In between sobs, I dimly registered the door to the toilets swinging open followed by soft footsteps. A pair of black boots appeared outside the cubicle door. I dropped my hands from my face as the boots waited.

"B-becca?" I managed to splutter out her name, even though it got caught on the phlegm in my throat.

"Hey A. Can I come in?" her voice was soft, and I knew she would be making puppy dog eyes at the closed door with her hands behind her back. It was her tactic to getting what she wanted, and it usually worked. Leaning forward, I slid the lock to the side, letting the door swing back on its own. I knew in my head that I looked a mess but that was confirmed by the momentary shock on Becca's face. She rushed in and knelt down in front of me, grabbing both of my hands, "Oh sweetie. I'm so sorry. When Jake and I heard, we drove over to yours. We didn't think you'd be at school today. Then your parents told us you'd come in and had seemed fine, so I knew something like this was gonna happen." I smiled at her through tear stained cheeks. They'd skipped school for me.

"You skipped school for me?" My voice trembled halfway through, but it was coherent at least. Becca nodded and pulled me in for a hug, evidently not caring (or, for my sake, not showing it) that she was now kneeling on the floor of a toilet cubicle.

"Of course we did A, you know we wouldn't let you be alone. In fact..." she bit her lip and looked back over your shoulder. "Jake's waiting outside for us. He wanted to come in, but I didn't know if you were the only person in here or not. I'll go get him." She pushed herself up from the floor and managed to almost successfully hide her grimace before spinning round so fast her boot squeaked. I watched her go before realising what she'd said.

"NO!" My yell surprised even me, "I mean, no he shouldn't come in the toilets. I don't need you two getting into more trouble. I'll come out." I wiped my eyes on the back of the jumper, pushing away the unbidden reminder that this was actually Eli's and stood up from the toilet seat. Becca had paused by the door, one hand extended to grab the handle but as I drew level with her, she grabbed my hand instead and gave it a squeeze. With her free hand, she grabbed the door and flung it open, ushering me out. Luckily everyone was in lessons now, so the only person out there was someone I didn't mind seeing. Jacob was leaning against the wall, arms crossed but as soon as the door opened, he jumped up. His eyes darted from my face to mine and Becca's hands to my jumper and in a matter of seconds I found myself enveloped in another hug. I dropped Becca's hand and returned the hug, the leather of his jacket cool against my wrists. We stayed like that for a few seconds, me breathing in the smell of his body wash, him with his chin resting on the top of my hair. Jacob and Becca had been my closest friends for as long as I could remember. We'd had playdates at each other's houses ages 2 through 10 and then we'd renamed it 'hanging out' and continued. I knew there were a lot of rumours around school about me dating Jacob or me dating Becca and yeah, if we weren't like family, I would have probably dated either one of them, but they were just like a part of me, and it worked. We never left anyone out, we teased each other equally about our crushes and we never left each other hurting. Next to Eli, they were my favourite people in the world. Feeling a bit better than the soul-crushing despair I'd been experiencing previously, I stepped back from Jacob's chest, cringing as I noticed the tearstains I'd left on his grey top. He looked down when he saw my face and shook his head,

"Don't worry about it A, it will dry. If I didn't know any better, I'd say you'd done it on purpose just to get my top off." I snorted despite myself and he grinned at me. Becca took my hand again and Jacob slung an easy arm around my shoulders, and they led me outside to one of the benches. I knew neither of them wanted to ask the question, so I beat them to it, looking down at my hands.

"The police think Eli was kidnapped." There

was a small intake of breath from Becca and I felt Jacob move closer to me, arm tightening on my shoulder, "I woke up this morning to my mum screaming and when I got to Eli's room, it was a mess. It looked like it had been torn apart. The police sent a forensics investigator round and he found a blood splatter and a used needle, which they think was used to drug Eli to get him out silently. I don't know why his room was such a tip if they drugged him though." I hadn't thought of it before, but now that I had, more questions kept piling up. "How did we not hear anything? How did they get a grown man out the window?" I trailed off and the questions hung in the air. Jacob was the first to respond,

"Maybe the room wasn't torn up in a struggle. Maybe it was torn up because they were looking for something." I turned to look at him,

"Like what? It's Eli! The only interesting thing he can do is draw. I seriously doubt they wanted pictures of lions that he drew for me years ago." But even as I said it, I thought of the notebook tucked away in my room. What if there was something in there that they wanted?

"I'm sure they'll find him A. They couldn't have had much of a head start." Becca rested her head on my shoulder. I nodded, even though I wasn't sure I believed it.

"Have they told you to do anything?" I shook

my head at Jacob.

"Apart from continue on with our routine as normal and tell them if Eli tries to contact me." Jacob's mouth twisted sympathetically, and he rubbed my shoulder. "I guess now all we can do is wait."

I guess now all we can do is wait.

Chapter 2

Three Years Later...

Waiting wasn't getting me anywhere. I looked up at the queue in front of me, then back at my watch. I wasn't even sure I had time for this. I was supposed to be meeting Becca and Jake in half an hour on the other side of town. The line moved an inch, the mousey-haired cashier looking perpetually bored as she rattled off the same spiel.

"Hi. Welcome to the Coffee Cup. Can I take your order?"

"Hi, yeah can I have a hot chocolate with whipped cream and..." Eli looked down at me, "What do you want Ari?" I glanced over at all the pictures of drinks on the board and pointed to the most colourful one. Eli sighed and shook his head, but he was grinning, "She'll have the Rainbow Smoothie please." He passed over some cash and nudged me, "Don't tell Mum okay, she'll freak. I'm pretty sure it's not fresh fruit." I laughed,

"I won't tell mum, I promise...iffffff..." I looked at him expectantly,

"If what?" The cashier handed him his change and he pocketed it, steering me towards the pick-up section.

"If you draw me a giraffe!" I grinned, bouncing up and down and he laughed again, ruffling up my hair even though I'd asked him not to do that anymore.

"Sure. I'll draw you one when we sit down, okay?"

"Miss? Miss are you okay?" I blinked, shaking my head as the cashier's bored voice invaded my thoughts. She was wearing a slightly concerned expression, though I suspect the concern was more based on her need to move the line along than actual human compassion.

Where the hell did that memory come from?

"Yeah, I'm fine, sorry. Can I get a passionfruit iced tea please? Large." I passed my card over the card reader, waiting for the beep and shoved it back in my purse before wandering down to the pick-up section. I had no idea where that memory had come from. Eli had been missing for almost three years now and I'd been in this café almost once a week. It had never happened before. I grabbed my iced tea and made my way over to one of the tables, still pondering the sudden flashback.

The police had pretty much given up the search for Eli after a couple of months. None of their leads turned up anything and the forensics team came up with jack shit. They'd told us they would continue looking but that we should be prepared that we might not find him. No one had contacted us either, for a ransom or to threaten us. It was like Eli had just disappeared off the face of the earth. Initially my parents refused to take the police's answer and they hired private investigators to keep searching for him. Twelve months of that, and one very hefty bill, and it seemed like all the fight had gone out of them. The most the PI's had been able to do was find a van that had been parked on our street that night, but by the time they located it, it had been dumped and abandoned. So, they'd given up as well. It had taken a while but even the town seemed to forget. We were hot gossip for near on a year and then, like a switch had been flicked, it was as if it never happened. Apparently, our tragedy gossip had a shelf life. I'd graduated school, Becca had gone to uni, Jake got a job in his dad's company and I... well I didn't do that much. Or at least, not that my parents knew about.

Since the PI's gave up, and the police only called every few months to half-heartedly update us, I figured it fell to me. My parents had simply redecorated around the elephant in the room. Literally. Eli's room was now an office. So, whilst they had been working and pretending they weren't missing a son, I had been searching on my own. I started where the PI's had left off, trying to find the owners of the van. I hadn't found much, but I'd managed to track it to a petrol station and that, at least, gave me something. So, for the past two years, I'd followed leads, each one never leading to much, but at least I was trying. I read and re-read Eli's notebook, the only thing I had left of him. I worked part-time at the local cinema, which was shit pay, but it meant I could fund my searching. I was even enrolled to an online university course; Forensics and Criminal Investigation, ironically. Maybe there is stock in the idea that if you want something done you should do it yourself. I carried on with my life, the entire time painfully aware that there was still an Eli shaped hole in it.

I told my parents I was fine. I told Becca and Jake that I was getting there. I told myself to keep searching.

I took a sip of the tea and winced as my teeth complained from the cold.

"Owww! Ow. Eli, I have brain freeze!" My voice screeched across the café, even though Eli was sat across from me. He shhhed me, taking away the Rainbow Smoothie that had been the cause of my outburst.

"Ari, you can't just scream about it." He was trying to sound harsh but we both knew he wasn't mad. I quietened though, sticking my tongue out to see if I could see the different colours. It mostly just looked dark green. Eli laughed at me then went back to his

notebook. He always carried one with him, although I didn't know why. He filled them with lots of writing and the occasional drawing. The drawings were mostly on my insistence; he was really good at drawing animals and I loved animals, so he would draw for me. Today it was a giraffe. Last week he'd drawn an entire herd of zebra running along the bottom of the page. It was like magic. I bounced in my seat as he shaded the last couple of spots on the giraffe's neck before turning the notebook round and sliding it over to me. I let out a squeal as I looked at the drawing, the giraffe eating branches with cartoonish eyes and an extra-long neck. Next to the drawing, Eli had scribbled down some words.

"G...eh...nah...eh?" *I frowned at the word at the top, hastily underlined. Eli took the notebook back from me,*

"It says 'gene' Ari. It's to do with DNA." He passed me back my smoothie, which I happily accepted, latching on to the straw and drinking as fast as I could, brain freeze already forgotten. Eli laughed at me again, then went back to his notebook.

I snapped out of the flashback as I ran out of iced tea, the slurping sound startling me.

Let's hope I didn't pull any weird faces during that...

Luckily, it didn't look like anyone cared. I breathed a sigh of relief, checking my phone...

Shit.

I had ten minutes to get to the bowling alley across town. Becca would never let me forget it if I was late again. Grabbing my bag and my jacket I raced out of the café and back to the car park.

I made it to the bowling alley with seconds to spare. Becca and Jacob were waiting outside for me, leaning up against Jake's Audi. Becca had her arms crossed and Jake was laughing as I swung haphazardly into a parking space and raced over to them.

"I'm here! I'm not late. I made it." I panted, watching Becca's eyebrows quirk as she tried to hold back the laughter.

"You cut it a bit close A. What if we'd missed our slot?" The raised eyebrow got me as Jake looked down with exaggerated disapproval, mimicking Becca. I broke into peals of laughter and it wasn't long before they both joined me. We made our way into the bowling alley, me in the middle, asking Becca about her journey back. She was at university in Wales, so she often chose to get a flight back rather than take the train or drive. Luckily, we made it in time for our slot and soon enough we'd squeezed our feet into suspiciously clean smelling bowling shoes and were typing names into the score board. I knew sometimes they both felt a little awkward around me when I brought up the topic of Eli; my 'refusing to move on' as my mum so kindly put it had caused a bit of a rift between us over the last year or so, especially since both Becca and Jake had gone on with their lives. I didn't want to lose the only friends I had so I tried my best to keep any Eli talk to a minimum, but I needed to tell someone about the random flashback, and it could hardly be my parents.

"So…I had a weird flashback in the middle of Coffee Cup today." I started as Jake finished entering our names. They both turned to look at me, so I continued, "It was a memory of me and Eli." Something flitted across Becca's face, but she covered it up quickly. I think she was concerned that I was spending too much time trying to find him. I never told them all of it, but they knew I'd been looking.

"A memory of what?" Jake asked as he started selecting his ball. I watched him pick up the heaviest one before wincing and putting it back down with careful concentration,

"A completely random one. We were in the Coffee Cup; I was about 8 so Eli was 14 and he'd taken me there to get drinks whilst our parents shopped. I had a Rainbow Smoothie and he drew me a giraffe in one of his notebooks." Jake picked up a different ball, a deep emerald and tested the weight,

"Okay? So?" I could feel Becca watching me

with concern as Jake got ready to bowl,

"So, it was weird. I haven't had a memory of Eli pop up in a while and I've been in the Coffee Cup so many times in the last three years. I couldn't help thinking that maybe it meant something." Becca put a hand on my knee.

"Maybe it meant that you want a Rainbow Smoothie." Jake remarked over his shoulder as he stepped up to bowl. I looked at Becca and she smiled at me,

"Was there anything else in the memory?" I smiled back, grateful she was attempting to take it seriously.

"Yeah, I remember seeing the word 'gene' written in one of Eli's notebooks. Obviously, I didn't know what it meant, but I didn't know he did either. Not at 14." Becca's eyebrows pulled together, a strand of hair falling across her face as she thought.

"Maybe it was for a school project?" she chewed her lip as she waited for my response.

I don't think it was.

"Maybe." I turned to look at the lane as Jake let out a whoop just in time to see him get his first strike of the night. It would be the first of many. I had spent a lot of time here with Jake and Becca over the years to know he would win. He strutted back over, flexing his muscles with a cocky grin,

"*That* is how it's...

done!" *Jake flashed me a dimpled smile as he dropped back down beside me. Becca stood up to bowl, muttering about people being big-headed.*

"*I'm sure she means that as a compliment.*" *Eli chimed in as we watched her throw a gutter ball. Jake high-fived Eli, who winked at me, then went back to his phone. Since we'd got here, he had been spending a lot of time looking at his emails. I leant over, trying to read the screen but he turned the phone away from me.*

"*Ari. What are you doing?*" *He said it with a smile but there was an undercurrent of something else there, something I hadn't seen before on my easy-going brother. I pulled back, confused.*

"*Why won't you let me see your phone?*" *His smile dropped. I crossed my arms as I waited for him to respond. On our lane, Becca had just harpooned the bowling ball towards the pins. It did not hit any of them. She skulked back to us, sulking as Jake jibed that she had proven how it was not done. Eli pocketed his phone,*

"*It's my turn.*" *He murmured to me, avoiding my eyes. I sat back against the hard, plastic bench as he went up to bowl. He didn't normally hide anything from me. I startled as I realised Jake was watching me.*

"*He's probably talking to a girl and doesn't want you to see, A. I wouldn't worry.*" *He shot me a small smile, and I felt myself smiling back, even though most of me didn't feel like it. Jake was good at that, making people feel happy despite themselves. A power he mercilessly abused on Becca, mostly when we were bowling so she didn't stay mad at him. I uncrossed my arms and grinned down at Becca who was pouting as she watched Eli knock her further down the leader board.*

"Don't stress Becca. I've got to go yet, and we all know I'm awful." Eli walked past and sat back in the seat, but I refused to look at him. Instead I stood up to take my turn, selecting a ball at random and chucking it with no amount of grace down the lane. Somehow, it hit one of the pins, toppling it over, edging me past Becca's score. I turned back with a guilty smile to see her mock-glaring at me. Jake high-fived me as I made my way to my seat on the bench. I still refused to look at Eli, even though I could feel him trying to get my attention. Becca spun round in her seat to have a go at me but stopped when she saw me resolutely ignoring Eli,

"A, are you...

okay?" I shook myself out of the memory to find Becca peering at me, one hand on my arm. Jake was behind her, watching with worried eyes. Our scoreboard blinked on the screen, the timer ticking down.

"Yeah, sorry. How long did I zone out for?" I forced a smile on my face but didn't miss the glance they shared. Jake checked the timer on the screen,

"About five minutes. We thought you'd fallen asleep with your eyes open at first."

"No. I just…I remembered another memory." They shared another glance and this time, it definitely wasn't as subtle.

"The same one?" Becca asked gently. I moved my arm out from under her hand, hating the look in her eyes. It looked like pity.

"No, this one was here. You two were both in it. It's when we went bowling with Eli just before the start of Year 13." Jake's face lit up,

"Oh yeah, I remember that! It was when we all wiped the floor with Becca. That was the last time we all hung ou…" he trailed off as he realised what he was saying, and Becca elbowed him in the stomach.

"Yeah, that was a couple of months before he disappeared. I've never even thought about that day since then, it was weird. But I was so mad at Eli, he wouldn't show me what was on his phone." Neither of them responded. I sighed, pulling at a lock of hair that had fallen in front of my face. "I know you guys are worried but I'm okay. Just confused as to why I'm suddenly remembering stuff from years ago." I smiled at them both and stood up, "Right. Time to bowl. I plan to wipe the floor with the both of you."

It wasn't until I was on my way home that I let the smile slip from my face. Something was bothering me about the memories. I rarely ever had flashbacks to Eli, not anymore. I think I'd gotten so used to everyone else pretending he never existed that I'd started to lose him too. But two flashbacks in one day, triggered by places I'd been to multiple times since his disappearance was definitely weird. I chewed my lip as I turned into the driveway, putting the handbrake on with more force than necessary. I didn't get out of the car straight away. Instead, I opened the glove compartment and took out the notebook I'd stashed in there when everyone had given up on finding Eli. It was battered now, the pages bent from my fingers flicking through them so many times. I'd read and re-read every page in this notebook over the past three years so often I probably could have recited it. Not that there was anyone I could recite it to. Most of what Eli wrote hadn't made any sense to me, but after the memory in Coffee Cup, I'd realised that one word had been repeated a lot. *Gene.* A lot of the time I didn't press what Eli had been doing, the research. I'd known it was to do with biology and he'd drawn a lot of animal diagrams, but he'd never decided to explain it to me. What I did remember was that, the things I had overheard, sounded like they probably weren't legal. Obviously, he was just researching it hypothetically, but that's why I'd kept it from the police three years ago. I didn't want him to come across as the villain in this, not for a hobby. I put the notebook in my backpack and climbed out of the car. My parents would be asleep by now, so I wasn't going to have to pretend to be okay in front of them at least. I walked through the house and up to my room quickly. The door shut with an audible *click...*

and I looked up to see Eli in my doorway. He wouldn't look at me; instead he was looking at the floor, one sock scuffing my carpet.

"What do you want Eli?" My words came out sharper than intended and I felt guilty as he flinched. Taking a deep breath, he looked up to meet my gaze. When he looked like this, I forgot he was the older sibling by almost six years. He was the one who was already at uni. But stood in my doorway he looked like a child.

"I'm sorry Ari. For turning my phone away from you. I know it's not a massive thing, but I know why you're upset. It made you feel like I don't trust you and I do. More than Mum and Dad, more than any of my friends. So, I'm sorry." I stared at him for a few more seconds before shifting so I was sat up on my bed and smiled at him. His shoulders softened. We both knew I wasn't mad at him anymore. When he made his way over to sit next to me seconds later, I could see he wanted to talk about something else but there was still something irking me,

"Why didn't you show me Eli? If you trust me, why

didn't you show me?" His shoulders hunched again, and I felt bad for making him uncomfortable, but I wanted to know. He was my brother. He shouldn't be hiding stuff from me.

"I don't know. It's not even that big of a deal. Look," he pulled out his phone, opening his inbox. I leant forward but his hand was covering most of the emails. Thinking he was going to show me, I reached for his phone, but he jerked it away, dropping his hand for a few seconds, enough for me to see the sender of the top email, the unopened one.

GAI.

With hurried fingers Eli selected the email and pressed delete before locking his phone screen and turning back to me.

"Why couldn't you just leave it alone Ari? Now it looks like I did that as a reaction, but I was going to delete it anyway, that's why I came in here." He pushed his hair back from his face, the curly gold locks growing too long again. I was stuck. I felt like I should apologise but I was still a little bit hurt. I decided to say nothing and eventually, Eli sighed and pushed himself off the bed. He walked to my door and paused with his hand on the handle.

"Ari...I'm still sorry..." The door opened, letting a sliver of the hallway light in.

"I'm sorry too Eli." I murmured as he slipped out. I don't know if he heard me. As soon as my door had closed again, I flopped back onto the bed, tell-

ing myself that he wouldn't be mad in the morning. I hoped not anyway. I heard him shuffling about in his room, the paper-thin walls letting far too much of the noise through. Instead of listening, I turned over and burrowed my head into the pillows.

Hopefully he'd forget about the email by morning.

The email. I wobbled as I settled back into reality, still stood by my door. On shaking legs, I made my way over to the bed, the memory another that I had apparently locked away. I'd completely forgotten how weird he'd acted over that email and the argument we'd had. He hadn't been mad the next day, but there was definitely something off. After that he kept his stuff a little more private. I never said anything about it and neither did he, but in those few months just before his disappearance, I definitely felt like he was hiding something important from me. Grabbing my laptop from where I'd abandoned it earlier in the day, I opened up my browser, tapping my fingers on the edge of the keyboard as I waited for it to load.

GAI.

I held my breath as I pressed search, the split second it took to appear feeling like an age.

GAI, also known as the Genetics Advancement Institute was created in the early 2000's by scientist Rick Laws. They have since been shut down due to legal and ethical violations.

Underneath it listed the date of closure as 2015. That was only a couple of months after Eli went missing. I continued scrolling, eyes flitting over various news articles that explained the reasons behind the company's closure. Most of them were vague, citing the same 'legal and ethical violations' as the summary had done and few expounded on what GAI actually did. Obviously, something to do with genetics but I couldn't understand why that would have led to them being shut down. From what I could tell there wasn't an official location connected with GAI; they could have been based anywhere. At the very bottom of the first page of search results was a blog entitled 'The Gene Guider'. Clicking on it, I was confronted with various screenshots of the now defunct GAI website.

GAI have come under fire again, and let's be honest, none of us are surprised. They are flying far too close to the radar. Their website, which cites research into the scientific possibilities of embryo and stem cells to aid human health issues, has been called out for not revealing all of their intentions. The company recently put out a call for new scientists to work at their facility and, it seems, they should have been a bit more concerned with who they were letting in. One of the potential occupants left after the first interview, saying they had seen experiments that were nothing to do with stem cell research. Whilst the newspaper never released the report on what those experiments were, and GAI didn't make an official statement, I think it's safe to say that it must have been bad. We at The Gene Guider have our own theories; maybe some hybridisation? Mutations of the embryo's? Let us know what you think in the comments!

The writer of the post had inserted more pictures from the GAI website and its founder below that and when I scrolled down, I saw there were thousands of comments. A quick glance revealed they weren't particularly positive. So why had the Genetic Advancement's Institute sent an email to Eli? I pushed the laptop away again and pulled out Eli's notebook, thumbing through the pages again. This time, another phrase stood out to me.

Stem cell research.

The rest of the writing underneath had faded but this phrase had clearly been indented into the page. Whatever Eli had written about it, he clearly felt it was important. I snapped the notebook shut and laid back onto the pillows. This was the first lead I'd had in over six months. I had no idea where to go with it though; with no location and a defunct company, there weren't many avenues to follow. If Eli had been approached by GAI during the last few months before he disappeared, that meant it had probably happened whilst he was at university. He seemed to know who they were, even though he hadn't opened the email. That's the only reason I could think of that he would have reacted the way he did. So, it would stand to reason that he had received at least one more correspondence whilst at uni.

I sat up again. What I needed was to talk to someone who would have been with Eli whilst he was at uni. Maybe someone in one of his classes or a lecturer. He was on a four-year course so they would all be in their final year, which meant that tracking one of them down wouldn't be that difficult.

But would he have opened his emails in a lecture?

No. He would have done it somewhere private, like his room. I gasped aloud as the realisation hit me, and also admonished myself for not thinking of it earlier; because of the shortage of accommodation at Eli's uni, he'd ended up with a roommate in first year. His roommate might have seen or heard something about GAI.

Okay, this is actually a solid lead!

I pulled out my own notebook with the research I'd been doing into Eli's disappearance. Once the police had done their investigation they had, unknowingly, provided me with a list of people who could have helped. They'd interviewed every person on the list but had come up with nothing.

Maybe it's a case of asking the right questions...

I quickly scanned the list, tracing my finger

down the column with the subjects' relation to Eli. Mostly they were lecturers, a few friends from home and employers, besides the family members, but on the back page were the words I'd been looking for.

Caden 'Cade' Thomas – University Roommate.

I grinned at the piece of paper in front of me. A quick search on my phone revealed that Caden had next to no security on any of his social media and, luckily for me, was still at the university, finishing his final year. Noting down his name and the dorm address, I put my notebook away and collapsed back onto the bed with a grin for the first time in a while.

I hope you can help me Caden Thomas.

Chapter 3

I stood outside the main entrance to the university, trying to ignore the nerves that were unfurling in my stomach. It wasn't like I hadn't done this before. In the first year of my search I'd spoken to most of the people on the police list, but they were all from my town. I kind of knew them. This guy, Caden, was a complete stranger. All I knew about him was his name, dorm room and, from a blurry picture Eli had sent me from the first week of uni, what he looked like three years ago. I could have delved deeper into his social media but if I turned up knowing everything about him and then asked him for help locating my missing brother, that might come across a little creepy. I figured I'd just start with the missing brother. According to the address the police had listed, Caden had stayed in the same hall for his entire degree, which meant I, at least, had a vague search area. Ignoring the fact he could be in lectures, or at work, or out…

It'll be fine. Stop worrying prematurely.

I stepped onto the campus, hoping I blended in.

I'd brought Eli's old jumper out from the depths of my wardrobe and then stuck pretty casual. Given what I'd seen as I'd arrived, I'd done a good job. No one afforded me a second glance as I strode through, too focussed on their coffees and friends. I paused for a moment as I took it in,

Maybe I should have done things differently and gone to uni rather than taking online courses.

I watched three girls stroll past, laughing at something one of them said and felt a pang in my chest before taking a deep breath and shaking it off.

Maybe if Eli hasn't disappeared it would be different…

I shook my head, banishing the rest of that thought. He *had* disappeared. I couldn't go back and change my decisions now, especially not when they might actually bring me closer to finding him. I brought up the campus map I'd downloaded on my phone. The place was so big they'd separated it into different 'villages'. I knew I needed the central village but, besides the safe guess that it was in the centre, I didn't know how to get there. Tapping my screen to zoom in on the map, I looked around for a building I could match up; every building I'd walked past had a little plaque somewhere on the outside with its name, so it shouldn't be that difficult. The nearest building to me was the Strathsbury building.

I found it on the map and grinned; I was only a couple of minutes from the central village and, hopefully, my next lead. Setting off past Strathsbury, I continued walking up the pathway until blocks of accommodation appeared, looming out of the horizon. From here I could see there were a lot of blocks, but I had a block number too; 18. It didn't take long to find 18, the same plaques on the accommodation blocks as on every other building I'd passed. As I considered my next move, a girl walked up to the block across from 18. She got to the door and passed something over a small box on the side which beeped and let her in.

Shit.

I hadn't even thought about the fact the accommodation blocks would require key cards of some kind. Of course they would. Otherwise, random weirdos would be able to get wherever they wanted.

You know you're the random weird in this scenario right?

I probably should have asked Becca before I got here but then she would have wanted to know why I wanted to know, and I didn't need her looking at me with concern again. There was no way I could get into the block without a card and I definitely didn't have one. Spotting a bench on the grass near the blocks I made my way over and sat there, keeping an eye on the doors of 18. If someone came out or someone went in, I could run over and grab the door, saying I'd forgot my key card. Crossing my arms, I settled back onto the bench, sincerely hoping it didn't take too long; the benches were decidedly uncomfortable. The minutes ticked by, as did my patience.

How much trouble would I get in for breaking a window and claiming I lost my keycard?

As I sat contemplating a potential felony, a harried-looking girl hurried up to the doors of 18, struggling with a stack of books. I shot to my feet immediately, thankful that the stack of books she was carrying meant she was fumbling for her key card, and sauntered over, Eventually, she managed to swipe her card and nudged the door open with her elbow.

She's in, go, go, go!

The door swung shut much quicker than it had opened clicking into place seconds before I reached it, panting.

"No!" I tried the handle, but the door wouldn't budge. Resting my forehead on the glass I tried to re-evaluate my plan. I couldn't just sit around all day waiting for someone to appear and let me in-

"You okay?" I spun around, already trying to come up with an excuse for whatever they'd seen, and froze.

Caden?

The guy in front of me was smirking, still waiting for an answer. His grey eyes watched me closely as I opened my mouth and floundered. That only increased the smirk. Taking a deep breath, aware that I needed to sound vaguely literate in order for this to work, I forced a smile,

"Hi. Um, no, I've actually lost my key card. This is my block, could you help me…?" I trailed off, making sure I dropped my gaze on the last bit. He snorted quietly and I looked up to see him holding back a laugh.

"That's some pretty great acting." He teased, propping his head on his fist and tilting it to one side with a smirk. The cocky look on his face was not endearing me to him.

"What are you talking about?! I'm just trying to get into my block!" My eyebrows knotted as I tried to keep most of the anger out of my voice. I didn't want him to walk away, given that he was my only lead.

"Trying so hard that you've been sat out here for two hours on that bench?" he gestured behind us to the grass and raised his eyebrow. My mouth dropped open for a second before I snapped it shut again, internally cursing.

"Were you watching me?" I could forget the helpless student act. It clearly wasn't working. I may have needed his help but at that moment I really wanted to storm away. He rubbed his hand over the stubble on his chin; that hadn't been in the picture from Eli. Caden had clearly decided shaving wasn't as important as he thought three years ago. I hated the fact that it was annoyingly attractive.

You are not here to like him. Just get the information.

Crossing my arms across my chest, and not missing how his eyes flicked down at the movement, I waited for his response. He drew out the silence, that half-smirk still at the corner of his mouth. Eventually he dropped his hand from his face,

"I mean, a pretty girl sat outside my accommodation with a look of pure murder on her face? Why wouldn't I?"

Who the hell does he think he is?

Sighing, I uncrossed my arms. I needed a new tactic.

He's caught you, might as well own up to it and hope he's not as much of an asshole as he looks. Just try and spin it in a way that'll make him feel like the hero.

Judging from the cocky grin, girls generally fell at his feet, so maybe that was the way to go?

Nope. Couldn't do it.

Just tell him the truth.

"Look, I'm sorry. I didn't mean to upset you." He

spoke before I could say anything else, his words startling me from my own thoughts. The smirk had dropped from his face completely. Now was my chance.

"It's okay, I just… um. You're right." He blinked in surprise but didn't say anything, "I don't live here. I don't even go to this university. I actually came here because I need to talk to you." More blinking. Clearly, he hadn't expected that. Point to me. "I was hoping to find you here since this is your accommodation, but I didn't realise you needed a key card to get in."

"Yeah, it keeps strange girls with questionable intentions and clumpy boots from getting into poor, innocent guys rooms." He leant forward, dropping his voice to a whisper, "I'm the poor innocent guy, in case you didn't notice." I rolled my eyes,

"Yeah, I got it. Though I seriously doubt you're poor or innocent." I snapped, pointedly looking at the shoes that I knew came with a hefty price tag and the beat-up leather jacket. Caden laughed,

"You know, you remind me of my old roommate." I stilled, watching his face very carefully as he continued, "He had the same personable attitude and a jumper exactly like that." He nodded to my jumper.

"You mean Eli?" my voice was quiet, the tension

in it almost palpable. He raised an eyebrow at the mention of Eli's name but, after a few seconds, he nodded. "That's actually why I came here. I'm Eli's sister and I'm really hoping you can help me find him." I held my breath as my words hung in the air between us. The rest of the world seemed to have gone very quiet, the background noises fading out as I waited for his response. His entire face softened as the words sunk in,

"You're Ari?" I nodded, "Eli told me about you. Heck, he never shut up about his little sister. He was so proud of you." Tears sprung to my eyes and I swallowed around the sudden lump in my throat. "I didn't realise he had disappeared until the police showed up. I'm sorry. Look..." he ran a hand through some stray hairs that had escaped the bun at the back of his head, moving wayward strands away from his face, "Do you wanna come up to my room? I'll help you if I can."

I nodded, still not trusting myself to speak. He swiped his key card over the door and pulled it open, holding it so I could duck under his arm. We made our way up the stairs in complete silence, the cocky attitude gone. When we reached his room, I made myself take a couple of breaths.

This would have been Eli's room.

He unlocked the door and pushed it open. Faded blue carpet greeted us as I cautiously stepped inside. The door shut behind me and clicked into place. Caden slipped past where I'd frozen in the doorway and sat on the bed on the left-hand side of the room. Looking around the room for the first time I noticed that it was completely bare in exactly one half of the room. Eli's side. The bed was empty, save for a mattress and the walls and drawers were uncluttered. By comparison, Caden's side of the room seemed like a bomb had hit it. Multiple times. Books were strewn across his desk, clothes piled in one corner next to a bin labelled 'Laundry' and water bottles littered the floor. I couldn't help raising an eyebrow and, when he saw me looking, he hastily kicked a couple of them under his bed. Unsure of what else to do, I took a seat on Eli's bed, the fabric of the bare mattress cold beneath my clammy palms. The room lapsed into silence, me unsure of how to ask and Caden watching me with an expression on his face that I couldn't quite read.

You need to say something. Get yourself together woman.

"So, Caden…" I tried to transition back into the line of questioning I'd used on people before. "You said you didn't even know Eli had disappeared? How is that possible? He was your roommate." Caden stared at me with an expression I couldn't read for a couple more seconds before answering.

"He told me he was going home for a few days,

which I figured was fair enough given it was right before exams and he was probably stressed. He didn't seem to be acting unusual and he only took enough stuff for a weekend, so I had no reason to suspect anything different. The first I knew of his disappearance was when the cops came around a few days later and said he'd vanished from his home." He kept eye contact the entire time. I nodded, having heard that from the police anyway.

"Eli didn't ever say anything to you about running away or about having ene...enemies?" I stumbled over the last word, hating the way my stomach seized when I thought about Eli ever possibly being hated by someone.

Caden shook his head,

"No. Everyone in the block liked Eli. He was charming, when he wanted to be, much like you I'd imagine, and he was never rude. We got on well." He sighed, "Look, this feels strange. You're Eli's little sister and we're sitting here like we're in an interrogation. I'll tell you everything I know about Eli, but I'd rather not do it whilst we face each other like a Mexican standoff." His comment made me suddenly aware that I had been sitting like I had a stick up my arse. I could see where Caden was coming from; this just felt weird, especially sat in Eli's old room.

"I agree. How would you prefer to talk to me?"

He flashed me a grin quickly and I could see the smartarse response formulating in his mind. Luckily, as I levelled a glare at him, he seemed to think better of it and stood up, walking over to a small box by his desk. When he opened it, I realised it was a mini fridge and couldn't help the snort as he pulled out two cans of fizzy drink. He gestured to the nearby desk chair which I took as an invitation. As I sat down, he handed me one of the cans before sitting back on his bed, far more relaxed than he had been a minute ago. I watched with raised eyebrows as he leant back on his pillows, grey t-shirt riding up slightly to reveal a toned, tanned stomach. He cracked open his can of drink and before I could say anything else, started talking,

"When I met Eli on the first day of uni, I knew we would get along. He came over to me and told me he was cool with having a mini fridge so long as I tidied up the cans," I glanced at the battlefield of bottles decorating the carpet and back at Caden with a raised eyebrow, "We aren't supposed to have fridges in our rooms, so I wasn't sure if he was messing with me or not, but he seemed cool. As soon as we got to know each other, heck even before we really knew each other, he'd told me about you. He was worried about whether you would be okay, now that he was at uni. I couldn't help picturing this adorable little sister whenever he talked about you." He grinned and looked me up and down, "I probably wouldn't call you adorable now having met you." I pretended to glare at him, but I was loving hearing about Eli after not talking about him for so long that I couldn't even pretend to be mad, "One thing I always noticed was that he carried a notebook around with him everywhere." I nodded, "When I asked him about them once, he said it was just a hobby, but he filled reams and reams of them. They took up most of the space on his desk and I was always tempted to have a peek when he went home, since he left most of them here, but I never did."

"Wait…" I interrupted Caden as a thought occurred to me, "He left most of his notebooks here?" Caden nodded, "Well where did they go after he disappeared? In fact, where did most of his stuff go? We never got it; or at least if we did, my parents hid it from me." Caden glanced over to Eli's side of the room,

"The police sent someone round to collect it all; they said it was evidence? I guess I assumed they would give it back to you when they were done." I shook my head,

"I'm ninety percent sure they never gave it back to us. Which probably means they still have it including the notebooks!" The chair squeaked as I shifted, resisting the urge to bounce up and down;

"What do his notebooks have to do with anything?" Caden sat up, propping one elbow on his faded jeans so he could look at me. I paused.

I probably shouldn't tell him anything. I don't actually know him at all and he could say something to someone else.

My teeth sought out my bottom lip, chewing and I noticed his eyes fall to them. I stopped quickly, licking my lip instead.

"His notebooks are the only thing he didn't let anyone see, so there might be something in there about who could be behind his disappearance. That's what I figure anyway." I couldn't tell him everything. Not when I really had no idea who this guy was. But it needed to be at least somewhat true to get him to believe me. He nodded,

"Well, the closest police station to your house is on Chestnut Street. That's the most likely place for them to be stored whilst they were conducting the investigation. I can... I can show you if you like? I kind of owe Eli that much." He muttered the last bit as he stood up, draining the last of his drink and throwing the can onto the desk. I stood up and moved next to him,

"What do you mean, you owe him that much?" He looked over his shoulder at me and sighed.

"I can't help but feel responsible for his disappearance sometimes. Like if I'd paid attention a bit more maybe I would have noticed if something was off or unusual. Or maybe he would have told me. It sucks that now everyone looks at me like I had something to do with it; they all know Eli went missing and it's like I've suddenly got the plague. I think that's why they never assigned anyone else to this room." He looked away from me but even from my position I could see the muscle in his jaw tick as he clenched his teeth. "So, if I have the chance to help his little sister find him, then I'll do what I can." I couldn't help but smile at him. Especially since it seemed that he had had people exclude him as well.

You don't have to show him what's in the notebooks. Just let him help you find them.

"I'd love your help, Caden." He grinned at me, the tension dissipating. Moving back over to his bed, he grabbed a backpack and threw things in there from around the room. I stood in the middle as he became a whirlwind around me, moving faster than I thought a guy in a leather jacket could do. Generally, they look at the world with an air of practised contempt and ease. Not veritable excitement. Once he was done, he came to a stop in front of me, backpack slung easily over one shoulder. I smirked at him.

"Why on earth do you need a pair of pliers and what appears to be a tub of hair gel? We're going to ask for Eli's notebooks, not break in." I hoped not anyway. I wasn't sure that would be the best way to go about getting evidence back. He shrugged.

"You never know what could come in handy. I've also got some tweezers, a protein bar and a bunch of string." He seemed proud of himself.

"I would ask why you have all of that to hand, but I'm not entirely sure I want to know the answer." It was weird how easy Caden was to talk to. I'd thought it would end up being awkward, like all the other people I'd talked to about Eli, but he just wasn't. I told myself to stop relaxing around him; I still didn't know this guy very well. But I knew at the back of mind that it was all because of Eli. Some part of me probably thought that, since Caden was my last connection to Eli, he was okay. I shrugged as Caden opened his door again, letting me past. As long as I didn't end up with an unwanted sidekick or, more accurately, as long as I didn't end up wanting a sidekick.

We walked back across campus towards my car. I'd suggested walking but Caden had simply raised his eyebrow at me and continued walking to the car park. When we got there, he hung back a step or two, letting me walk over to my car.

"Really?" I turned to see him staring at my Hyundai i10 in disbelief, "*This* is your car? I didn't take you for a teeny tiny car kind of person. I was expecting something casually cool with a hint of disdain. This is definitely more cute and preppy." I glared at him over her hood.

"I don't see you offering up a car, so shut up and get in." Yanking open the driver's side door, I deposited my phone in the console and put the keys in the ignition. After a couple of seconds Caden opened the passenger door and made a big deal of folding himself over to get into the seat. "Oh, give over, you're hardly Dwayne Johnson." Once he'd shut the door I slammed my foot down, ignoring his startled yell as he was thrown into the door. I may have smirked.

"Just so you know, in order for me to get you to the police station, I have to be conscious and, you know, *alive*." The mutter came from behind a pained grimace. I didn't bother replying. Instead I slowed down to a crawl, waiting for directions. With a sigh, he told me to turn left and then straight over the roundabout. The radio was the only sound for a while, save for occasional instructions and the blaring of my own thoughts. The closer we got to the police station, the more I started to feel apprehensive. Why hadn't they given us back Eli's stuff? I wasn't sure it was going to be that easy to get it now, especially given it had been three years. In the console, my phone buzzed, the screen lit up to tell me it was Jake. Caden saw it too, his eyes lighting up as he saw the 'x' after the text, the same way Eli's used to before he teased me. Another pang hit my chest.

"Don't." I snapped on reflex, even though it had

been years since Eli, or anyone besides Becca and Jake had tried teasing me. It came out sharper than I'd intended, a leftover from the ache in my chest, cutting through the air before he could say anything; he sunk back into his seat, pouting. "He's not my boyfriend, he's one of my closest friends and he's probably worried about me. I acted kind of weird earlier this week." I didn't know why I was telling Caden this. He didn't seem bothered, choosing to ignore most of what I'd said,

"Ooooh, 'close friends'. The friendzone, poor guy… Is he not your type?" he teased "Maybe you need more of a charming, funny, gorgeous kind of guy." He gestured a hand up and down the length of his body. I snorted, making the next turn. "So gorgeous isn't your type, either huh?" Another text lit up my phone, this one from Becca. Caden fell quiet for a few seconds, "Or am I fighting a losing battle because guys aren't your type at all?" I tried to hide my smirk,

"Both Becca and Jake are both my closest friends. Or, were anyway. We haven't been that close recently…" I trailed off getting lost in that thought. Caden shifted and I snapped back to the present, "Not that it's any of your business, but since I can see this is going to go on for a while if I don't answer you, guys *and* girls are my type. I'm bi. So if I don't like you, that's a problem with you, not your gender." I enjoyed the moment of silence in the car as he processed that information. When I snuck a glance out of the corner of my eye, I could see a smile playing on the edges of his lips. "What?"

"Eli was right. Take a left here." I swung around the corner, trying to concentrate on the road but failing pretty miserably.

"Eli was right about what?!" I'd never told Eli I was bi because it hadn't come up. I didn't think he would treat me any differently and, given that I hadn't ever had a serious relationship, it wasn't like I really needed to tell him. Sometimes I felt a bit bad because it seemed like I was keeping it a secret from him, but it had never been that. It was more that I didn't see the point of making a big deal out of it when I didn't need to. Caden seemed to know that I was entertaining my own internal monologue.

"Eli said to me once that he thought you were bi but since you hadn't said anything to him, you clearly didn't want to make a big deal out of it. So, he never asked." I couldn't keep the smile off my face, even as my chest lurched at the memory of him. I was glad to know he hadn't been upset. Wait…

"Why were you discussing my sexuality?" I hadn't meant it to come out sounding so aggressive, but I'd snapped before I realised. Caden looked away. Was he blushing?

"I-I'd asked if you were seeing anyone. Eli showed me a picture of the two of you from when he went home for a weekend and you looked cute." Well, now I was blushing too. At least mine was hidden by my hair. We lapsed back into silence until Caden yelled for me to turn right. I swore under my breath and yanked the steering wheel round, barely missing the curb. Up ahead I could see the sign for the police station.

Probably shouldn't be driving like a maniac in front of a police station. It's not gonna make a great first impression.

Righting myself so that I was no longer in danger of mounting the curb, I pulled up in the nearest space before turning the ignition off. We both sat there for a few seconds, neither one of us quite sure what to do now that we were here. Eventually I turned to face Caden, the seatbelt cutting into my neck as I did.

"I think we should just go in there and tell the truth."

"What that you're the sister of a missing kid from three years ago and just today you tracked down his university roommate who you then coerced into going to the local police station to get back notebooks that were taken from his room in an investigation that never fully closed?" I didn't appreciate the sarcasm.

"Well, not that exactly. But I'll go in and say that I'm Eli's sister and that I was hoping to claim his possessions that were taken into evidence." I grabbed my phone from the console, making a mental note to reply to Becca and Jake later. Providing I didn't end up in police custody or something. Caden pulled his backpack from the back seat and got out of the car. Once I'd locked up, we started walking down the street. I was trying my best to stay relaxed but the same nerves I'd been feeling all day were back. As we walked through the sliding doors the receptionist looked up with a smile,

"Hi guys, how can I help you?" I leant on the counter and smiled back. Caden hung back behind me and I hoped he didn't look too much like a hardened criminal.

"Hi. I was hoping you could help me recover some family items that were taken into evidence." She seemed taken aback but recovered quickly, keeping the smile on her face.

"I'll definitely see what I can do. First off I need some more information…?" She trailed off, giving me the opportunity to fill in the blanks. I nodded,

"Okay. Um, my brother, Eli Farrow disappeared three years ago and as part of the investigation the contents of his university room were seized. These items were never returned to us after the investigation threw up nothing and I was hoping to be able to get them back now as they included a lot of personal items." I finished. She nodded at me and started typing; I shot a glance over my shoulder at Caden who shrugged. After a couple of minutes, in which the only sound was the tapping of her keyboard, she looked up at me and gave me a half smile.

"I've found your brothers case here. We do still have the evidence however our database says the case is still open so I cannot surrender the evidence to you."

"What?! That's ridiculous. You haven't done anything to further my brother's case in over two years! How can you-" I could feel Caden's hand in the small of my back applying a small amount of pressure, I presume to get me to calm down. I was livid. I stopped and took a breath, waiting for the anger to subside a little, "Is there nothing you can do? Even putting us through to a supervisor so we could have this discussion with them?" Her eyes darted back to the screen and she shook her head,

"I'm sorry, I don't think there's anything we can do to help you. Your best bet would be to appeal to have the case closed at court. Then all possessions could be returned to your family." The phone on her desk started ringing and she shot me an apologetic look, "I'm sorry, I have to take this." Caden pulled me away by my elbow, standing me next to a large potted plant. My hands shook, the need to yell at someone simmering just below the surface. After all this time and my only lead had been cut short by a *database.* I blew out a frustrated breath, moving some strands of hair off of my face and then noticed that Caden still had his hand on my arm. He seemed to notice at the same time and quickly dropped it.

"What do we do?" I hissed, "I'm hardly just going to leave the notebooks here when it's the only chance I have." Caden glanced around then leant in,

"Look, I have a plan. I can probably get into the evidence locker if you can distract the front desk. I brought a couple of tools with me and I have a bit of experience disabling magnetic locks, which is what most police stations use." He wouldn't meet my eyes and despite my anger, I couldn't resist,

"So, you are a no-good bad boy! I knew you weren't innocent." I stuck my tongue out at him, not really caring about the whole breaking the law part of this plan. The adrenaline had taken over now, I was *so close.* "Okay I'll go back over and have a breakdown. Hopefully, she'll be so flustered trying to calm me down that she won't notice if you slip back there." I nodded to the door marked staff only which was the only likely route. "Please don't get caught." I added.

"Oh why? Are you concerned for me?" the cocky smirk was back.

"Not for you. For myself. Everyone saw me come in here with you and if you get arrested, so will I. Or, at least detained and that's not going to get either of us very far. Now go wander off to the toilet or something." I pushed him back and then closed my eyes, trying to make myself cry. It wasn't that difficult; letting in all the fears I had over Eli was something I tried to avoid but if the situation called for it… well, I was about to cause a monumental distraction. As the tears started pricking my eyes, I turned and walked back over to the desk. The receptionist had put down the phone and was now back on the computer. She looked up as I walked over and quickly realised that I was crying.

"Oh, are you okay?"

Generally someone breaking down in tears in public is an indication that they're very much not okay.

I shook my head and let the tears fall faster, adding in a couple of sobs that got caught in my throat.

"I…I'm s-sorry…I jus-st…I just mi-ss my b-b-brother!" Time to wail. Out of the corner of my eye I noticed Caden slip past, as the receptionist stood up and started fussing over me. Hands on my shoulders, she gently steered me over to the seating area, grabbing a box of tissues as she did so. I kept the tears coming, letting my sobs get a bit more hysterical each time. I could see from her face that she didn't know what to do and I did feel bad for a few seconds. Then I saw Caden slip back out of the 'Staff Only' door with his backpack slung over his shoulder.

Shit. That was fast.

He gave me a thumbs up and meandered out of the front door. Sniffling, I wiped away the tears and sat up, giving the receptionist a watery smile.

"I think... I think I'll be okay now...thank you." She smiled back and patted me on the arm, before standing up and walking back to her desk. Using a tissue, I blew my nose and stood up as well making my way to the front door. I made sure to sniff again just before I left. As soon as I was outside, I walked back to the car where Caden was waiting, arms crossed.

"What took you so long? I was about to break in to your matchbox of a car." I shook my head at him and unlocked the doors. After we'd climbed in and I'd started the car I couldn't keep the question in any longer,

"Did you get them? Please tell me you got them. I can't do that again. I'm not the experienced criminal that you are." He shot me a glare but unzipped his backpack to reveal a cluster of notebooks. I let out a high-pitched squeak, ignoring the incredulous look he shot me. "So, no one saw you? What if they notice?" He sighed,

"No, no one saw me. I think they would have stopped me. They won't notice because I took a load of notebooks I found lying in a storage box on my way there and replaced them. I doubt they've actually read through them and, if like you said, they haven't worked on the case in over two years, they aren't going to start again now." I grabbed the backpack off of him and took out the notebooks. They were all the same brown leather with blank covers, but I knew inside they would be full of Eli's drawings and notes.

"Thank you, Caden. I really appreciate this. I'm sorry I dragged you into a potentially illegal situation." He shrugged,

"It's okay, it's not like I was doing anything else today. I mean I have a lecture this afternoon but…" he trailed off and looked at the clock "Shit. Could I please ask that you put this tin can into the highest gear it has and get me back in time for my lecture. I really can't miss another one." I threw the notebooks into the back and grabbed my seatbelt, before peeling away from the kerb. Again, probably shouldn't be doing that in front of a police station but I did kind of owe Caden.

I dropped him off at the main entrance with minutes to spare and laughed as he sprinted off into the distance. Then I glanced back at the notebooks in the back seat.

I really hope you were worth it.

Chapter 4

I couldn't bring myself to open them. I'd been sat staring at the notebooks for nearly an hour. They were all laid out on the bed in front of me, along with the original notebook I already had. I'd skipped dinner when I got back, going straight to my room with every intention of pouring over the notebooks but for some reason as soon as I'd sat down, I'd been absolutely terrified to open them.

So here I was, an hour later, still staring at them. I didn't even know if what was in them was still legible. This was my best chance at finding Eli, or at the very least finding out what happened to him. Setting my shoulders, I reached for the closest notebook, the leather cover soft to touch in my palms.

You need to do this.

Carefully, I unwrapped the cord that held the notebook closed, my stomach tightening with each loosening coil. The front cover fell open as soon as I removed the last coil, the soft leather refusing to hold. The first page was covered completely in Eli's handwriting, the spiked letters jumping off the page. Seeing his writing again was like being transported back three years. Bolder now, I started flicking through the rest of the pages, the musty smell of the paper wafting around my room. Most of the pages were covered in writing but a few diagrams dotted the paper here and there. No giraffes or lions though. A lot of the same words jumped out at me as with the first notebook; 'gene' and 'hybrid' the most noticeable, but nothing in here seemed to have any connection to GAI. Or, if it did, Eli hadn't made the leap.

I discarded that notebook and picked up the next one, unwrapping the cord and leafing through. The same theme arose; the same words and a few diagrams but nothing else.

This is just another dead end.

The anticipation of opening the notebooks was replaced by a slowly forming rock in my stomach. My fingers flew through the next few, their pages not giving up any secrets and by the time I reached the last one, I'd pretty much given up. As expected, it just talked about the same things as all the others. Towards the back, a thicker set of pages halted my progress. Eli had stapled some printouts of articles looking at stem cell research onto them. I paused.

Could this actually be something useful?

The first mentioned something called the HFEA. I grabbed my phone to look it up, but all it came up with was the Human Fertilisation and Embryology Authority. The second article referred to an ASAP database, which was talking about an Alternative Splicing Annotation Project. Neither of these seemed to have any connections to GAI even though they were in the right field. Eli had scrawled some notes around each article, but it was mostly incomprehensible to me and after another couple of minutes of reading, I flopped back onto my pillows with a sigh.

This is useless.

Beside me, my phone buzzed.

Wanna get some coffee at CC? x

Jake. Becca had gone back to uni now, probably mad at me because I hadn't responded to her texts from earlier, but Jake would have just finished work and there was no way I could avoid him. I'd just have to make sure I didn't let slip what I'd been up to today.

Sure, I'll meet you there in half an hour? X

I didn't bother to wait for the reply. Jake was always late. Instead I grabbed the notebook with the articles stapled in, shoved it in my backpack and picked up my car keys before heading out of the house.

Even with traffic, it took me less than 10 minutes to get to Coffee Cup, so I ordered my usual drink and sat down at a table near the back to wait for Jake. It was busier than usual, and I resisted the urge to glare at the mother next to me whose kids were screaming. After a couple of minutes of people watching, I went back to the notebook and the articles at the back. It was probably a good idea to read them again. Halfway through the second article, a pair of boots appeared in front of me and waited. Irritated, I glanced up, only to have my mouth drop open instead,

"Caden? What are you doing here?" he grinned at me and pulled out a chair, looking annoyingly at ease. I guess after risking jail for me (or for Eli), I couldn't really complain about him sitting down.

"Hey. Nice to see you too. Whatcha drinking?" he grabbed my cup before I could protest and took a slurp, wrinkling his nose. "God, that's awful. What is it?" I snatched it off of him and set it back down in front of me, carefully avoiding dripping condensation over the notebooks.

"It's iced tea and it's mine so stop drinking it." Out of defiance, I took an even longer slurp, smacking my lips and staring Caden down. His chuckle was almost too low to hear above the surrounding din. "Why are you here, Caden?" I asked, glancing towards the door in case Jake had decided to be early for the first time in his life. Luckily, or unluckily depending on Caden's response, there was no sign of him yet.

"Besides to have a lovely conversation with you? It's because I found this in my backpack and figured it probably came from the notebooks and that you might want to have a look at it. Of course, you didn't exactly stick around after our earlier adventure, so I had to get creative to find you. I remembered Eli saying you used to come to the Coffee Cup a lot, so I figured I'd give it a try. I don't know why you can't live without that crap though." He wrinkled his nose at my iced tea before handing over a folded slip of paper. It was the same kind of texture as the paper in the notebooks. Caden watched as I opened the folded square; there was barely anything on it, just one line scrawled in Eli's writing.

Columbia Industrial Estate, Bedfordshire, MK** 2**

Confused, I pulled out my phone. It looked like an address. I quickly typed it into Google Maps.

"No way." I breathed, zooming in on the results. Caden leant over, crowding my shoulder as he tried to glance at my screen.

"What?" His mouth was close to my ear, raising the hair on the back of my neck as he spoke. I looked up at him, trying to contain the excitement I could feel bubbling underneath the surface.

"This is an address. For an industrial estate." He

stared at me blankly, "I bet it has something to do with Eli's disappearance! Why else would he have this address? It looks like it's for an empty warehouse as well, so it would make sense." Realisation slowly dawned on his face,

"Riiight. Well, what are we going to do?" I stilled, searching his face,

"We? What makes you think you're invited?" He tried to cover the flash of hurt that crossed his features by pouting but I still saw it... and I still felt like an arsehole.

"After everything I risked for you today and I don't even get to come along to the fun part?"

Tell him yes, that's right. Tell him to go home. He's already risked jail.

"I guess I could use the help," The words were out of my mouth before my brain had even processed them.

Well done. You really told him.

Caden grinned and grabbed my phone from me,

"Hey! -" I protested but he just flapped a hand at my face.

"I'm just giving you my phone number. That way you can let me know when you're gonna go to investigate and I can come with you, rather than me awkwardly stalking you so I don't miss all the fun," He handed me my phone back with a grin just as I spotted a familiar face walk through the door.

"Oh, crap, um my friend is here, and I haven't told him anything about today so you kind of need to...go," I finished, flapping my hands much the way he had done seconds earlier. Caden chuckled and pushed himself up from the table,

"No worries, buttercup. Just shoot me a text when you're ready to go. Don't stand me up!" The slight twang of his accent seemed especially prominent and I could feel the flush starting at my ears as I registered what he'd called me. As I floundered, he turned and sauntered out of the café, passing Jake on the way. They nodded at each other before Jake hurried over to me, still in his suit, jacket slung over the crook of his arm. I forced a smile onto my face as my heart tried to do the tango in my chest.

"Hey! How are you?" I greeted, leaning over to give him a hug. He returned the hug but when I pulled back, he was looking at me strangely. "What?"

"Who was that?" He glanced back over his shoulder to where Caden had been. I started to shrug but knew he wouldn't let it go just like that.

"That was Caden. I met him earlier today...he's nice." Lame, I know, but I couldn't think of what else to say.

"Nice? He looks like trouble, A." Jake looked concerned, so I laughed it off.

"You'

"You're just jealous!" I teased, moving the conversation on, even as I couldn't stop thinking about how his chuckle had sent thrills across my body.

He does look like trouble.

***

I glanced at my phone again, the neon numbers blinking at me. Caden should have been meeting me, well…now. From my position, huddled in the front seat of my car, I could see most of the street. I don't know why I felt so shifty; we were simply going to look at the warehouse and see if there were any clues. Caden thought we were looking for clues about Eli, but I was looking for intel on GAI. If Eli had written that address down it was important. I was willing to bet that it had something to do with that email. I checked my phone again.

21:31.

Even though I knew I was being harsh, I couldn't help but be annoyed. Caden had tracked me down to the Coffee Cup to give me a piece of paper and his number and then couldn't even be bothered to be on time.

As I was grumbling to myself, a figure walked past my wing mirror, causing the grumbling to dry up in my throat. A couple of seconds later the figure appeared by my door and leant down. With a sigh of relief, I realised it was Caden in a black hoodie. He looked like he was about to rob a bank. Darting a glance at my own all-black outfit, I realised I didn't look much different. The door opening sounded so much harsher in the darkness. As he folded himself into the passenger seat, he shot me a grin that I didn't return.

"Hey. What's up?" he asked, closing the door softly. I huffed and glared at him,

"You're late." He pushed his hood down from his face, revealing his long, dark hair no longer caught up in the loose bun from earlier. I watched the frown cross his face as he looked at the dashboard clock.

"Yeah, by two minutes. Are you seriously mad about that?"

Why am I mad?

I didn't know what I was mad about, I just needed to be mad at him. Turning away instead of answering, I shoved the key in the ignition and started the car. I'd already got the route ready on my phone, so I didn't need to talk and right now I was thankful for that. We sat in silence as I pulled away from the curb and started down the road. The streets were empty at this time, even though it was still a little light; there wasn't exactly a bustling nightlife scene. As we drove along, curtains twitched and shadows graced the windows.

Probably the local neighbourhood watch outraged that someone dared to drive down the street.

The atmosphere in the car was about as welcoming as the houses outside. Part of me felt bad for snapping at Caden for being two minutes late; he didn't deserve it. But I was trying very hard to fight against the fact that I was beginning to like him, in case this all turned out to be nothing but another dead end. I was sure once the adventure disappeared, so would he. We passed the last of the houses, pulling out onto the main road which was thankfully pretty empty. I saw two cars go the other way, their headlights momentarily blinding me before fading into the shadows and leaving us alone in our bubble. Clearly it was a good night for sneaking around.

The silence stretched on as Caden resolutely stared out of the window. I was itching to say something but instead I turned on the radio. The car was filled with an awful screeching sound, causing us both to jump, followed by static. My hand scrabbled as I frantically tried to turn it off. Eventually, Caden reached over and pressed the button, returning us to our bubble of solitude. I half smiled, hands back on the steering wheel, checking the sat nav.

"Your destination is ahead on the right," The tinny voice of the sat nav filled the heavy silence.

It only took another couple of minutes and we were pulling into the industrial estate. Caden sat up from his slouch, looking around at the buildings we passed. I, on the other hand, was scanning for any witnesses. Luckily, I didn't see anyone as we reached the building we needed and seconds later I had turned off the car, plunging us into dreary darkness. Neither me or Caden moved, the only sound our breathing. I could feel the tension building up as he stewed.

This whole night will be a bust if neither of you talk to each other. Get it together, Ari.

Unbuckling my seatbelt, I turned to face him with my leg tucked underneath me, one knee leaning on the handbrake. Even in the low light I saw his eyes flick over to me and then back to the dash.

"I'm sorry." Now that I'd said it, I couldn't take it back. There was another moment of charged silence, the air in the car seeming to move like molasses before his shoulders relaxed.

"It's okay." We didn't say anything else. I grabbed my backpack from the back seat and opened the car door, careful to shut it quietly. Everything seemed to echo in the open space, even footsteps. As Caden walked around the car to meet me, his steps ricocheted off the concrete. Together we slunk towards the building. From the outside it looked pretty unremarkable, a large grey cube with metal panelled siding and no windows. As we approached, I pulled my torch out of my backpack to shine on the door. The doors were also metal, secured with a chain and padlock which didn't seem particularly high tech.

Maybe this is just another empty warehouse. It doesn't seem like a high-tech underground research facility.

Caden stopped at the door, fumbling with something in his pocket while I started walking around the rest of the building, looking for any kind of clue as to what was in here. At the back of the building, looking out onto fields, a bunch of material had been dumped. Kicking at it with my feet, I identified some chicken wire and a bunch of old padlocks. Nothing was branded and nothing gave any indication that Eli or GAI had ever been here. Suddenly, the air was shattered by a loud clang followed by a clattering of metal. I stilled, the sound echoin across the space, waiting for the ensuing cars or people to come running. The rest of the world stayed silent. After a couple of breaths, I made my way to the front of the building. Caden was nowhere to be seen. I jogged forward, ready to start yelling his name when I saw the padlock and chain in a heap on the floor. The front doors were slightly ajar and inside I could see a flickering light. Turning off the torch I slipped through the doors, my backpack dangling by my waist so it didn't get caught. As soon as I was through, a hand shot out and grabbed my wrist.

"Shiii...!"

"Shhh. You wanna get us caught?" Caden's voice came from the darkness, the eerie space around us making it all the more creepy. I prayed my heart would stay in my chest as I answered,

"You're the one who broke into a building!" I snapped, making sure to keep my voice low. Caden released my wrist and stepped forward, coming into the staccato of the flickering light. Shadows danced across his face, slightly green hued as he grinned at me. In this light even his All-American smile looked creepy, stretched by the sporadic flashes from the bulb.

"You wanted to know what was in here didn't you? Now you can." I tried to tell myself I should walk out and leave the building, and Caden, behind but I couldn't do it. Now that we were in, the desire to look around was growing.

"How did you even get in?" I hissed. He held up a contorted paperclip and winked.

I don't want to know how he learnt that.

Instead of interrogating Caden on his previous lockpicking antics, I walked forwards. Scuttling accompanied my footsteps, most likely rats, and

I prayed they wouldn't scuttle over my feet. I was balanced on a razor's edge with my nerves as it was. The room seemed mostly full of old, damp cardboard boxes littered on metal tables. At the far end of the room was, weirdly, another room erected from plywood boards. I could hear Caden picking his way across the floor behind me, catching his feet every so often on some of the metal wiring that had been strewn across the floor. The flicking light was at the far end of the building, a single bulb that was clinging on to life, illuminating tiny blasts of the room every couple of seconds. Everything had a damp feel to it, a musty smell, the darkness more cloying than the star-guarded air outside. I did not like it. But there had to be something in here. I was sure of it now. Caden appeared by my shoulder as I paused to look at the smaller room; he tapped my arm and I turned to face him.

"I'll start looking in the boxes. You take that room." I nodded and made my way to the rectangle in the plywood that appeared to be a door. There was no padlock on this one but there also wasn't a handle. I shoved my shoulder against it and felt the wood give way a little. On the next shove, I heard a splintering sound.

I'm gonna go crashing through this door, I can see it. I hope there's not a rats' nest or something the other side.

Taking a deep breath, I shoved the door a final

time and felt it completely give way, sending me tumbling through. There was no light whatsoever managing to filter into this room and the smell had only increased. Wrinkling my nose, I shone the torch around and suppressed a whimper. Most of the room was taken up by another metal table, but this one seemed to be stained a rusted colour that looked decidedly like dried blood. With a hand over my mouth, I edged forward, careful to avoid touching the table itself. Up close I could see the blood splatters, now completely oxidised. Next to the metal table was a stand with a tray. As I looked at the tray, my breath caught in my throat. On it sat a handful of needles, the exact same as the one that was found in Eli's room.

Please don't let that be his blood.

My stomach churned at the thought. Moving around the stand, I started towards the back of the room, torchlight shaking as I tried not to look at the table again. The very back of the room contained a small workbench, again made from metal. On it was a stack of papers and something covered in black material. I wedged the torch into a gap between some of the equipment so it was shining on the papers and pulled some gloves out of my pocket.

It would be just my luck that I'd pick up something nasty.

The top paper was the same article I'd found in Eli's notebook, talking about the HFEA. I moved that one aside and rifled through the rest of the stack; a lot of them were similar articles, focussing on the use of rats in embryo research. I paused at the last piece of paper, eyes straining to make out the words. Unlike the other papers, all of which seemed to be printed off articles, this one looked handwritten; or at least a photocopy of something handwritten. The only words I could make out from the scrawled writing were 'Test Subject 1' and 'not viable'; the rest was illegible, the scrawl more like a bunch of wiggly lines. Going to return it to the pile, I passed over the beam of the torch, one word standing out on the back of the last paper. Turning it over, I couldn't help the small grin that tugged at my lips.

'Genetics Advancement Institute' was written across the top of the page, along with the address of this industrial estate. It looked like headed paper of some kind, although most of the header had faded. I tried to make out the rest but it was too degraded.

But, this proves GAI were connected to Eli's disappearance. Maybe I should take this as evidence... Although, if anyone comes back to check on this place and sees anything out of place, they might go too far underground for me to find again.

I replaced it at the bottom of the stack, making

sure they were as neatly lined up as they had been when I came in. The only other thing left unturned in the room was the covered box to my right. I almost left it, since I'd at least gotten something useful already but the niggling voice in the back of my head told me it could have been important. As soon as I moved a corner of the fabric covering it, an intense, musty smell wafted up. There was an undertone of something mixed in, almost sweet but still *wrong* somehow. I couldn't quite make it out. Before I changed my mind, I flicked the fabric away from the box and realised it wasn't a box at all.

It was a cage.

The bottom was covered in sawdust and there was a food bowl and water bottle tucked in the corner. Whatever had been in here had clearly been a rodent of some kind, judging by the droppings… and the smell. As I went to cover the cage back up, something tucked in the far back corner caught my eye. I was trying to make it out when the realisation hit me.

Don't throw up. Do not throw up in here.

A dead rat was curled in the back corner, starting to decay, finally putting a name to that sweet-but-off smell. But it wasn't completely normal. Even from outside the cage, I could see that the tail wasn't bare skin as normal rats' tails were but covered in scales and bony feathers stuck from the very end. It didn't take much to come to the conclusion that the rat had been used for some kind of experiment. My mouth twisted in sympathy and I covered the cage back up. I'd seen enough. Quickly, I made my way back around the table and out into the main room. I could see Caden's shadow moving over by the furthest wall, so I began to make my way over there. I didn't know how much to tell him. I couldn't tell him about GAI, not when I barely knew about them or what they meant. I was still chewing my lip as I walked within reach of him. He paused as he heard my footsteps, his hands rifling through one of the cardboard boxes. I hoped he had gloves on.

"Did you find anything?" he whispered, even though we were the only ones in here. I got it though; I didn't want to talk loudly. I felt like we were being watched.

"Kind of." *How much should I tell him?* "I found needles that were exactly the same as the one the police found in Eli's room." I trailed off, letting him take that in. His shoulders tightened and he paused for a moment before he turned around and pulled me in for a hug. My brain short-circuited briefly before I hugged him back. When he pulled away, I couldn't see his face.

"I'm sorry, Ari." Hearing him call me Ari was a bit of a punch in the gut. Eli was the only person who had called me Ari. "I know it must be hard finding all of this." It wasn't great but I'd been searching for so long, part of me was actually happy to find something, even if it was a metal table covered in blood and a deformed rat. Not that Caden needed to know about that. I mumbled something non-committal, thankful that most of my face would be in darkness then cleared my throat,

"Did you find anything?" Looking around at the reams of cardboard boxes, I was hopeful he had found at least one more piece of the puzzle.

"I found a lot of medical equipment, like the vacuum-packed sterile stuff, and some really old food."

Oh.

"Oh. Well at least I found the needle, that means we're on the right track." He murmured in agreement and closed the cardboard box he'd been looking through. "Let's get out of here. I don't think we're going to find much else." I tugged on his sleeve and we started walking towards the door. Checking my phone, I was relieved to see we'd only been here for an hour which meant we could get back and I could get in the house before my parents asked any questions. Outside, the sky was completely dark, the moon barely a slither. Caden shut the doors and locked the building back up, the padlock clicking easily into place like we'd never been here. As I waited for him, I looked out over the fields that surrounded the industrial estate. Without the light pollution from the streets, the stars were really easy to see. Looking up at them felt more peaceful than I'd been in years. I didn't even realise that Caden had walked up next to me until he touched my arm. I jumped, flashing him a quick smile but I couldn't drag my eyes away from the stars.

"Eli used to point out all the stars to me when we were little. We'd go into the garden after we thought our parents had gone to sleep and sit on the grass and then make shapes out of the stars. I'm pretty sure my parents knew but they never stopped us." I hugged my arms to my chest at the memory, surprised when Caden's arm came around me as well.

"My little brother loved learning all the constellations. He was so good at it." I stilled, not wanting to say anything and interrupt him. I didn't know anything about Caden's personal life and I didn't want him to clam up now. "He even won a prize for a model he made of them. I was never that smart." His voice was so soft and wistful, and I didn't need to see his face to know he was smiling. He hugged my shoulders once before dropping his arm and walking towards my car. I waited a few seconds before I followed him, hating how my shoulders felt cold now.

Do I feel like this because I trust him or because I

like him?

He'd risked his life for me twice and now he'd talked to me about his family. Plus, the more I was around him, the more I could see why he and Eli got on. I told myself I liked Caden because he reminded me of Eli but as he made another joke about the size of my car, I wondered if maybe I liked him for himself.

Chapter 5

I spent the weekend researching everything I could find about GAI. They were difficult to pin down, with nowhere listing an address or any credible information really. If it hadn't been for Eli's notebook, I would never have found the industrial estate. That, it seemed, was the only helpful thing in the notebooks though. I'd leafed through each one, back to front, and so far, all I'd concluded was that Eli really needed to work on his penmanship. It was almost as bad as the writing I'd found in GAI's old building. I sat back in my desk chair, spinning it around as I tried to figure out my next move. I couldn't go back to the building, not this soon, but as it was, I didn't have any more leads. I'd even researched experimentation on rats but that had brought me back in a full circle to the articles in Eli's journal talking about embryo and stem cell research. There was nothing about rats with scales and feathers, although I doubt there would have been. From what I'd read, even the embryo research was strictly monitored by multiple agencies because of moral concerns raised by the public, so rats that had been modified to have scales would definitely have come under fire.

I glanced at my phone again as I spun around but the screen was still black. Caden hadn't contacted me since I dropped him off at the campus over three days ago. Given the possibly illegal activities and the sharing of personal memories, I had *at least* expected a text. Maybe even a phone call. But no, I'd had zilch. He'd been quiet on the way back in the car, playing with the sleeve of his hoodie and only talking when I directly asked a question. It was almost like telling me about his brother had made him take a giant step in the other direction. Weirdly, I felt the exact opposite; I'd had a lot of time to think whilst he hadn't been texting me and everything he'd done had shown that I could trust him. I was bursting to tell him the other stuff I'd found in the building, but first I needed to tell him everything I hadn't said originally and for that, I needed to talk to him. I stopped spinning around on the chair with a jerk, staring at my phone. Maybe if I concentrated enough… the screen lit up with a buzz and I leapt towards it only to slump backwards when I realised it was just a text from Becca. She was talking to me again, but I knew she was worried I was getting too wrapped up in looking for Eli. Obviously, she didn't know the half of what I'd done but she could tell I was doing more than just sifting through my own memories.

Throwing my phone back on the desk, I stood up, stretching. I had barely stood up today and my muscles were letting me know. Even my desk chair had taken on a butt-shaped imprint. Padding across my carpet, I grabbed a clean top out of my wardrobe and wandered to the bathroom, wanting to feel at least a little bit refreshed even if I had no plans to leave my room for the rest of the day. I caught sight of my own face in the bathroom mirror as I splashed water on my arms and neck. Did I look like Eli? I could kind of see the sibling resemblance between us but where he was harsh, I was soft. He had obvious cheekbones and a strong jaw, and my face was rounded with a button nose. His hair had always been short, a messy halo around his head in a sunlight-dappled blonde whereas my hair fell in dark waves to my chest. He was tall, I was short, he was toned, I was curvy. The only thing that we had exactly the same were our eyes, both a sea green colour. The longer it was, the harder it got to remember him, but I knew his eyes. He used to tell me that we could talk to each other in our minds because of our eyes and, up until I went to secondary school, I believed him. Shaking away the memory and wiping the water off my arms, I pulled my old t-shirt off and put the clean one on before walking back to my room. The t-shirt went in the laundry basket and a purple pillow from my bed joined the campout at the desk (to save my butt and the chair). Sinking back into the chair, I cast a quick glance at my phone and paused when I saw the little light flashing that told me I had a message.

It's probably just another text from Becca.

As likely as that was, curiosity got the better of me and I unlocked the screen. There was another message from Becca but underneath that, three tiny letters, was a message from Caden.

Hey.

Hey. That was it?! I'd waited three days for a hey. Grumbling to myself, I typed the same thing back and pressed send, forcing myself to turn back to my computer screen, trying to ignore the sudden spike in my heart rate. Only seconds later my phone buzzed again and I pounced on it.

Did you want to come over? I might have found something more about Eli.

I tried to type slowly but my fingers flew across the keys. I was only replying because I wanted whatever he had on Eli. Nothing else. No awkward shoulder hugs. Nope.

A couple of seconds later I was shoving my laptop in my bag and walking out my door, glad that I'd at least changed my shirt. The drive over to the university campus seemed to take an age as I caught, it seemed, every red light in existence. I'd almost chewed through my lip by the time I parked and started the walk to Block 18. Caden was sat on the bench I'd been sat on the first time we'd met, and he smiled when he saw me, getting up.

"Hey." There was that word again. I was beginning to hate it.

"Hi..." We walked the rest of the way to his block together in awkward silence. It seemed strange that I'd only walked up these stairs for the first time a little over a week ago. When we reached his room, I sat on his desk chair instead of Eli's bed. I don't know why. He lounged on his bed again and the room descended into an awkward silence. I looked at my lap.

Say something. Anything. This is so awkward.

Eventually Caden cleared his throat and my eyes snapped up to meet his so fast I almost gave myself whiplash.

"So, I found something this weekend. I was going through Eli's side of the room, in case the police missed anything, and I found this." He held out another folded sheet of paper. I took it, holding the paper gingerly before unfolding it. My eyes widened at the words imprinted across the paper.

'Genetics Advancement Institute'

It's the same as the paper I found in the warehouse.

This was more than just a piece of headed paper though; I started reading:

Dear Elliott Farrow,

My name is Amelie Starling and I am the Head of Administration at the Genetics Advancement Institute. We are a relatively small company and, due to the nature of our research, have kept ourselves out of the public eye. However, we have recently been made aware of your research and we would like to discuss it with you. We are very interested in the hypothesis you have been assembling and would like to offer you a place to advance your study with us here at GAI. Please find attached some more information about our company and the place we are offering you. We hope to hear from you soon.

Yours Sincerely,

Amelie Starling

I put the piece of paper down on Caden's desk, my mind racing. GAI had offered Eli a place at their company. Had he said no? Is that why they'd kidnapped him? I was willing to bet that the email they'd sent was another attempt to get him to respond. That's probably why he was so cagey about it, especially if he wasn't sure what to do about it. I could see Caden watching me and I knew my face had probably revealed too much,

"Did you read it?" I asked him in a small voice. He nodded curtly,

"I was shocked to learn of something called the Genetics Advancement Institute even existing but judging by your lack of confusion, I don't think I can say the same for you." I looked away, aware that I appeared even more guilty but in reality, I was. I hadn't told him.

"I'm sorry. I'd only just met you, I didn't know if I could trust you with everything that I'd found out." His mouth tightened and I felt even worse, "I know that I can trust you now." He let out a snort,

"Oh, so it only took me risking my life twice to convince you. I'm so glad." The words dripped with sarcasm and I felt my heart drop a little. I took a breath and tried again,

"Look, Caden, I'm really sorry. I'd made up my mind to tell you today but then you showed me that before I could. I know it will be difficult to believe me now, but I promise you, I was going to tell you what I know. Please don't hate me." *I hated me.*

Why do I care what Eli's roommate thinks of me? I shouldn't... And, when did I stop thinking of Caden as Eli's roommate?

He stared at me for a couple more seconds, arms crossed but then his face softened, and a hint of a smile tugged at the corner of his mouth.

"Weirdly, I do believe you were going to tell me." He stood up, crowding the space in front of me. I pushed myself up out of the chair, my head only reaching his shoulders, wary of what was coming next.

Before I could say anything else, he was hugging me, my face pressed against the soft cotton of his shirt. I breathed in, enjoying the smell of his clothes. He smelt like the woodland after heavy rain. I relaxed into the hug, my arms linking around his waist, trying to ignore the thrill that ran through my veins as my arm lifted his t-shirt and brushed against the warm skin of his hip.

After what felt like no time at all, Caden pulled back, snapping my pine-trees-and-hormones haze. Reluctantly, I craned my head up, immediately wishing I hadn't. His eyes bored into mine with an intensity that made every part of me blush. "I can see now why Eli was so protective of you. You're very easy to like." He murmured, voice husky as he stared down at me, a half-smile pulling one side of his mouth up. My brain wouldn't let my mouth form words, the racing of my heart competing with the racing of thoughts that threatened to overwhelm me.

The room around us seemed to suspend in time as I tried to regain control of my own body and form some kind of comment. I didn't get chance. Something changed in his eyes, something like hunger. Less than a breath later, his lips were on mine, soft and teasing. I kissed him back, dimly wondering at the back of my mind how I had ended up in this situation. I couldn't really concentrate on that right now, not when he tasted of vanilla and cinnamon and when the feel of his mouth against mine was sending a fever dream of fireworks through my blood. Every part of me felt as if it was about to burst into flames and I didn't care. I wanted to, if it meant this moment could continue.

Far too soon, he stepped backwards, breaking the kiss and I blinked after him, my brain apparently having short-circuited. His grin threatened to split his face in two, eyes creasing at the corners, the grey sparkling like a winter ocean.

Okay, now is the part where you say something. Literally anything. Even blinking would be preferable to staring at him like a rabbit in the headlights. Come ON.

He chuckled, the sound breaking the heavy silence, and flopped back down on his bed. I (finally) regained control of my own body and forced myself to sit back in the desk chair, hoping my face wasn't as red as it felt. I think it probably was. I could tell he was enjoying this way too much, running a hand through his hair, the muscles in his forearm jumping as he did so.

The arms that were around you just a minute ago... Focus Ari.

Shutting the flytrap my mouth had become and pulling my brain out of the gutter it had fallen into, I shifted my attention back towards the letter on the desk and slowly the shock from the kiss wore away, replaced now by excitement from this new information.

"So..." his voice, still a little husky before he

cleared his throat, sent a tingle across my arms, "Are you gonna fill me in?" I nodded, psyching myself up.

"A few days ago, I had some flashbacks to memories with Eli. In one of those memories, Eli received an email from GAI." Caden's eyebrows rose but he didn't interrupt, "He was really cagey about it and wouldn't let me see the rest of the email. When I tried, he deleted the email entirely. That was only a couple of months before he disappeared, and I figured that email wouldn't be the first piece of correspondence he'd had. That's why I contacted you because the most likely place he would have received it would have been at uni and he would have probably waited until he was in his room to open it-"

"So, it made sense that I might have heard or seen something…" Caden finished. I nodded and continued,

"Obviously you hadn't but when you mentioned his notebooks, I really hoped they might say something and then you found that address. Whilst we were there… whilst we were there, I found more than just needles I also found a stack of papers with articles on embryo's and stem cell research, the same stuff as in Eli's journal and one of the papers was on the same GAI headed paper. There was also…" I shuddered at the memory, "a dead rat in a cage in that room. It had scales and feathers, like it had been experimented on, and there was a lot of dried blood." Caden shuddered as I described the room. "I don't know what it means, or if there is anything that can lead us to Eli, but that's what I found and that's what I didn't tell you. I am really sorry." I smiled hopefully at him, relieved when he offered a tentative smile in return, although he looked a little pale.

"I can understand why you didn't tell me, I was just a bit hurt, I guess. I'd kind of…" as he trailed off, my thumping heart filled the silence. "Well, I like you Ari and I thought you felt the same way but when I found out you kept that from me, I thought you thought of me as just a means to an end. My fragile masculinity was a tad dented." I laughed, enjoying the warm feeling that was spreading across my body. Given the kiss, and my reaction to it, I couldn't exactly pretend I didn't like him. We grinned at each other like idiots for a few more seconds, the room lapsing into a comfortable silence. Then, something flitted across Caden's face and he frowned, looking behind me to the beige of Eli's side of the room.

"What?" Hopefully this wasn't where he told me he could see dead people. If that was the case, I was out of here. Good kiss or not. He considered me for a couple of seconds,

"What do we do now? I mean, we know that GAI are the key but, unless you're keeping more intel from me," he winked, "We don't have any idea where they are or what to do next to find Eli."

I'd been thinking the same thing the entire weekend.

"The only thing I can think of is going back to the building in the industrial estate and seeing if there's any more information there about where they might have moved their lab to? We could go tonight." I picked at the fading upholstery of the desk chair, pulling the now-grey threading as I waited for him to answer.

"Sure." Risking a glance, I was relieved to see him smiling, "I'll meet you at the Coffee Cup this time? That way it won't look weird that you drive off with a strange man two nights in a row. I'm sure the curtain-twitchers are still abuzz with gossip from the last time." So, he'd noticed. The joys of living in a neighbourhood where everyone knew everyone.

"Are you gonna be okay dealing with my *tin can* of a car?"

"I'll have to manage. After all the owner of the tin can is very pretty, so that's a bonus." He followed up, with another contagious grin and a wink. I could feel the blush that I'd just managed to get under control creeping back up my neck and my ears, so I pulled my hair in front of my face, standing abruptly before I embarrassed myself any further. The bed sheets rustled as Caden stood up but I kept my focus on the door.

"Okay, so I'll see you tonight? About 8?" The words rushed out of my mouth, garbled as I attempted to leave before I made any more of a fool of myself.

"Yeah sure-" I slipped out of the door before he could flash me another grin. I was definitely feeling embarrassed. It was like my brain no longer knew how to act around him now that I'd decided to trust him.

The door shut behind me and I breathed a sigh of relief, my shoulders relaxing. Shifting my backpack so it was more comfortable on my shoulders, I started making my way down the stairs, feet thudding on the worn-out carpet.

I should probably reply to Becca.

My hand went to my pocket to grab my phone, only to be met with the coarse material of my jeans. As realisation dawned, I let out a groan and spun around on the stairs.

Right. Act normal. Or less weird. Okay.

Back outside of Caden's room, I stopped. His voice filtered through the door, talking to someone so I paused, hand falling back down to my side. Content to wait until he was done, I leant against the wall and tried not to listen until I heard my name come up. My stomach filled with butterflies.

"No, I know this wasn't the plan but it's how it's happened. Yes, I'm being careful. No, I don't think she knows." Knows what? Who was he talking to? *"She didn't even question the letter and the address. She has no idea I planted them. Don't worry, she won't be finding Eli any time soon."*

The worn-out carpet beneath my feet was suddenly a lot closer. I blinked at the floor, realising my legs had given out. My stomach felt like a chunk of lead, all the butterflies crushed into dust and the heat in my face swept away as numbness hit. It didn't take much to put the pieces together and realise what he was talking about.

Caden *worked* for GAI.

"I'm not going to be able to get out as early as I thought though. Yeah. I know. Look, I'll do my best here and wrap it up in time to meet you guys in Kincraig." Kincraig? I filed that away. Right now, I had bigger problems. Like the anger that was coiling in my chest; I tried to ignore it, tried to shut off the emotions that pressed in from all sides. I could use this information to my advantage. Unbidden, the kiss from only minutes before flashed into my head, the words he'd whispered.

That bastard.

Yeah, okay, I couldn't ignore all the anger. I was *pissed.* He'd manipulated me into thinking

I could trust him; worse he'd made me actually *like* him. The kiss had likely been a way to seal the deal; take advantage of the desperate girl with the missing brother that he...that he probably had something to do with. I suppressed a scream as my anger spiked, the coils curling deep and needling into my blood. I couldn't believe I'd let myself fall for it; Jake had said he looked like trouble and he'd been more right than he realised.

My nails dug into my palms, indenting half-moons as I scrambled for a solution. At the moment, he was leaking information to them, so anything else I had, any other intel had to be kept to myself. I wasn't even sure if what I'd seen at the industrial estate was real. He'd looked shocked but he was clearly a good actor. First things first, I had to get my phone back. I definitely didn't want to leave him alone with it now. What if he'd already bugged it?

The room behind the door was silent again, phone call now finished so I took a deep breath, pasted a smile on my face, tamped down the rage and stabbing hurt and knocked. There was surprised shuffling from behind the door and seconds later his head poked out. A frown crossed his features as he realised who it was, and I could almost see him wondering if I'd heard, but he quickly returned my smile and stepped back.

"Back for more?" he teased. I raised an eyebrow

at him.

You have no idea.

"Missing my phone. Figured I must have left it on the desk. Is it there?" My voice was even, unwavering, even though I felt like screaming at him and I was proud of myself for that. Luckily it didn't seem like he suspected I'd heard him.

Probably because any sane person would be screaming at him. Or running in the opposite direction.

The door swung open as he wandered over to his desk and returned seconds later with my phone in his hand. I held out my palm for it, resisting the urge to flinch as our hands touched. It's amazing what back-stabbing betrayal can do for... whatever we had been doing. His fingers stayed touching mine for a couple of seconds as he flashed me another grin and I made myself grin back, gritting my teeth against a wave of nausea. In my mind I was already down the stairs and out the door.

"I'll see you tonight." The wink that followed, that minutes before would have probably caused another blush, now made my skin crawl. Nodding, I grabbed my phone and turned on my heel, escaping to the comfort of the white-painted hallway. Even the stairs seemed appealing, the grey-specked carpet a welcome sight as I rounded the corner. By the time I'd trekked across campus, the groups of people fading into the background, and made it back to my car, I was close to crying. It wasn't because I was sad; I was hurt, yeah. I'd given my first kiss, my first proper feelings to an arsehole. But more than the hurt, I was fuming mad, but short of turning back and punching him, I couldn't do much else.

Or can I?

On the phone he'd mentioned joining them in Kincraig. I didn't know exactly where that was, but I could find out. If I prevented that, that would no doubt cause some issues. I wasn't going to kill him, obviously, but detaining by imprisonment seemed like a good way to go. Revenge for the broken hearted and all that. A smile began to spread across my face as a plan formed in my head. I had the advantage of surprise; he had no idea I knew he was working for GAI. Plus, we were heading to an abandoned industrial estate building. I'd need to stop at B&Q. With a chuckle, I reversed out of the parking space and headed back towards town.

Revenge is a bitch.

***

My fingers tapped on the sticky table top of my corner booth at Coffee Cup, eyes fixed on the door. I'd order an iced tea, but it sat, untouched, creating ripples of condensation on the lacquer.

The café wasn't particularly busy but, even so, I'd chosen the seat furthest from the door, backed up against a wall. I guess you could say I wanted to cover my own back now that I knew someone wanted to stick a knife in it.

A couple of minutes before we were due to meet, I saw Caden saunter up the side of the café; he'd ditched the hoodie and gone back to his leather jacket, warm skin standing out against the black material, his strong jaw holding up another one of his cocky grins. I hated that it looked good. I hated that I had a reaction. I hated that he couldn't have just been a decent guy.

He walked in, glancing around the café until his eyes fell on me huddled at the back of the café. I sat up, taking a long gulp of my drink so I could get my rage under control before I talked to him. When he slid into the seat, it took everything in me not kick the chair out from under him. Instead I kept drinking, the sharp bite of the iced tea making my teeth tingle. Caden leant on the table, catching my gaze and I smiled around the straw, biting down. The rest of the café seemed quieter, all my attention now focussed on pretending I didn't hate him. I had no idea how he'd been able to act for so long so easily. This shit was hard.

"Hey." When he spoke, his voice grated in my ears, the previous attraction I'd felt for him stripped away. Have you ever had that? Where a voice feels like grit and needles in your ear drums? Yeah, it's not particularly pleasant. I realised I hadn't replied when he kept talking. "You ready to go?" His hand reached out to touch mine, one calloused finger stroking the back of my hand. I jerked my hand away then realised my mistake as his brow furrowed,

"Sorry. It tickled." That seemed to appease him at least. Standing up, I grabbed my drink and walked towards the door, heels of my boots clacking on the fake wood floors. The scuff of his shoes followed mine. In the pocket of my jacket, my phone vibrated. I knew without looking that it was from Jake. He'd been messaging me near constantly today; it was like he knew I was about to do something pretty stupid that could possibly backfire. I clicked it on to silent, just so Caden couldn't hear the relentless buzzing, and shouldered open the door. Outside, the weather had taken a turn for stormy, a faint mist of rain in the air with the promise of downpours.

Pathetic fallacy at it's finest. My old English teachers would be so proud.

I hoped it would at least hold off until we got to the industrial estate and, for once, I had some luck on my side since it did. As we pulled in to the concreted parking, the first of the storm clouds rolled in overhead, an ever-darkening grey. I heard Caden mutter about getting his jacket wet as we got out and rolled my eyes. The padlock and chain were still in place from the last time, the building looking just as desolate from the outside as I knew it looked within.

"I'm going to check there's no one nearby" I muttered, stalking off towards the back of the building. I honestly wasn't sure whether Caden had actually broken in or if he had a key and I didn't want to find out. It would just rub more salt in the I-was-duped wound. The chicken wire was still bundled in a haphazard ball at the back. I bent down to rifle through, checking any of debris for more information or possible weaponry. I found a cockroach. When I reached the front of the building again, my footsteps sending echoes across the concrete, the doors were open, padlock and chain in a heap on the ground. The same green-hued flickering light sparked between the open doorway. For all I knew that was fake too. I stepped into the room, the damp, stagnant air immediately enveloping me. Caden was waiting just inside the door, hands in his pockets.

"Where did you want to start? I'd suggest we stay away from the dead-rat-and-blood room. I didn't get the chance to check out those boxes last time." He gestured to the far wall that ran up to the edge of the plywood room. I nodded, making my way over to the first table and opening the box. The air inside had apparently turned to dust, billows puffing out into the already cloying atmosphere. Coughing, I fanned it away, smirking when it wafted directly into Caden's face. The box was filled with pads of paper, petri dishes and syringes. I pushed it to the side and grabbed the next one, working through methodically, each box presenting more of the same thing. Even though GAI didn't exactly have a mission statement, it was becoming clear that they had a dispensable income. Caden worked through his boxes as well, the only sound in the room a faint buzzing from the persistent light bulb. Eventually all the boxes had been opened and pushed to the side; I glanced around the rest of the dimly lit room, but there didn't seem to be much more to investigate. I guess that meant it was time to put my plan into action. With a smile, I grabbed Caden's hand, enjoying the look of surprise on his face.

Just wait. You'll be even more surprised in a minute.

In the centre of the room was an old desk chair, the kind with the scratchy fabric. It seemed to be missing all of its wheels, which was even better for me, and no doubt it was slightly mouldy. When we reached it, I pushed Caden back until he sat down, long legs folding, then straddled him. I could only see half his face, the light from the doors letting in a fair amount of moonlight, but it was enough to see that his infuriating smirk was back. I held on to both his wrists as I leant down to kiss him, his stubble rough against my face. The kissing was still, annoyingly, pretty good but this time my mind was clear. I released one hand to reach into my jacket pocket, grabbing one of the cable ties I'd put in there earlier.

The hand I had let go of moved to my waist, fingers resting in the curve of my waist as he deepened the kiss. I tried not to smile. I braced my free hand behind his head, cable tie curled tightly in my fist until I was sure he was completely distracted. I took my time, moving my kisses down his neck, so my torso was in line with his hips, and when he tilted his head back to let out a little moan, I wrapped the cable tie around one wrist and the arm of the chair, pulling it tight. His head instantly whipped up, hair flying round, the desire replaced by confusion. His momentary pause gave me enough time to tie his other wrist; as I tightened that cable tie, he seemed to realise I wasn't playing, and his entire face changed.

The grey eyes that had once been open and welcoming, clouded to storm-cloud grey until they almost disappeared in the dim light. Anger worked its way across in waves, his lips curling and eyebrows dipping. He began to twist on the chair underneath me, the strength in his legs alone enough to buck me off. I stumbled backwards onto the concrete, satisfied that I'd managed to restrain his arms. If I'd cocked up the cable ties, I'd been pretty sure I wouldn't have had a chance; he would have easily overpowered me and I didn't even want to think about what would have happened then. In the back of my mind, I was aware that this had been a risk. Or, as Jake probably would have called it, a terrible, absolutely stupid idea. But, the first part had worked. I still had to subdue him in order to get away safely. I had one of the syringes I'd found in a box in my other pocket, along with some mild sedatives.

The first couple of weeks after Eli had disappeared, my mother had suffered an understandable breakdown and had ended up being hospitalised. In order to help her and to help us keep her from injuring herself, the hospital had given us a few doses of liquid sedatives, meant to be taken diluted in a glass of water. I figured injecting them into the bloodstream would make them work that bit faster. As I pulled the syringe out, Caden started yelling,

"What the hell are you doing you crazy-" I snorted, interrupting his tirade

"Oh, I'm the crazy one? I'm not the one who helped kidnap their own roommate and then, three years later, tricked his sister so she couldn't find him by trying to sleep with her. I don't think I'm the crazy one in this scenario." He stilled. I could see the cogs turning, the need to find a way out of this situation written all over his face. He knew I knew and that meant he also knew I wasn't planning on letting him get out for a little while at least. Sure enough, that mask of charm fell over him again, the confident smirk spreading across his face. It was, objectively, fascinating to watch but I hated how easily I'd fallen for it.

"Look, I know what I did was wrong, but I did really like you. I was only trying to help Eli-"

"HELP HIM? You fucking kidnapped him you psycho and then covered it up and stayed here in case you needed to cover it up some more. You planted shit so I would play along in your little game. What were you planning to do, kidnap me as well? I imagine you would have if I'd got too close to finding out where GAI had taken him." The charm disappeared with a roll of his eyes.

"I was supposed to lead you to a dead end. Then I could leave. Not before I'd had my fun of course." The words were spat at me, the merciless grin a clear indication of what fun he had had in mind. I began filling up the syringe with the sedative, refusing to respond to his comment. He watched me with barely disguised hatred burning in his eyes. Once the vial was empty, I dropped it on the ground, the glass tinkling as it rolled across the floor, glad for the second time that the chair didn't have wheels. In my rage fuelled haze of planning, I hadn't taken into account how I would get the sedative into him before he managed to spin the chair and kick me but since the chair couldn't easily be moved, I was feeling a bit more confident that this would work.

His eyes followed me and as soon as I went behind his back, he twisted, trying to scrape the chair around. The plastic against the concrete floor was not a nice sound. I waited a couple more seconds, part of me enjoying this a little too much, then grasped the back of his neck and plunged the needle in just to the right of his spinal cord. He jerked, trying to leap away from me but, with his hands tied, he couldn't do much other than squirm. Once the syringe was empty, I let it fall to the floor, the same as the vial. It wasn't that I wasn't worried about him escaping. I knew he would eventually, but by then I would be way ahead of him. I just knew that he wouldn't go to the police when he was working for a company that shouldn't legally exist. He would have a hard time explaining that. Not to mention he broke into an evidence room and this building. We both knew I had a lot of stuff against him. So, I wasn't worried about fingerprints, not really. Within seconds, the sedative had begun to take effect, his head lolling forward, the struggling stopping. I moved back around to the front of him, his lidded glare still resolutely focussed on me; crouching down in front of him, I placed a hand under his chin, tilting his head up. Even his eyes were struggling to stay open now; I only had a couple of seconds.

"Anything you want me to pass on to your coworkers when I find them?" He tried to snap his head back but only succeeded in dropping his chin to his chest. As his eyes closed, I didn't think he would answer but before the sedative claimed him, he muttered,

"You won't find them. They're under lock and key…" the rest of the sentence melted away, his head now completely unable to support its weight. I shrugged, standing up. That would knock him out for a while. I knew he had a phone in his jeans, and it didn't take me long to find it, pocketing it so he couldn't contact anyone when he came to. Another scrap of paper fell out with it; I opened it to find what I guessed to be another red herring he had been planning to plant. I crumpled that up and threw it on the floor; then, because I'm not a complete bitch, I took out a bottle of water and a cereal bar and left them at his feet. Hopefully by the time he came to and got out of the cable ties, I would be a lot further ahead, maybe already with Eli before he could alert them. Satisfied, I made my way out of the building. The rain was hammering down outside, soaking the concrete to a dusky black and in the distance, I could hear claps of thunder. I closed the doors and looped the chain back through the handles, clicking the padlock into place before running over to my car.

Once I'd climbed in, soaked to the skin even though it was only a short run, the reality of what I'd done began to hit me. Part of me, the part that recognised this was a point of no return, debated going back and bringing him with me, hoping he didn't find some way to overpower me and contact GAI. The other part, the part that was vengeful on behalf of her brother and herself, told me he was lucky I didn't do anything worse. I wasn't sure which part of me was right.

Focus. Kincraig.

I took a couple of deep breaths, the rain-damp air clinging to my throat and backed the car out of the carpark.

I'm gonna find you Eli, I promise.

Part Two
Scotland

Chapter 6

There was no time to waste. As soon as I got back, my damp, dusty clothes shoved into a corner of the wardrobe, I opened up my browser. It turned out that figuring out what Kincraig meant wasn't the difficult bit. A quick search revealed that it was a village in the Scottish Highlands about an hour from Inverness. A village was still a vague location and, unfortunately, there was no neon flashing arrow labelled 'GAI Secret HQ'.

I spent an hour looking at satellite imaging, trying to identify where you would stash an underground organisation headquarters. I doubted it would be based in the village pub. Nothing on the imaging filled me with confidence. As far as I could tell, it was a quaint village with a few shops, some pubs and a wildlife park next door. Frustrated, I turned my attention to searching for abandoned buildings in the nearby area or old industrial buildings, but again, there was nothing. I was 99% sure Kincraig was actual intel and not another red herring. Caden hadn't had any idea I was listening to his conversation, so I had to be missing something. Like a really big something.

Grabbing a notepad and paper, I decided to start over. Whenever I'd had a big school project, Eli had always told me to start by looking at the big picture, then narrowing it down until you figured it out. I had spent a lot of time stressing about essays because I would always get bogged down in the details; most of the time Eli would find me at 3am, banging my head on the kitchen table and would have to lead me gently to my bed before telling me he would help me with it in the morning. He always did. So that, Eli's logic, was my best bet.

I had two big pictures; GAI and Scotland. The company and the only location I had to go by. I started first with GAI; they were ostracised, funded by a billionaire and hadn't been heard from publicly since 2016. Some of their research included animals, stem cell research and embryos. I sat and stared at the paper for ten minutes, trying to find something in what I knew about GAI to spark some inspiration.

Nothing.

Sighing, I turned onto a new page and wrote Scotland.

Think bigger picture. What is special about Scotland, particularly the Scottish Highlands, that would make it useful to GAI? It's remote, that's for sure. Not easily accessible in the winter months. Lots of free roaming wildlife. Lochs, mountains... wait.

I thought back to what Caden had said before he fell unconscious, something about GAI being 'under lock and key'. Given how cocky he was it would make sense that he would try and say something cryptic. His clear lack of faith regarding my intelligence meant he probably expected I would have taken lock and key to mean a physical lock and key, but it could have been a homonym. Loch would have more relevance to Scotland. I feverishly began to search for Lochs near Kincraig, my fingers flying over the keyboard, the prospect of getting one step closer to GAI spiking excitement through me. Unsurprisingly, that excitement fast came to a close when I realised just how many Loch's were near Kincraig. If you went as far as Inverness, even more.

This was hopeless-

"It's never hopeless Ari!" Eli laughed at me from the other side of the kitchen table, pages of notes spread around us. I glared at him from behind the curtain of hair I'd pulled over my face. The rest of the house was dark, the clock on the oven blinking neon grin numbers at us. It was 3am. I had less than 6 hours to get this finished and I had nothing.

"Sometimes things are hopeless Eli. I should just accept it. This essay is doomed!" I rested my head on the kitchen table, back in the same position Eli had

found me in half an hour ago. There was silence for a moment before I heard the chair scrape against the kitchen floor. Seconds later the notebook was pulled out from under my face, smushing my nose into the wood table. "Hey, ow!" I cried, sitting up and rubbing the end of my nose.

"You're fine Ari, don't be dramatic," *his eyes were skipping over my notes, the same intensity he had when working on a project reflected in his face now. Eli was only ever serious when he was figuring out a problem and right now, the problem was his little sister's inability to plan her essays in time for the deadline. He flipped the page over and grabbed a pen from the table, feverishly scratching at the paper. I already knew I wasn't going to be able to decipher his notes but also knew that Eli would stay with me until the whole essay was written. He'd probably write some of it himself.*

"Okay, so, you've got a start here. But you've focussed on the wrong topic to use as your main point. If you spin this quote this way you can focus on a bigger picture and have a lot more evidence to use. It won't be the most individual essay ever but it'll be decent and easy enough to write…" *I stared down at the paragraph of spiked handwriting that, actually, did make some sense.*

Maybe there was some hope if Eli was involved.

"Ari? You okay with this? You've only got a few hours to write it," *he interrupted my train of thought. I blinked up at him for a brief moment before grinning.*

"*Yeah, this is great Eli. Thank you. I don't know what I'd do half the time without you here to help me. Even if you are annoying the other half of the time,*" *I stuck my tongue out as Eli shot me an easy grin.*

"*Anytime sis. I'd go to the ends of the Earth to help you. Well, maybe to the end of Scotland,*" *he teased.*

"*Hmm, I might go to, say, Yorkshire for you,*" *I shot back, letting out a yell when he flipped my hair back into my face.* "*Oi! What was that for, you idiot?*"

"*You're the one being an idiot. We both know you'd go to the ends of the Earth too,*"

"*Maybe,*" *I relented,* "*But don't tell Mum and Dad. We can't be siblings who actually like each other...*" *Eli laughed and handed me a pen.*

"*Get writing. I'll get us some snacks...*"

I snapped out of the flashback with an ache in my chest, one hand reaching up to brush away a tear that threatened to fall. Even if it was hopeless, I was still going to give it everything I had. If that meant searching every damn loch near Kincraig, then so be it.

I guess I'm going to Scotland.

Maybe, once I was there, I would find something else to help me figure out which Loch had some connection to GAI.

Working quickly, I found the next flights up to Inverness; there was one leaving in the afternoon of the next day, so I booked it, hoping this wasn't going to turn out to be some wild goose chase. The route from Inverness to Kincraig seemed pretty straight forward by car so I added car hire to my flight and closed down the browser. As I was hunting for a suitcase, my phone began to buzz. I clambered over the bed to reach it; the screen lit up with Jake's picture. Guilt twisted my gut as I realised I had never replied to his multiple text messages. I slid to answer and waited for the onslaught. Silence.

"Hi." My voice came out as a whisper, the complete silence throwing me off more than the yelling would have done.

"So, you're alive then." He was not impressed.

As it stands, yes.

"I'm sorry I didn't respond to your messages. I got caught up in work and completely blanked. I'm a terrible friend, I know." Best to start the grovelling early. There was a sigh at the other end of the phone and even though I couldn't see him, I knew he would be pinching his eyebrows together,

"You are. But that's not why I'm called A. I want to know why you drove to an industrial estate with that guy from Coffee Cup and then drove back an hour later *without* him." I froze.

Oh, crap.

"I, um…did you follow me?" Silence. "Jake, why did you follow me?" I could hear him awkwardly clear his throat on the other end of the phone,

"I…we are worried about you. Ever since we went bowling, you've been acting really weird. We thought you'd put this obsession with finding Eli behind you. But then you disappear for almost a week, not even answering our texts and end up spending a load of time with a random guy who, and I feel like we do need to come back to this, you either just abandoned in a warehouse or killed. I say it as a joke, but I'm not that sure anymore." I swallowed, knowing I was going to have to lie left, right and centre to one of my best friends. Best start with something resembling the truth.

"That guy, the one you saw in the Coffee Cup, he's Eli's old university roommate. I contacted him after I remembered some weird stuff Eli had been going through just before he disappeared. He was helping me try to find out more about what happened to him. I know you and Becca want me to let this go, but he is my brother Jake, I can't just forget about him, even if everyone else has." Jake didn't say anything, so I carried on, "We found out some information about a company who had been contacting him before his disappearance and decided to check out an old address they had listed. That's the warehouse. I left Caden at the warehouse because we had an argument and I decided he could find his own way back." I'd just left out the mutated rats, dried blood, kissing, backstabbing and illegal activity. There was a few more seconds of silence as Jake contemplated everything I'd said before a frustrated huff crackled through the phone.

"Okay. Since I'm not a complete idiot, I know you're probably keeping some stuff from me, but I believe the rest of it. I'm sorry that you felt like you couldn't tell us any of this." Relief broke over me, my happiness at not losing my friends momentarily replacing the worry and impending (and probably insane) trip to Scotland.

"It's okay. I'm sorry too. I do have a favour to ask you though…" I paused, aware that this would probably raise more questions. "Could you drive me to the airport tomorrow morning? I have an afternoon flight to Scotland." There was a long hesitation on the other end, followed by another sigh.

"I want to ask why but I don't think I want to know the answer. Yes, I'll drive you, even though you have your own car and are perfectly capable." *Yes, but if Caden got out, he'd probably be looking for my car.* Not that I could tell Jake that. "Just… be careful please A? Whatever you're doing. If you need help, you can actually ask for it." It was strange how happy someone kind of telling me off made me. I quickly told him a time and hung up before he could ask any more questions. An hour and a half in the car with him tomorrow would be enough time for that. Shutting my laptop, I spun the chair back around to face the open suitcase on my bed.

Right. What do I pack to go track down my missing brother in the Scottish Highlands?

***

I was outside my house well before Jake was due to pick me up the next day, suitcase resting by my legs. I'd been nervous all night, barely able to sleep and I'd woken up well before my alarm. My parents thought I was going to stay with Becca, so I'd dodged any further questions. Now I was stood on the cracked pavement, playing with the tassel on my hoodie. I'd ended up packing enough layers to last me probably a whole winter in Scotland, but I'd been so unsure what I needed that I'd panicked. So, in went the Disney-themed wraparound scarf that I hadn't actually worn in years. By the time Jake pulled up I was reconsidering my entire suitcase. I smiled as he got out of the car, grey peacoat looking far too fashionable next to my black jeans and hoodie. He returned my smile, but I could see that he was wary; his hug was half-hearted as he grabbed the handle of my suitcase and threw it into the back of his car. I clambered into the passenger seat, unsure of what to say to him for the first time in my life. If he knew all the shit I'd actually done over the past few days, I doubted he would want to be friends with me at all. Best keep that quiet. The radio was already on, filling the interior of his car with a thumping bass; I didn't know if he'd done that deliberately, he didn't seem all that interested in talking as he pulled away from my house. As soon as we'd joined the main road however, his hand went to the volume dial, turning down the music until the most prominent thing was the road noise.

I looked over at him, waiting for the questions. He didn't look at me, eyes fixed on the road, but I could see the muscle in his jaw working and his hands fidgeting on the steering wheel; all classic signs that he was nervous. The last time I'd seen him this nervous, it was before the Year 11 prom when he told me and Becca that he was bailing on our idea to go as a group because Sadie had asked him to go with her. Back then we'd teased him mercilessly, making kissing faces whenever Sadie had walked in the room. I didn't think that would go over too well now, especially given that I was the one who was bailing. Around us, road signs sped past, telling me the airport was 40 miles away. That's a lot of time for awkward silence. Eventually, just as I was debating tucking and rolling out of the car onto the motorway, he seemed to make a decision,

"Please just tell me you're not in danger, because this feels a lot like a 'trying to escape the country' kind of deal." I could hear the concern in his voice, covered up by a façade of irritation. I knew he would stay mad at me for a bit, even though we'd talked it out on the phone last night. That's just how Jake worked. But underneath he was just worried.

"I'm not in danger." I mean, strictly, that was true. I wasn't at this precise moment in time. Whether I would be in the future wasn't the same question. "I'm also not trying to escape the country." Unless Caden escaped before I found Eli. Then I might need to make a whole new identity and move to Brazil. Hoping none of my thoughts were showing on my face, I shot Jake a smile, relieved when his hands relaxed on the steering wheel and his shoulders dropped. We went through a tunnel, the sporadic lights casting shadows across the car. Any other time I would have pulled faces. As we re-emerged into daylight, I saw his lips curl into a grin,

"So, Caden." I ignored the twang in my stomach, "I know you said he's just Eli's roommate, but I saw the way he looked at you in the Coffee Cup."

Yeah, with eyes full of deceit.

"He was definitely interested in you. Did anything happen? Is that why you had the argument?"

Not quite.

"God you're so nosy. It's hardly like I'm going to say I fell madly in love with him." Just in like. "But, since you have to know, he did kiss me." Again, true. Jake made a suggestive noise as he waggled his eyebrows at me. I rolled my eyes and stuck my tongue out.

"I knew it. You won't kiss me, someone you've known for years with amazing abs and a hilarious sense of humour, but you'll lock lips with someone you've known for like two days because he wears a leather jacket, has an American accent, some gorgeous features and has amazing long hair." Way to rub in my stupidity Jake, thanks. I cringed inside as I relived the stupid (or, more accurately, the many stupid) decisions I'd made over the past two days.

"Hey, don't put yourself down. You have amazing hair too. Plus, we both know you would never have been able to handle me." I poked his side, enjoying his surprised laugh as he shied away from my hand, then reprimanded me for distracting the driver. We lapsed into a comfortable silence, any tension from earlier melting away.

"What did you argue about?" It was a gentle question. He knew me well enough that it must have been something pretty bad.

Well, you see, I found out he was a deceitful bastard working for the company that kidnapped Eli and I just kind of snapped. I tied him up in a chair and drugged him then locked him in the warehouse.

Probably not a good idea to reveal that. It was only when Jake continued talking that I realised I'd been silent for too long.

"You don't have to tell me." Every best friend's guilt-ridden trump card. I pulled a lock of hair out from the ponytail I'd hurriedly tied this morning and began to twirl it around my finger. I had to think of something to tell him that didn't involve illegal activity.

"He...he was seeing someone else at the same time as he kissed me. I flipped out about it, probably overreacted a bit, but he'd been so cocky, and it really pissed me off that he'd hidden it from me. So, I called him a dick and told him he could find his own way back. I feel a bit bad about it now."

No, I don't. He deserved it.

Jake gave me a sympathetic look and began talking about the girl he'd been on a date with last week in an attempt to distract me. It didn't quite work but I appreciated the effort and before I knew it, we were pulling into the drop off area of the airport parking. Jake grabbed my suitcase from the boot as I made my way around the car and pulled me into a hug.

"I meant what I said okay? If you need help, ask for it." I nodded into his shoulder, breathing in the smell of his body spray and ignoring the lump that had appeared in my throat. When he pulled back, I held on for a couple of seconds before swallowing and grabbing my suitcase handle.

"I'll see you soon Jake." He nodded, leaning against the side of his car as I began to walk into the Departures terminal. I waved before I went through the sliding doors, hoping that this didn't all come back to bite me on the arse and that I *would* see him soon. He waved back and got into his car, leaving me to take a deep breath and walk into the throngs of people.

I've always had a weird relationship with airports. On one hand, I loved the fact that they could literally take you anywhere in the world. Reality seemed to warp inside the terminals, with people going to different places, on different journeys, feeling different things, all in one place existing with each other. It was kind of cool. On the other hand, I absolutely hated the crowds, the noise, the overpriced food and the apparent inability of people to follow the simple directions at security. It was the same effect as bank holidays; everyone left their common sense at home with their sun cream.

As I stood in the centre of Departures, it was like its own ecosystem. Families with screaming children rushed past, the mothers glaring at the fathers for forgetting the iPad. Businessmen sauntered in herds, holding coffee cups and wearing permanently disdainful expressions. Stag and hen dos found everything hilarious, attracting the gaze of everyone with their pink fluorescent tutu's and penis boppers. I was always one of the ones who managed to slip through the crowds unnoticed, blending in to the background. Today was no different. I wheeled my suitcase around the groups of people, heading straight for security. I'd made sure I only had a hand luggage sized suitcase, even with the seeming mountain of clothes I'd packed, so I didn't have to wait at the baggage carousel when I got to Inverness. I was in and out quickly, through to duty free and into the departures lounge with more than enough time to spare. It seemed so mundane, queueing up for a Starbucks as I waited to journey up to Scotland to potentially find my brother's kidnapper and my brother, all while possibly being chased by a revenge-bent bastard.

As I began to queue for boarding, my phone buzzed. I pulled it out to see I had a text from Jake.

Let me know when you land x

I smiled at the message as the queue in front of me began to board the plane so I rushed a reply before pocketing my phone, boarding pass at the ready. Luckily, I was one of the first to board, so I secured a space in the overhead locker for my suitcase without having to fight Mum-zillas or disgruntled businessmen in ill-fitting suits and slid into my seat. I was by the window which meant I only had to deal with one person being next to me; they took their time, being amongst the last to board. I kept my gaze pointedly out the window, watching the crew load in the bags and finish fuelling the plane. It was only when my new neighbour elbowed me in the side that I turned. Given the fact that she continued moving around, faded red hair pulled into a bun at the back of her head, it was clear she hadn't even realised she'd elbowed me, more concerned with arranging the tiny pillow just right behind her back. I rolled my eyes, resisting the urge to grumble under my breath and went back to looking out of the window.

Before long we were ready to take off. I leant back in my seat and closed my eyes, breathing in the sharp smell of the airplane. There was a constant background noise of rustling interspersed with the occasional cough. My neighbour seemed to have calmed down, the taxi-ing of the plane stopped her constant fidgeting. I hoped she wasn't a talker. The flight was just over an hour, so as soon as we were in the air, I grabbed the magazine on Inverness that I'd picked up at the airport and began flicking through, trying to figure out which Loch to head to first.

"Oooh, you're going to sae the Lochs!" She was

a talker. Her pastel blue eyes were locked onto mine as she grinned. Pasting on a smile, I nodded, hoping that would be the end of our conversation. It was not. "If yer ask me, Loch Ness is overrated. So many tourists! Aye, an the boats, they're just so overpriced? Payin' over £20 to do a circle, an' you dinnae even stop at Urquhart! Such a rip-off…" As she babbled, I realised she was Scottish.

"Do you live in Inverness?" I asked, interrupting her rambling. She paused, clearly shocked I had responded.

"Och aye, now. Moved there a few years back. Every year I watch tourists flock to Loch Ness in search o' Nessie. Course, they all leave scunnered but still put a wee good review on TripAdvisor. I canny understand it." Maybe my new friend could be helpful.

"So, what Lochs would you suggest visiting? Quieter ones perhaps?" I couldn't imagine GAI would set up shop next to somewhere overflowing with tourists. I couldn't even figure out why they would choose a Loch but my gut told me they had. My neighbour beamed at me, delighted.

"You asked the right person! You could try Loch Morlich or Loch Insh. They'll be a wee bit busy but nowhere near Loch Ness. Or, if you want even quieter maybe Loch an Eilein or Loch A'an.

You won't be able to drive to A'an, you have to walk or ride." I started scribbling down names, stopping her a couple of times to ask about the spelling. The earlier elbowing was forgotten, and we began our descent into Inverness before I even realised the hour had passed. As we got off the plane, I thanked her. The answering smile creased the lines at the edges of her eyes, and she shocked me by giving me a hug before wandering off to the baggage carousel. I walked straight through, and out into the car park to collect my hire car. I laughed as they showed me to it, the familiar badge of the Hyundai i10 greeting me. It wasn't the exact colour of my own car; this one was a metallic blue but at least I knew how to drive it.

With my suitcase in the back, I slid behind the wheel, the reality of the fact that I was actually in Scotland starting to hit me. I pulled out the notepad with the Lochs on, looking each one up on my phone to figure out how far they were from Kincraig. Since that was the only location, I had definite knowledge that GAI were connected to, I still wanted to start there and look around the village and Loch Insh before I tried any of the other Lochs. Typing in the address of a B&B I'd found, I threw my phone onto the seat next to me and drove out of the rental parking lot. Halfway through my journey to Kincraig, it buzzed, and I realised I'd forgotten to tell Jake I'd arrived.

Good start. Well done. Should probably update the only person who knows where you've gone.

All around me were sheer mountain cliffs and trees, the bones of the Cairngorms. Occasionally I'd passed small car parks, so I figured they would have a few more. Sure enough, about five minutes later, as I rounded a corner that opened out into breath-taking mountain views, I saw another parking sign. Pulling in, I grabbed my phone to see that I had 2 messages. The first was from Jake, which I answered quickly before heading back to look at the second message. The sender was listed as 'Unknown'. Puzzled, and trying to figure out if I'd signed up to any dodgy sites recently, I opened it.

I hope you enjoyed your head start. I'll see you soon, bitch. Caden xxx

My stomach dropped to the floor, all the blood rushing to my ears. I let the phone fall onto the seat, the screen still open and glaring at me. I'd only just got to Scotland and Caden was already on my tail. The skies overhead darkened and the first drops of rain hit my windshield, blurring the crisp mountain landscape into a watercolour. I took a couple of deep breaths, trying to slow my heart rate, to force it back down from my ears.

This is bad, this is bad, this is bad.

I shook my head violently, trying to shake away the crippling doubt that was pounding through my body.

It's not that bad. Now, you're just working to a time limit. So, get moving.

Gritting my teeth, I pulled back out onto the main road, the rain hitting the windscreen in a tsunami now. I was only twenty minutes from the first Loch, and I wasn't going to stop now, not after I'd come all the way to Scotland. Caden was an issue for future Ari. The rain continued to buffer the car as I sped into the mountains.

Time to hunt some monsters.

Chapter 7

Myths and legends are funny things. For the sake of either one we'll give up our money and our time, spending hours and days fixated on something that might not even exist and then trekking across land and ocean to find out if it does. I guess that's the appeal of it, the draw; it's that possibility of discovering something magical, something that people tell their children in a fairy-tale but don't actually believe. For some people it becomes an obsession, the need to prove one of these mythical beings exists as strong as blood calling to blood. In reality, it was probably made up by a farmer who had drunk too much homemade beer whilst walking his fields and hallucinated a giant, furry man. Most people who chase legends return home empty-handed, with muddled dreams, barren pockets and the commemorative t-shirt. The lucky few will snap a blurry picture and get their fifteen minutes of fame. It's definitely a fool's game.

I look up from my internal monologue to gaze, or squint rather, through the mist and across the Loch. I couldn't really judge legend chasers when I was sat on a freezing cold, moss-covered rock in the Scottish drizzle staring determinedly at a Loch. Like I had been for the last five hours. For the last two days. Really it wasn't important how long I'd been here.

With a sigh, I opened the notebook I'd been shielding on my lap, covering the battered pages with the edges of my sleeves in an attempt to prevent any water damage. As it was, the ink on the pages had faded to a sea-foam grey, years of wear and tear, of fingers running over the same lines, rubbing away all but the faint indent. It didn't matter though, I knew the words on the pages by heart, having re-read them countless times in the last three years. I traced a finger over a drawing that took up half the page, or at least it did once, fluttering over phantom curved lines and razor points. The drawing was annotated, my brother's handwriting sticking out in spiked peaks even on the faded paper suspended, it seemed, in mid-air. I smiled at the shadows of the doodles sprinkled in the margins, cartoonish animals grinning back at me. He drew them for me, back when I hounded him every second of every day to pay me attention. Instead, he found a way to distract me, drawing tiny landscapes on scrap pieces of paper, punctuated with their animal counterparts. As I turned the page now, a lion bared its teeth in an over-the-top grin. My brother had never been that interested in animals that actually existed, but they provided entertainment for his annoying kid sister, so pretty soon they were cropping up everywhere. Now, most of his drawings in the house had been covered up, an attempt on the part of my parents to forget him and move on but these drawings, the ones in his notebook were mine and mine alone.

A sudden crack of thunder in the distance made me jump, the booming sound ricocheting off the landscape in waves until it broke over my head. I closed the notebook quickly, passing the thin leather cord around the cover once, twice, three times before looping it over the tarnished catch. With a final glance at the Loch in front of me, I pushed myself up from the slimy rock, my knees cracking as I stood, protesting against the movement with a groaning symphony that rivalled even the approaching storm. Grabbing my backpack from the ground next to the rock I hastily shoved the notebook inside, tucking it between a wool hat and my crumpled map. Zipping it up, I threw the pack over my shoulder and began to make my way back up the trail I had all but slipped down earlier. The near constant drizzle, the same drizzle that had been going on for days now, had bogged down the path, watery-brown patches of mud sucking at my boots as I picked my way through the mossy undergrowth. The only good thing about this rain was its ability to get rid of every bug in the vicinity. Much more effective than Deet! Overhead, the thunder clouds continued to roll in, their blackened shadows turning the landscape a grey ombré. With a grimace, I pulled my hood tighter around my face, the toggles dangling at my chin as I stomped through the sludge.

Can your eyes get frostbite? It certainly feels like it.

The drizzle was slowly giving way to rain, fat, heavy droplets interspersed in the mist. You could hear them audibly hit the leaves and branches as their tempo picked up, becoming an overwhelming melody. Another clap of thunder broke the horizon, though this time I felt it before it hit my ears, that low rumble carrying through the soles of my shoes and up my arms in a goosebump wave. There was only time for a few breaths before it rolled again, this time accompanied by blue-white lightning that lit up the trail around me. For a brief moment, tree branches seemed to reach out, arthritic fingers twisted in the eye of the storm. Shadows that had previously crept along the ground, slinking over roots and around rocks now leapt forward, edges sharp against their barked backdrop. I stumbled over an outstretched limb, the paranoia of being alone in the storm shooting up my spine. Taking a breath, I forced my feet to stop, my panicked soles protesting as I leant against the trunk of a tree, closing my eyes against the elements. Almost as quickly as it had come, the lightning faded and the thunder remained silent coaxing the landscape to settle back into its charming, albeit slightly soggy, façade. The heartbeat that had been hammering in my throat relented, calmly sitting back in my chest. For a few seconds there was a peaceful hum, the kind of sound that comes from nothing but things existing.

Then, with the fanfare of a brass band, the thunder and lightning resumed their schedule, the blazing electric light casting a blanket of white fire over the trail. I pushed off from the tree, my feet squelching in the mud. In the surrounding chaos, the edges of the trail seemed to scurry away. My shoes began to slide, the boggy ground too loose to keep any kind of traction. I felt my left leg go out from beneath me, flying to the side as the path became more and more of a river. Instead of the resounding squelch of more mud, my foot met air, the edges of the narrow trail apparently closer than I had realised. With a cry that was quickly gobbled up by the storm, I slid off into the foliage, my ankle rolling as it dragged along the edge of the rocky ground. The vegetation hid a slope that seemed to drag me down, my balance forfeited way back in the mud and I felt my shoulder hit the ground with a thud as I careened down the hill. Each limb was met by a rock or root; new bruises marked under the surface, ready to flourish in a matter of hours. My hands scrabbled, trying to grab hold of anything I could reach but my cold, wet fingers simply washed off of any solid object. Slowly the hill levelled out, the slip n' slide of mud making way for a boggy swamp instead.

I juddered to a stop, now the same colour as the rest of the landscape. I had no idea how far down I'd fallen, or how far off the trail I'd ended up and the raging storm overhead showed no signs of stopping. Gritting my teeth at the pain in my shoulder and my ankle and, well, almost every part of my body, I scrambled up with all the grace of a very muddy new-born giraffe and tried to see through the torrential rain. Ahead of me, trees curved like giants, their branches knotted together to form a sort of canopy; although it may not have been the safest solution for the lightning, I needed to get out of the rain so I could try to get my bearings. There was no way I could do that with a waterfall running down my face.

With shaking footsteps, I made my way over, arms outstretched in a desperate attempt to keep my balance. Once I was under, the rain eased, the leaves catching most of the droplets; I wiped away the torrent of water that was still running from my scalp, distantly hoping none of it was blood and had a better look around. The trees here seemed to stretch on for a while, their trunks thick and old, lining what appeared to be various pathways. Or, at least, they had once been pathways but were now so overgrown with brambles and nettles that they seemed more like vague suggestions of trails. The largest path took me deeper into the forest, most of the path fading into shadows. Glancing back over my shoulder I tried to decide if I could climb back up the hill, but the incline told me I'd probably break my neck trying. Shuffling my backpack, which had somehow clung on during my rapid descent, higher onto my back I turned back to the path in front of me, hoping no lightning decided to hit.

Although the sodden dirt was still squelching underfoot, the soft covering of grass combined with the fact this clearly wasn't a well-trodden path, meant I could walk quickly, still mostly sheltered from the rain. The thunder still rumbled behind me and every so often the trees would spark with lightning but, as I walked further into the canopy of trees, the sounds from the storm dimmed, buffeted by the foliage.

A glint caught my eye, nestled in between the large leaves of a plant at the edge of the path. Stopping, I crouched down so I could see the mystery object in better detail. A curved piece of metal gleamed at me, almost meeting in a perfect circle. Despite being sat in the undergrowth, there was no tarnishing, no rust, only a couple of bits of debris. Pushing the leaves aside I wrestled the metal out from the soil. It was the size of a dinner plate, with holes notched on one side of and pins on the other. I pulled the two ends of the metal together with more force than necessary since I'd expected at least a little resistance, then pushed the closest pin into the closest hole. It slid in smoothly, fastening with a satisfying *click.* I stared at it for another few seconds, trying to equate the lush forest around me with the cold metal in my hands.

It looks like a collar... But what kind of animal would be wearing a collar this size?

I didn't even want to think about it. As I went to drop it back in the grass, something stopped me; for some unknown reason I found myself unzipping my sodden backpack and dropping it in, the weight pulling down the bottom of the bag.

Keep going, you still need to find shelter.

I walked back into the centre of the path and continued through the trees. It was only another minute or two of walking before the wide mouth of a cave appeared on my left, sprouting out of the surrounding foliage without warning. Ahead, the path continued but I couldn't see where it ended or even if it ended at all. The storm was still raging in the distance and fat droplets still made their way through the canopy every now and then. Without any other option, I stepped up to the mouth of the cave. Cool gusts of air hustled at the entrance, but the cave itself was dark and somewhat muggy; I could make out the vague shape and didn't see any creatures who had lost their giant metal collar waiting in there to eat me, so I stepped off of the spongy grass, feet meeting the dusty cave floor. The furthest wall looked the most inviting (and least damp) so I slumped against it, back sliding down the smooth mounds of stone until I felt my butt hit the ground. The thumping pain from each bruise was making itself known, my shoulder and ankle loudest of all. Tilting my head back, I rested it against a bump in the stone, relaxing as I did.

Click.

My eyes flew open as the wall seemed to disappear from behind my back. I tumbled over, landing hard on another piece of stone that hadn't been there a few seconds ago. In the shadows, a flickering light buzzed to life, pulsing like it hadn't been used in a while. Forcing myself upright, I realised that the wall had, in fact, disappeared. Well, swung to the side. Instead of cave, I was now faced with dark, slightly stale smelling air accompanied by a faint buzzing.

I mean I'm kind of done with adventure for today.

I was already on my feet. My body might have been done with adventure, but clearly my mind wasn't. Hands extended into the darkness, I stepped in, following the flickering and the buzzing. The space got wider, the walls either side of me falling away, opening into a larger cavern.

Fumbling, I grabbed a torch and shone it around in front of me.

Maybe I've got a concussion.

Instead of another chamber of the cave, as I had been expecting, I was greeted by what appeared to be a lab. Inside a cave. In the back and beyond of Scotland. Swinging the beam of the torch back across the walls I had just walked past, I noticed a small set of switches embedded in the stone. Hobbling over, I flicked them all on, waiting to hear any kind of reaction. Nothing.

Were you really expecting them to work? I mean this place could be decades...

The faint buzzing suddenly got louder, accompanied by a series of clicks, like machines turning themselves on. The flickering light on the ceiling slowed down, casting a tiny halo of light for a few seconds at a time. Then, with a loud *whirring*, the cave around me was flooded with light, bulbs that had been hidden in crags in the stone coming to life, casting bright LEDS across the room.

What the hell is this place?

I shuffled forwards, towards the centre of the room and the lab equipment abandoned there. Stainless steel tables supported microscopes and monitors, full of machines that I'd never seen before. As I reached the centre of the room I spun, trying to take it all in. At the far side, the room opened up into a cavernous ceiling, grey rock laying perfectly flat.

Weirdly flat.

Spurred by the need to *figure this place out*, I hurried over, placing a hand on the rock, looking for another button hidden somewhere, anywhere. The stone was cool beneath my palm, feeling almost damp but there was no actual water on it. I continued running my fingers along the smooth surface, but it remained unblemished, expanding at least fifty metres across. Eventually, the rock merged back into the craggy cave wall and as I reached it, I saw another switch hidden in the shadows. Stomach fluttering, I flipped it, hoping it opened another door whilst at the same time, really hoping it didn't. Clanging noises filled the air, a rattling sound that groaned and wheezed. Painfully slowly, the flat piece of rock split in the middle, pulling back like a pair of curtains. I stepped backwards, hitting one of the tables, mouth open, as it continued to pull back, somehow disappearing into the cave wall. Behind the flat surface, glints of murky blue and green sparkled. My stomach dropped. Even before the wall had finished moving, I could see tiny schools of fish darting about behind a pane of glass. Kelp danced at the bottom, fronds floating on a watery breeze. There was no obvious end to the water, no outer wall that could be seen through the murky grey-blue depths. Every so often, the water lit up and seemed to vibrate.

The storm. That's the storm.

I stepped up to the glass again, placing my hands on it, still unable to believe what I was seeing.

"It's the Loch." The words slipped out before I could stop them, falling into the stagnant air around me for no one else to hear. As soon as I said it though, I knew it was true. Somehow, this lab, this underground cave lab, had a viewing window into the Loch. Lightheaded, I moved backwards again, arms searching for a chair, a table, somewhere to sit so I didn't fall over. As I found another table, I felt something soft hit my palm. Turning around, I picked it up.

A notebook?

The leather was pliant under my fingers. Unwrapping the cord tied tight around it once, twice, three times, I let the front cover drop away over my wrist. My breath caught in my throat as familiar spiked handwriting, handwriting I hadn't seen for three years, stared back at me. My fingers turned the pages, slowly at first, then faster until the writing became a blur, until I reached the back cover. A small sob worked its way up my throat as I stared at his name, scratched into the leather with a black BIC, the same place as always.

Oh brother, what have you done?

I looked around the lab again, then back at his notebook. He had been here. I was sure of it. Something akin to excitement washed over me, the realisation that I was *this close* to finding him; it was also the realisation that he was still alive. Or he had been when he was in here, and that couldn't have been long ago given the lack of dust on the sparkling tables. Grinning, I took another look around the lab. I needed to find out where he had gone and maybe, whilst I was at it, what GAI were actually involved in. My first step, I figured, was the notebook. Since it was here it meant it was probably one of his most recent ones and would maybe have some more information than the ones I had looked through.

I pulled a metal stool out from under one of the benches, the legs screeching across the stone floor and sat on it, facing out into the Loch. The fact that they had installed a sliding wall into the cave indicated that the Loch, or something in it, was pretty important. I opened Eli's notebook back at the first page, my hands loving the familiar feel of the soft leather. The first few pages were much the same as his other notebooks, more research into genetics but nothing specific; a few pages in however there was a break and then his writing began again, more scrawled and frantic than it had been before. I squinted at the pages, trying to decipher some of the letters that he had haphazardly strewn across the page. The first phrase I could identify was halfway down, next to a diagram of a DNA molecule.

Transgenic animals.

I'd never come across that phrase before and, as far as I knew, Eli hadn't used it in any of his previous notebooks. I took another look at the DNA molecule, the vague recollections of secondary school science coming back to me and realised it didn't look quite right. There seemed to be some gaps in the sequence, and some filled in with odd colours. Puzzled, I turned the page. There was another break, the blank pages stark white compared to the muddled scrawl of the previous. When I found more notes, it was easy to see another difference from Eli's original writing. Most of his notebooks seemed to be a continuous stream of text, no breaks and no organisation but now, underlined in thick marker, was the title 'Methods'. Underneath, bullet points dotted the page like gunshot wounds, the black ink bleeding out from its assigned circle.

Can we use microinjection to transfer the recombinant DNA into the embryo nuclei?

I blinked. Not a word of that made sense to me. Further down, more bullet points posed questions,

Somatic cell nuclear transfer?

Gene-targeted zinc-finger nucleases?

The further down the page, the more detailed the notes became, with answers to the questions scribbled across margins. I flipped through more pages, the diagrams becoming more complex. Whatever Eli had been working on, it was well beyond the research he'd been doing before he was kidnapped. Not to mention well beyond my ability to comprehend it. A lot of the pages had boxes outlined at the top with a note:

See Report A9 /B7/F5

I looked up from the notebook, scanning around the lab to see if I could find any obvious places to keep reports. Mostly, I just saw my face reflected and mutated in the various different surfaces. I sighed and kept turning pages in Eli's notebook. Towards the back, another block of pages were separated from the rest, these ones entitled 'Nessie'.

Nessie?

Way to theme your weird research to Scotland, Eli.

As I went to turn the page, a huge wave crashed into the glass wall, the sound reverberating around the lab. I jumped, dropping the notebook on the floor, briefly wondering if I should close the sliding wall in case the storm caused the glass to break. Jumping down off of the stool, I made my way back over to the panel. As I went to press the button, I paused, my eyes drawn to another oddly-shaped piece of cave directly underneath the first panel. Running my fingers over it, I quickly found a latch and flipped the cover up, revealing another panel of buttons. These ones had symbols drawn on them. The first was three semi circles, one on top of the other, like part of a Wi-fi symbol. The second showed a cluster of fish and the third was a skull. I frowned, trying to figure out what they could be. My fingers hovered over all three, hesitating. I needed some idea of what was going on here, but I didn't want to press unknown buttons, especially ones with skulls on.

Drawing in a breath, I quickly pressed the one with the fish on before I could change my mind. In front of me, in the Loch, a hatch opened and a bunch of fish were propelled into the water on a cloud of bubbles. They floated in front of the glass, the iridescent silver of their scales sparkling even through the thick wall of glass. I waited a couple of seconds, to see if anything else happened. It didn't. Shrugging, I turned away from the panels. Something in here must be able to tell me where GAI went. The only place I hadn't walked through yet was the far side of the room which was mostly in shadow. Most of the tables were also bare, though you could make out the dust patterns of pieces of equipment that had been on them until recently.

At the far end of the wall, almost hidden behind a craggy outcropping were storage containers.

They all opened easily, and I was relieved to see they actually had something in them. The first container was full of plastic boxes containing the same syringes I'd found in the warehouse. At the bottom there were crates of tubing and Petri dishes scattered haphazardly. Strange, but nothing that could help me. The second storage container's lid was wedged shut by a small piece of the cave wall that pressed down onto it. Grabbing the sides, I jostled the container until it moved out from its place, flush against the wall before opening it up, crossing my fingers for more than just Petri dishes. I was in luck. This container seemed to be full of filing boxes; I began pulling them out and dumping them on a nearby desk until I reached the bottom of the container. Three piles of filing boxes waited on the desk, each pile nearly six boxes high.

This might take a while.

Grabbing another stool, I pulled down the first filing box, surprised at how light it felt. They didn't seem to have any kind of organisation system on the side but as soon as I opened it, I realised why. The first three boxes only held a single of paper, each a different article about GAI, the same ones I had seen on the internet. From the dented seams of the boxes, I knew there had been more paper in here, but it seemed they had taken it with them before they had left the lab. My shoulders slumped.

This might be nothing but another dead end after all.

Half-heartedly, I tugged open the fourth box, expecting to see only a single piece of paper; instead I was greeted by a half-filled box. On the very top piece of paper was a Post-It note; my heart jumped as I recognised Eli's writing again.

Transgenic Animal Case Studies Part 1

Pulling off the Post-It and sticking it to the table, I began to rifle through the rest of the box. Some were printed articles and others were typed reports. One title jumped out at me, 'Beltsville Pigs', so I slid that piece out from the rest and brought it to the table in front of me. Most of the report was in note form, but I was pretty sure Eli had written it; it read the same as his notebooks.

Beltsville Pigs – possible area of initial research. Pigs given human growth hormone to accelerate their growth which was successful however this led to humanoid diseases – arthritis, partial blindness and ulcers. Look at finding an animal-based growth accelerant for subjects?

Should be noted that researchers tried to use the same hormone in fish growth acceleration with less side effects – could this be mammalian only? Would avoid the human-animal chimaera so not technically breaking any laws.

I could understand most of it, hypothetically,

but I had no idea what pigs had to do with Eli. The next report seemed be only notes, no references made to outside research as far as I could tell.

Odontocetes have no fused neck vertebrae – could this be used to give the movement to the Test Subject that has previously been an issue? Focus on Beluga initially as they have 180-degree sensitivity underwater which would make it easy to train them to respond to the stimuli. Cons – Beluga melon is not a good acoustic receiver so this may become problematic over longer distances and leave room for error.

Where the hell had Belugas come from? The rest of the pile of reports all seemed to look at different animals with Eli's notes outlining the pros and cons of each. Nothing in the reports gave any indication of where the research had moved to. I pushed the stack away, wondering if I should try a different approach. Leaving the rest of the piles on the table, I started another lap of the room, keeping close to the wall to try and see if there were any more panels like the one by the glass wall. Just to the left of the door I had come in through, the cave wall petered out into a smooth, almost shiny, area. I ran my hands across it, waiting for the tell-tale feel of a panel cover. Sure enough, my fingers brushed over a small latch and, with a triumphant smile, I flipped it open. This panel only had one button, the kind that you had in lifts to open the doors.

Looking along the smooth area of the wall, I realised a line ran down the middle, almost like a seam.

Maybe I'll have more luck in there.

Running back to my bag, I grabbed the torch, thankful it hadn't run out of batteries yet, then moved back to the panel. Closing my eyes, I pushed the button. A tiny *hiss* came from behind the panel before the wall began clicking and whirring. As I watched, torch in hand, the seam split and moved outwards. Once they had stopped moving, I peered into the darkness. There was a definite smell coming from the room, a sawdust kind of musk and I wrinkled my nose as I stood at the entrance. The torch beam illuminated the ground in front of me, enough to see another set of stairs leading even further down into the ground.

I really hope this isn't some Indiana Jones shit where the door shuts as soon as I walk through.

I stepped over the doorway and onto the wobbly metal steps that led down into darkness.

Chapter 8

The first thing I noticed was the humidity. Everything around me was sticky, the air clinging to my skin and invading my nostrils. It made the smell I'd clocked at the doorway ten times worse. Down here, mixed with the sawdust, I could smell something sweet and cloying mixed with the smell cow pats. Wrinkling my nose, I held a palm over my face as I continued forward. Once I'd reached the bottom of the stairs, I had tried to find the wall, hoping I would also find a light switch. So far it seemed as though the wall stretched on indefinitely. I took hesitant, shuffling steps forward, my feet brushing across some kind of sediment that seemed to coat the floor. From the beam of the torch it just looked like a film, knocked aside in trails. The further into the room I edged, the more the air seemed to press down on me.

Shffff.

I froze, the torch wobbling slightly in my hand.

Did… did something just move?

The silence seemed to stretch around me, my

ears and eyes disorientated by the almost pitch black. After another couple of seconds, I heard the sound again.

Shfff.

A squeak tried to claw its way up my throat as my heart hammered against my ribcage. *Something* was in here with me.

I really hope it's in a cage.

The room lapsed into a heavy silence again. I took a few more steps forward, waiting for my hand or leg to brush up against whatever was in here. I couldn't get my bearing at all, the only meagre light coming from the open doorway up the stairs and my tiny torch. Whatever had been making the sound remained quiet; I was sure it was listening to the staccato of my heartbeat. I dragged in a lungful of air, trying to calm my shaking hands and, before I could back out, swung the torch beam up and away from the floor. Flashes of metal illuminated under the direct beam; they filtered across the back wall. As I stopped swinging the beam about and focussed, I realised they were almost as thick as my forearm.

They look like prison bars... or cages.

The realisation dawned. I swung around, pointing the light behind me, back to the entrance and slowly panned across. The entire room was lined with cages, each one stretching up to the ceiling. I could barely see where one finished and the next one started, the only indication coming from the panels of metal that broke the bars in two. I kept turning, senses on high alert, waiting for my torch to land on a pair of eyes. It didn't happen. From the swing of my torch I could see the room was a long rectangle, the cages taking up most of the space. In the centre of the room, just to the right of where I was standing was another hastily erected plywood box, about six foot tall and wide. My stomach tightened, flashing back to the industrial estate and the same sweet, cloying smell. I quickly averted my eyes, not wanting to find another table covered in blood. Instead I stepped towards the nearest cage. Clipped to the bars was a whiteboard, the letters smeared in someone's attempt to wipe away whatever had been written on there. I could make out the last few letters, neatly printed in blue marker.

CHI

The rest of the letters were indistinguishable and, without anything else, CHI could mean anything. Inside, the cage looked empty, but piles of something were stacked up on the floor. It didn't take much of leap to realise that it was some kind of animal dung. Looking up, I could see multiple platforms suspended in mid-air, some with rotting fruit clinging on to the edges. The dung and the fruit made me think of bats but the platforms, and the cage, were far too big. Frowning, I moved along to the next cage. As the light swung over the bars, I caught a glimpse of something grey and soft. My heart leapt in my chest as I stilled the beam. It was definitely fur. I didn't dare breathe, waiting for it to move, to leap at the bars. It was only when seconds passed, and I realised that maybe I should breathe before I passed out, that it became clear that whatever had been in there was dead. I leant closer to the bars, trying to stretch my light and gasped.

Curled on the floor was something unlike anything I had ever seen before. Its face was turned towards me, eyes vacant and milky. The snout and ears reminded me of a wolf, but the size and shape of the body more closely resembled a bear. Every inch of it was covered in fur, apart from its back which shone with the iridescence of scales, not dissimilar to the fish in the Loch. Nothing about it was natural, not even the position it was laying in, head thrown back at an angle seemingly detached from the body. This one had a whiteboard too, but no one had bothered to erase the notes on it. At the top of the whiteboard was a code,

POL214BCAR

Not viable. Showed signs of degeneration after its first two weeks. Accelerated growth caused partial internal organ failure. Developed secondary traits from recombinant DNA that were unexpected including venom and hibernation. Suggested termin-

ation.

Had they...had they *made* it? My mind scrambled as I tried to understand how that would even be possible. Eager to move along, I hurried to the next cage. This one was full of foliage, and rocks and in the middle was a large pool of water. Above the cage, a humidifier was humming, pumping out jets of warm air. I began to make my way to the whiteboard, part of me hoping it had been rubbed off so I didn't have to find another dead... *thing* but the other part of me really wanted to know what the hell was going on. As I approached the cage, I heard the sound again.

Shfffff.

I paused, still a few feet from the whiteboard.

Please let that have come from inside the cage.

When it didn't happen again, I shuffled forward until I was in front of the whiteboard. It wasn't wiped out. A tiny ball of anxiety formed in the pit of my stomach. I was pretty sure that meant something was in here, whether it was dead or alive.

OTT103ACAR

Not viable. Most successful subject from litter but showed signs of being unsuitable after separation from litter mates. Made multiple attempts to socialise with the handlers displaying a need for comfort behaviour. No known secondary traits. Possible use as template for future subjects but would need to reduce the social need of the subject before implementing field tests.

At least they hadn't suggested terminating this one; although, if it was still alive, they had basically left it for dead anyway.

Bastards.

I peered into the cage, taking in the small portion of slowly decomposing fish in a heap by the pool. A few heavy seconds ticked by as I waited to see if anything to see if anything would move, but it remained silent. Shrugging, and altogether relieved, I decided to move on.

Let's just get out of whatever the hell this place is.

Shffffff.

My shoes squeaked against the concrete floor as I spun back around, eyes frantically searching the space in front of me.

Nothing was moving.

As I turned away again to keep moving, the torch beam swept over the bottom corner near the whiteboard and I jumped back with a cry. A pair of yellow eyes watched me, barely a couple of feet from the ground. A few steps back I finally shuddered to a stop and took a couple of breaths.

It's inside the cage. It's not getting out. Breathe.

When my heart had dropped back into my chest, I moved the torch beam up, trying to ignore how violently it was shaking. As soon as the light settled over the pair of eyes, I couldn't help but laugh. At the sound, the animal squeaked at me, revealing tiny canines. Slowly I moved closer, crouching down so I could get a better look. For all purposes, the creature in front of me looked like...an otter. He watched me, letting out tiny mewing sounds as I scanned over his body. He was a couple of feet long, with a broad tail and webbed feet. The only anomaly I could see was his colour; instead of the brown I was expecting, he had thick grey and white mottled fur. He seemed to wiggle, almost like a dog wagging his tail, as I leant even closer to the bars. It was only when he turned his head that I noticed the ridges running along the fur. As he took a breath in, they fluttered.

They're gills.

So, he wasn't just an otter. I felt my chest tighten as I looked at him, my eyes resting on the colour of his fur again, wondering what else had been done. He didn't seem as affected as I was, sticking his wet nose through the bars and letting out a stream of chattering sounds. He seemed thrilled to see me. My thoughts drifted back to the whiteboard and the note that said he had attempted to socialise with his handlers.

"Hey..." I pushed aside the voice in my head that pointed out I was talking to an animal, "Hey little guy." He pipped at me, a short sound that almost sounded like a responding greeting. His yellow eyes were bright as he regarded me, "I bet you were lonely, huh? They left you, didn't they? You poor thing." Another pip and a chirp followed by some more chatter. I smiled despite myself, sitting down on the floor and crossing my legs. He followed suit, laying down on the dirt ground of his cage, never taking his eyes off of me. "What did they do to you?" He stuck his nose through the bars again, sniffing the air in front of me and blinked. Without thinking I stuck my hand out and stroked him on the nose. He let out a squeal, leaping up and running a couple of small circles before he came back to me and poked his nose through again. I laughed, tapping him gently on the nose, enjoying the way he wriggled as I did. When I stopped, he let out a loud squeak and shoved his nose as far through the cage bars as he could.

It's like he's communicating.

"What do you want?" I pitched my voice as though I was talking to a dog, using the up and down tone and leaning so close that our noses were almost touching. Really, I should have been getting out of this lab as quickly as I could, but, even if this little guy couldn't help me find Eli, I couldn't just walk away and leave him here. As I leant in, he let out a soft chirp, almost like a purr. "I think we need to give you a name." I paused and he vigorously chattered, filling the otherwise silent air. "Okay! What about…Pip?" I said, thinking of the sounds he'd been making. There was a pause and then he began to make the exact sound I'd been referring too, wiggling about behind the bars.

Whoever left him here must have been completely heartless. Sounds about right.

As I sat there, I realised I couldn't leave him locked up. I might not know exactly what he was, but he didn't seem dangerous and he definitely didn't deserve to live in this hell hole. "Right Pip, I think we need to figure out how to open this door. Do you agree?" He chirped and I nodded, getting up from my sitting position and scanning the room for any kind of electric system. The walls seemed bare but from my position I could see a window looking into the plywood room. It would make sense to have a control centre to operate the cages from. Hoping that I wasn't about to see more nightmare fuel (or more so than I already had), I walked over and peered into the plexiglass window. It seemed that, unlike the one in the warehouse, this room was split into two. The window only overlooked part of it but, as I had guessed, it appeared to be a control room. Buttons stretched across a desk, each one with a code written underneath it. Feeling a surge of determination, I looked back over my shoulder to Pip's cage,

"Don't worry buddy, I'm gonna get you out of there." I whispered before grabbing the handle of the door and wrenching it open, half-expecting it to be locked. The switch board took up most of the room and, after a quick glance over the buttons, I landed on one at the top that said 'Lights'. I flicked that one on, relieved when overhead halogens began to stutter to life, their bulbs fizzing. After a couple of seconds, there was enough light that I didn't need the torch anymore. I scanned back over the rest of the switchboard. Even with the ink faded it was easy to figure out which one opened Pip's cage. It had the same code as on his whiteboard.

Are you sure about this? You have literally no idea what he is.

I looked back over to his cage, with his eager face pressed up against the bars, little nose snuffling the air. There was no way I could leave him here, even if it meant possibly opening up a can of mutated worms. Setting my jaw, I flicked the switch on the board, hoping it was still connected to whatever system was running the humidifier. There was a second of silence before a loud buzzing filled the room. I covered my ears at it reverberated around the booth, the plywood shaking slightly. Eventually the buzzing stopped, though I could still hear an echo in my ears, and a loud click came from Pip's cage. Slowly, the door began to slide back, the bars dissecting the inside of the enclosure. Pip danced around by the edge of the door, his eyes watching the sliding. I watched him from inside the booth, wondering why he didn't just dart out. The door came to a juddering stop, clanging as it hit the sheet metal wall. Pip was still dancing just outside of the now open space, his tiny paws leaving wet pawprints on the concrete.

Puzzled, I stepped out of the booth, walking back over to the cage. As soon as I came within touching distance, Pip stilled. I stepped out, ready to walk into the enclosure, when he let out a series of high-pitched screeches, tiny pointed teeth bared. I stepped back, trying to ignore the fact that my hair was standing on end, slithers of fear racing up and down my arms. Everything went back to an uncomfortable silence, the humidifier whirring in the background. Pip calmed down when I stepped away from the cage entrance but still didn't make a move to come out. Probably a minute after I had released the door, a loud alarm sounded, blaring through the underground level and, from what I could hear, the upper level as well. The open space in front of the door began to hiss, suddenly sparking bright blue for a few seconds before shutting off. Looking closer I could see charge points on the inside of the door and the wall.

It must have been electrified as a precaution.

I shivered, hoping the faint smell of burning flesh was just my imagination. If Pip hadn't screeched at me, I would probably be a bit crispier right now. When the sparks died down, another shorter alarm sounded, three times in a row. Pip cocked his head. As soon as the alarm finished, he wiggled forwards, leaping at me. I stumbled backwards, laughing as he placed his paws on my knees,

"Okay, okay!" Kneeling down, I let him sniff my hands and crawl into my lap, marvelling at how excited he was to have human company. With what sounded like a contented sigh, he curled up on my legs, tucking his head under one grey speckled paw, his soft, rounded ears, flicking at the sound of my voice. I couldn't understand how anyone could have left him here. I knew he wasn't quite normal, but nothing about him screamed dangerous. If anything, he seemed like a large ferret with incredibly soft fur. After a couple of minutes, I gently tapped his nose. He lifted his head, blinking up at me with almond-shaped eyes.

"You're very cute, but I can't stay down here." I thought of the rest of the boxes back in the main lab. I had to find out what they were doing here; maybe that would tell me where they were going next. Pip squeaked at me, a tiny, mewling sound that scattered into the air. I grinned, far too aware that I was getting rather attached to this creature. "I have to find my brother." I whispered, leaning in to let him in on the secret. "I think he was here; I found his notebook upstairs. I really miss him, and I need to find him." Even though I was telling myself that there was no way Pip could understand me, something in his eyes, the way he was watching my facial expressions, told me that maybe he could understand at least a bit of it. He snuggled back into my arm, pressing his cold little nose into the crook of my elbow. Even though Eli, and just exactly what he was tangled up in, was still playing on my mind, I could feel myself fighting the urge to grin.

"Alright then buddy." I put a hand under his belly, surprised by how smooth it felt, and lifted him up from my lap, "If you're not gonna move, I guess you're coming with me." He wiggled again, cuddling into my chest as I heaved myself off the floor, one hand still under his belly. As soon as I was standing, I tucked my other hand under his tail, cradling him in my arms. Together, we made our way back to the rickety stairs. If I couldn't find anything else in the main lab, I was going to have to come back down here, but for now, I'd seen enough of GAI's private zoo. The stairs felt even more wobbly under foot going up, the banisters shaking with every step. I hurried up the last few, somewhat relieved to be back in the clinical light of the main area. Or at least, pretty confident I wasn't going to find any half-wolf, half-polar-bear corpses in here.

I put Pip down when we reached the top, laughing as he scampered about. As he sniffed everything, I realised that he probably hadn't seen anything but that cage for his entire life. I watched him for a couple more seconds then began to walk over to the boxes I'd left piled on the far table. As soon as I moved, he let out an alarm whistle and pottered after me, his nails clicking on the concrete floor. I stopped when I reached the stool and he careened into the back of my leg, falling into a heap by my feet. As soon as he realised I wasn't going anywhere, he circled a couple of times, like a dog, and curled in a doughnut shape. I grinned at my new sidekick and pulled the next filing box towards me. Like the first few that I'd come to, this had barely anything left in it, just a couple of spare scraps of GAI letter headed paper. Another bout of frustration hit. Instead of throwing it across the floor, which is what I really wanted to do, I pushed it down the desk. As I began to open the next box, a strange tapping noise filled the air.

I stopped what I was doing, peering down at Pip curled by my feet. He blinked back up at me but didn't move. The noises petered out, the lab descending back into silence so I shrugged, continuing with the next box. The second I pulled the lid back, the tapping began again, like something was taunting me. This time Pip leapt up from under my feet, tilting his head as he glanced around the lab. Following suite, I slid off the stool, glancing back over to the open door of the

'Zoo Room' but nothing seemed to have changed. As I was about to settle back into my seat something moved in my peripheral vision. I stilled.

Go back to the boxes. Whatever you just saw is not going to be anything good.

I couldn't do it.

One… Two… Three…

My mouth dropped open in a silence scream, throat convulsing as I tried desperately not to make any noise. A pair of large, slitted eyes watched me, unblinking. Pip crawled between my legs, making a chattering noise as he spotted the creature. Even if I hadn't been frozen in fear, I would have stayed perfectly still. It's eyes never moved from me, the deep black of the pupil reflecting the silver metal in the room around us, giving the impression of staring into an oil spill. My heartbeat hammered in my chest and rushed to my ears in waves.

That can't be possible…it's…not even real…

As the whooshing in my ears increased, my eyes travelled down the length of *its* body, blinking against the image in front of me. Its head was rounded, leading to a long sinewy neck. Most of its body was smooth but it had a whip-like extended tail. Pectoral fins jutted from three points of its body, rounded and flat. Its entire body seemed to shimmer, catching the colours that were thrown around in the water by the storm.

Under the iridescence I could see spots of grey, almost like blossoms, appearing over its entire body. There was a hump in its back, reminiscent of a top fin; I felt like I'd seen that shape somewhere before. Along its neck was a feathery piece of flesh; everything screamed 'predator'. It shifted in the water behind the glass, the currents from the waves moving it along the window, but its head remained completely stationary.

On the one hand, it looked like a dinosaur, the prehistoric fins, the immense size of it but on the other hand, it looked almost exactly like something I had seen recently. I realised, as the grey began to haze the edges of my vision, that I'd been too focussed on what was in front of me to realise what was going on inside of me. The panic began to set in, forcing small, panting breaths into my lungs. The humming in my ears grew louder and soon the world had narrowed to a pinpoint; the only thing I could see was the creature. As I began to pass out, my mind provided the missing answer. I crumpled to the floor, distantly aware of Pip's frantic squeaks, but the only thought in my head, spinning over and over was a creature I'd seen posted everywhere on my way up here;

Loch Ness Monster.

***

Four Years Ago...

I pulled the blanket tighter around my neck as, on screen, a storm raged. It might have been fictional, but the room definitely felt colder than it had in the previous scene. Eli laughed at me, throwing a piece of buttered popcorn at my head from the other side of the L-shaped sofa.

"You're such a wuss Ari. You'd probably pass out if you ever saw a monster." I caught the piece of popcorn before it hit my forehead, popping it in my mouth with a deliberate crunch, ignoring Eli's comment. He knew it had irritated me though. He threw more popcorn at me, a handful this time, the kernels scattering over the sofa cushion around me. None of them hit me.

"That was a terrible shot Eli. You'd probably pass out if you ever had to play sports." I gathered up the spilt popcorn into one palm and started munching on it, my eyes still fixed on the tv. In high-definition the hapless heroine scrambled away from the monster, constantly looking over her shoulder as she tried to escape. I rolled my eyes, finishing the last piece of popcorn and muttered,

"She's useless. No one is going to escape a monster looking in the opposite direction to where she's running." Pushing myself up from the sofa, I grabbed the now-empty bowl from Eli and wandered into the kitchen, leaving the heroine screaming in fear. Shoving another bag of popcorn in the microwave, I

leant on the kitchen counter, listening to the crashing and screeching from the other room. Accompanied by the pops of the corn, it was almost musical. The microwave beeped at me, snapping me out of my daze and I quickly emptied the bag into the bowl, licking my fingers to get rid of the residual butter. As I wandered back from the kitchen, I snorted to see Eli cuddled up under the blanket I'd vacated. He peered up at me guiltily, only his eyes and eyebrows visible over the trim of the blanket. Casually, I swung my legs over the arm of the sofa and flopped next to him, hugging the popcorn to my chest. Eli pushed the blanket away from his face, stretching an arm out to try and grab the popcorn. I pulled it away from him, pretending to look angry,

"If you want popcorn, give me my blanket back. Otherwise this popcorn is mine." The ultimate ultimatum. I hid my grin as he considered, eyes darting back and forth between the popcorn and the warmth of the blanket. On screen our heroine was still running, somehow not exhausted even though she was in heels. The monster was still chasing her; much like all horror films, both monster and victim seemed to have the stamina of long-distance runners. After a few seconds of deliberation, Eli threw the blanket off with a flourish. I grinned fully now, not trying to hide my amusement. Handing him the bowl of popcorn, after securing a handful for myself, I pulled my blanket back over me, settling into the cushions. We watched the film in silence for

a few more minutes, one of us snorting every now and then as the heroine did something particularly stupid. The monster appeared back on screen, relentlessly giving chase. He must be getting so much cardio. Even high-definition couldn't hide the awkwardly stitched together costume that accompanied all good bad horror films.

"I think I can actually see the guy in the suits hair. They haven't even sewn the head on right." Eli tutted at the screen. He cocked his head to one side; a sign I had seen enough over the years to know he wasn't focused on the film anymore. I waited. My aforementioned experience with Eli's process meant I knew he would let me in on his thoughts sooner or later. As I watched the heroine screaming in the clutches of the monster only a few minutes later, I saw Eli make the decision to tell me. I grabbed the remote and pressed pause as the monster leant down to devour the shrieking woman.

"What?" Best move the process along where I could.

"Do you think it would actually be possible to make monsters?" He didn't say it loudly but without the near constant screeching from the tv, it seemed to echo around the large room.

"Make monsters in what way?" I was thinking Play-doh. Eli gave me a look; the same one he always gave me when I said something sarcastic. Like I wasn't taking this seriously. I mean I wasn't, but

that was beside the point.

"Like, werewolves and krakens and the Loch Ness monster. Do you think somebody could make them? Not Frankenstein's monster make them but create creatures that looked like all these monsters and creatures of myths and legends?" It might have seemed like a strange question to anyone else, but I was also used to how Eli's brain thought. So, I shrugged,

"I mean, I don't see why not? If you were smart enough and had the right tools, it would probably be possible...I'm not sure you could fit the Loch Ness monster in our bathtub though Eli. Maybe start smaller." I stuck my tongue out at him, but he wasn't looking. His eyes were far away and before I knew it, he was up and retrieving a notebook from his room. When he sat back down, he nodded to me to start the film again. I sighed, knowing I was going to be watching this by myself. Whenever he got an idea in his head, even if it wasn't something entirely plausible, he had to write it down and plan it out. It was just what Eli did. I grabbed the popcorn bowl off of him, snuggling back, ready to watch the rest of the film, but all I could hear, just below the screaming and roaring was the repetitive scratch of Eli's pen on the thick paper as he scribbled down his newest idea...

***

I came to, finding Pip frantically licking my

face, his smooth tongue leaving slobbery trails across my face. I spluttered, rolling over; my head spun as I tried to sit up, a pin point of pain radiating from the back.

What happened?

From the tender spot at the back of my head, I was pretty sure I'd cracked my skull on something. I winced as my fingers probed the spot, trying to feel for bleeding. Luckily it just felt like swelling but I would have to be careful. The rest of my head was throbbing and, as I blinked blearily at Pip, I realised I must have passed out. I hadn't passed out in years, the last even close call being the night Eli disappeared.

What the hell made me pass out?

I looked around, my back propped up by the stool. The lab was clear, as was the window.

But it wasn't.

The memories rushed back in, bombarding me again with the image of the monstrous creature I'd seen behind the glass. Now the water seemed calm, the storm overhead apparently having calmed. But I couldn't get the image of its eyes out of my head, the predatory way they had watched me, unblinking. It looked almost exactly like the images of the Loch Ness monster I'd seen plastered in every gift shop except very real and very terrifying. Pip had curled up next to me, his face resting on my knee, every now and then letting out little chirping sounds, as if to make sure I was still conscious. Absently, I stroked his head, burrowing my hands into his soft fur, my eyes still focussed on the glass window.

After a few minutes, my head stopped spinning. Shakily, I pushed myself up until I was standing, one hand grasping the edge of the table; then, when I was fairly confident I wouldn't pass out again, I gingerly made my way over to the window, Pip at my heels. As I reached the left-hand side, where the panels were hidden, I leant against the cave wall, scanning the open water. A few fronds of kelp floated near the glass and I could see a small school of fish in the distance, but other than that the water seemed undisturbed.

"Where do you hide something that size?" I mused, looking down at Pip. He chittered at me, staring out into the water as well. "What even made it come out of hiding in the first place?" There didn't seem to be anything that would attract it this way. Given the way it was looking at me, it had looked hungry…

The fish.

I looked over to the panel of buttons, remembering that I had released some fish into the water earlier. Unless they had floated into the distance, I didn't think they were here anymore. Curious, I pulled back the cover of the panel again, scanning the buttons. Since a skull was never good news for anyone, I immediately moved away from that one. I didn't know what the three lines meant, so I decided to press the fish button again; hopefully it would attract the creature back. As terrifying as it had been, a niggling feeling in my head was telling me that it was pretty important. There was a burst of bubbles as the fish were propelled into the water again; they floated near the middle of the window. I watched the water, but I wasn't expecting an instantaneous reaction; nothing had happened immediately last time. Relaxing my shoulders, I slide down the cave wall, prepared to wait.

No sooner than my butt had hit the floor did I see a flash of grey down near the bottom right-hand corner of the window. Before I even had time to pull myself back up, the creature had reappeared, opening its wide jaws to snap up the entire group of fish in one mouthful. I could feel my heart rate pick up, but I forced myself to take deep breaths, eyes fixed on the creature. Pip had scurried behind my legs, his eyes also following the creature behind the glass. I could feel his pulse racing as he hid and my hand reached out on autopilot, gently stroking the length of his body.

Once the creature had eaten the fish, its head

and neck snaked round, 180 degrees to its body and stared through the glass again. This close to it, I could see that it didn't seem to have any eyelids, its pupils constantly staring, like a shark and its head was elongated with a large gaping mouth filled with rows of teeth. It looked horrific. The main bulk of its body was streamlined, mostly taken up by the huge pectoral fins, each with thin, fan-like additions at the end, and its tail seemed to jut upwards; from here it looked like it could be six foot or more in length, even with the water and glass distortion. Under the long, whip-like portion of its tail was another fluke, smaller and pointed. It seemed to interrupt the flow of its body, almost like it had been placed there by accident. As I took in all the details, it swung its head to the side and noticed me, curled by the corner of the glass. In less than a second, its head was directly in front of me, one eye pressed close to the glass, mouth dropping open slightly to reveal more of its teeth. I resisted the urge to scramble away, even as Pip began to whimper. I was so close that I could get a real sense of its size, its head bigger than my entire body. Its tail whipped across its body every now and then, forcing the water out of its way. The resulting currents smashed into the glass.

I really hope they reinforced that glass.

After a couple of seconds, it seemed to get bored, flipping around and swimming down into the bottom of the Loch, past where the window could view. Even after the water returned to normal, my brain was spinning.

Eli, what the hell were you involved in?!

As I stared out into the water, I remembered there was another button on the panel. Standing up, my fingers hovered over it.

I mean, we're already knee deep in the impossible. Why not?

Squaring my shoulders, I pressed the button. To begin with I thought nothing had happened. The water remained calm and there was no sign of the creature. It was only when I realised the ringing in my ears wasn't actually in my ears that I understood what the button did. It was some kind of signal or sonar. The ringing got louder until it was piercing, forcing my hands over my ears. Beside me Pip was keening, rubbing his head into the floor. After a couple more seconds of ringing, the sound went higher than I could hear. I lowered my hands from my ears, breathing a sigh of relief as Pip stopped headbutting the floor. A couple of seconds after the ringing went above my hearing range, the floor began to judder. A low rumble was radiating from below the window; the flash of grey alerted me to the creature again but this time it didn't slow down as it swam, heading straight for the glass. I stumbled backwards as I realised it wasn't going to stop,

Pips claws skittering backwards with me. With a powerful flick of its tail, the creature rammed directly into the glass, jaw open wide.

Oh shit.

The entire wall shuddered. I couldn't tell if the ringing was still going but the creature had pulled back for a second attack. It rammed the window again, the glass shuddering under the pressure. I kept walking backwards, stopping when my back hit the nearest table. The creature swam backwards for another hit but just before it reached the glass, a loud bell rang out across the lab and it stopped dead, snaking its neck along the glass but not attacking. There was silence, heavy with tension. Then, with a whip of its tail, it disappeared again.

I will not be pressing that button again. Nessie is far too friendly a name for that thing. It's definitely a monster…wait…Nessie.

I grinned, running back over to where Eli's notebook had fallen earlier, the pages open and splayed on the floor. Picking it up, I leafed through to the section entitled 'Nessie'.

Maybe Nessie is the key to figuring out what the hell is going on in this place.

Eli's Journal

Nessie

They've assigned me a new project. They won't tell me much, but I think they want to try for something even bigger after I successfully created OTT103ACAR. I get the impression that this is what they were leading up to, the entire reason GAI was created. We're moving up to a lab in Scotland; Kincraig. That's where I'm supposed to conduct the initial research. They've called the project 'Nessie'.

***

We've reached the new lab in Scotland. Now that we're here, they've told me some more about the project. They want to create a replica of the Loch Ness Monster. They still won't tell me why, but it doesn't take a genius to figure out that you could make a lot of money off of something like that. There is a lot more equipment up here; we're directly under a Loch. They've actually built the lab into the Loch. It's insane. Ari would flip if she saw it. For now, I have to find viable subjects to build the DNA with, but I know the main issue is going to be the size. They want this thing huge. Like twenty to thirty feet long. I don't know how I'm going to do that without growth hormones.

***

I've found a possible base genome; if I use a beluga whale as the base, I can hopefully create the snaking head movement they're looking for. Belugas don't have fused neck vertebrae. I don't know what creature I would use for the neck. From the description they gave me, they want it to look very similar to a Plesiosaur or Pistosaurus but without access to their fossilised DNA, I'm not sure it will be possible. For the rest of the DNA I'll have to use quite a few marine animals. As far as I can tell, the thresher shark is the best bet for the tail. It seems to have the ability to use it as a whip to startle prey, which might add to the wow factor. I've also identified blue shark DNA for the pectorals and cuttlefish genes to help with camouflage in the Loch will be the most viable option.

The scientists here want to know how I'm going to select the genes I want. I suppose it seems simple to me. I've identified a few possible methods. The OTT103ACAR hybrid did not involve multiple incoming DNA strands so it was relatively simple, however on a project of this scale I will need to be prepared to try more methods. My immediate idea is to use a microinjection in the embryo nuclei to transfer the recombinant DNA, which will allow me to transfer small pieces of genetic information. With this method however, I have to ensure that the appropriate molecular modifications are made to ensure that the chosen gene has the desired effect on the embryo. This will likely require more than one attempt. From the information I studied on this method, it has only been conducted in small mammals, so I may encounter issues when transferring this method to larger animals; it may also lead to psychological abnormalities. Most of the research into splicing embryos was forcibly halted before the embryo formed a central nervous system so I cannot guess how the development will progress after this stage.

I may also have the option of using gene-targeted zinc finger nucleases via a microinjection of plasmid. This will allow me to target specific deletions and modifications in the DNA sequence. Prior research in this area has revealed the hybrid molecules often result in consequent mutations in the subject. The tests have so far been conducted on rats which will not equate when transferred to a larger subject. My final option to use in this project is TLA (Targeted locus amplification). So far this method, which allows us to selectively amplify and sequence genes, has proven predominantly successful. TLA has identified the CRISPR-Cas 9 nucleus; I can design targeted genome editing in many biological sequences. CRISPR- Cas 9 has had more success in a larger panel of species than any other method.

***

BEL502BCET has failed. This is the 5th revision of this experiment that has failed. I think it's time to move on to a new model. I have attempted all methods of mutation but separately, they don't seem to be working as well as I had hoped. One issue that has arisen is the docility of the subject; the overseers of the project are unhappy with a subject that lacks curiosity and predatory nature, something I will have to rectify. The largest concern is the consequent mutations in the text subjects. Most were unable to develop past infancy, even with the growth accelerant. I believe it is to do with the hybridisation of mammals and fish. This worked in my earlier experiments but does not seem to be supported in such a large-scale project. I have decided to change the make-up of the subject to use only fish genes. The new experiment will use the base genome of a blue shark. I will still keep the thresher shark tail but will also take elements from conger eels and coelacanth for the physical appearance. One of the technicians was able to secure me a viable coelacanth subject to use, which was the most difficult element to procure. I have also included common octopus genes in order to allow the subject to change shape and colour and sea mouse genes to give the creature iridescent setae in order to blend in to the Loch. My immediate concern is keeping the subject under control, if it makes it to the release stage.

***

The 2nd run of the newest model worked! BLU201ACAR has progressed steadily past the stages the previous experiments failed to survive. Our next step is to release it into the Loch to see how it functions in a larger body of water. So far there have been no adverse effects from the accelerants I gave it in order to aid and support the gene splicing. The overseers have shown interest but also dislike of the small fluke that has grown under the main tail, a part of the thresher shark DNA but, if this works, I am confident I would be able to rectify this issue… they mentioned Ari today. Talking amongst themselves. I heard them saying that Caden was still in place to prevent any issues… I don't want him to hurt Ari. I've just got to keep my head down, produce the results they want. I'll keep her safe.

***

BLU201ACAR has progressed better than expected. The release into the Loch has shown no issues and the subject has grown exponentially, even past my initial estimates. I have come up with a use for OOT103ACAR whilst studying the subject. In order to keep the predatory nature in control when the subject is released into a larger Loch, we have created a sonar signal that should incapacitate it, should the situation arise, however the overseers have expressed a desire to have a secondary system in place should this not work. I recently read some research about Otters attacking Conger Eels and believe we could use the base genome of OTT103ACAR to provoke and move the subject away from any future issues. So far, I have not suggested this to the overseers as OTT103ACAR would need training to follow commands. I will move forward with this idea once I have studying the subject's reaction to sonar… Caden called one of the overseers today. Ari has contacted him. I miss her so much; I hate that I can't talk to her. I don't trust that bastard not to hurt her.

***

BLU201ACAR has been declared 'not viable' due to the additional fluke. I believe they're being twats. But I have been instructed to conduct another run of the experiment, this time using ZFNs to remove the additional fluke. They told me to eliminate BLU201ACAR, but I made the case that we should study it further. This is the first successful experiment and I will not allow them to destroy it on the grounds of a purely aesthetic issue. I've come too far and too close. They're already talking about the next project. They want to move us to Europe. If I move to Europe, I don't think I'll ever be coming back. I don't want to leave Ari. I have begun on the newest batch of subjects, but they will still take a few weeks to fully mature, so I won't be able to leave this lab until they do. They told me they have a release site lined up for the next successful subject, but I don't know where it is. They want to release it as a juvenile. It might not survive.

I have begun my training of OTT103ACAR. Most of it is conducted in secret, when the rest of the scientists are asleep. I don't sleep much anymore. I don't need to. I think one of the overseers knows what I am doing but they won't get rid of me. I'm too valuable. So far, he is responding well, but is becoming attached to me. I cannot allow myself to feel emotion in this place; it feels like if I do, everything will fall apart.

***

They're moving us. Caden called again, saying Ari knew about GAI. I couldn't help but smile. She's always been incredibly smart and determined when she wants something. But they made me pack up my lab and the juveniles. They eliminated some of the other preliminary subjects. I saved BLU201ACAR and OTT103ACAR, but I couldn't bring them with me. I am leaving the secondary generator on to allow them to survive for as long as I can. I am not sure the juveniles will survive the move. The overseers are saying Ari is close to figuring out where this lab is. I hope she does. I know my sister; she'll be able to find it and when she does, she'll give them all hell. Then I can go home. I don't know if I'll be able to go back to the boy I was before this, but at least I can be with my parents and Ari. I never got to say goodbye to them.

***

In case Ari finds the lab, I'm leaving this notebook here. I've transferred all my research to another file.

Ari,

I love you. Please don't give up on me. I'm still in here, I'm still your brother. I'll be waiting for you.

Love,

Eli

I love you too Eli. I'll find you, I promise.

Chapter 9

I put down the notebook with reluctance, the final few entries hitting a bit too close. Part of me was glad Eli had thought about us, his family but the other part felt all the more guilty that I had taken this long to find a solid lead and had then missed him by a couple of days. If I hadn't fallen prey to Caden, believed him, *trusted* him, he would never have know I knew about GAI. Maybe I could have got here before they panicked and moved everything. I was *so close.*

With renewed determination, I tore through the rest of the boxes, every now and then glancing over to the glass window to see if Nessie had reappeared. I couldn't have imagined something like that but clearly Eli had. I was struck for a second at how smart he was. Why hadn't my parents kept looking for him? Pip twisted himself around my feet, chattering to himself as I moved box after box aside. I opened the last box hoping I would find at least something helpful but this one didn't have a single sheet of paper in it. With a cry of frustration, I swept all of the boxes off of the desk, sending them clattering to the floor. Pip yelped as they hit, scurrying backwards. Bending down, I scooped him up and held him to my chest, stroking his soft fur until he calmed down.

"I'm sorry buddy, I'm just frustrated. I've searched everywhere and there is nothing that tells me where they could have gone. Where they've taken Eli." I looked around the lab, at the mostly bare tables and the storage containers I'd already searched. Even if they had left in a hurry, they'd done a pretty good job. As I scanned the lab, my eyes fell on the doorway leading off to the room of cages. My mind went back to the plywood box that had been split in half. I'd only been in one half of it.

"There might be something in the other part of that room." I mused to Pip, who blinked up at me. Setting him down on the floor, I cautiously made my way over to the entrance to that room. I didn't want to go back down there, especially not now that I knew there might be more mutated creatures. But, and it was a large but, that room was the only place I hadn't searched. It might have something, it might not but there was no way I could give up now after reading Eli's journal. Pip was dancing at the doorway, little paws padding up and down the entrance but never going further. Not giving myself a chance to bow out, I put one foot on the wobbly staircase. Pip let out a squeak and I turned to give him a pat.

"Stay here. I don't need to be worried about

you down there as well as myself." I didn't know how he understood exactly but he laid down, head resting on his paws. I made my way down the rest of the steps, glad that the lights had remained on. Entering the room in the light was definitely more comfortable, although the reality of what I was looking at was harrowing. I could only assume that they had taken some of the creatures with them, judging by the obvious use in some of the cages but a lack of creature or body. I tried not to let my eyes linger on the wolf-polar bear hybrid cage but even in the bright halogen light, something about its eyes, staring vacantly into the distance, was still creepy. I'd left the door open to the control room, the thin plywood swinging on its hinges, every so often letting out a small creak. There was no window into the other half of the room, and, on closer inspection, I realised the only way in was through an almost invisible door in the control room. I took one more look around outside, the cages still silent. I couldn't help but feel like something was watching me. Jolting, it suddenly dawned on me that there could be camera's in here, still functioning, if they ran on the same loop as everything else.

Well shit. It's a bit too late to do anything about that.

Hurrying back inside the room, I shut the door, hoping they hadn't thought to install any cameras in here. Then I started trying to get into the separate room. The door itself didn't appear to have a handle or a lock; it was just a completely smooth line in the door. Cursing, I looked back at the switchboard. The last door I'd needed to open had been on there. There was a good chance this one was too. I quickly scanned the codes, eyes skipping anything that looked like a creature code. The bottom line of switches were the only ones with written names instead of codes. The first was 'Main door' which I presumed was the door I'd come in through, although why anyone would want to lock themselves in here was beyond me. The next seemed to be an override for the electricity circuits and an override for all the doors. I carefully avoided those.

The final two seemed the most promising. They were labelled 'Door 1' and 'Door 2'; to me that seemed a tad vague and unhelpful. Granted they had probably known which was which. I hadn't looked at the other side of the room, but I was willing to bet one of those was a fire escape in case of total chaos, which didn't seem like it could be all that dangerous. I mean, surely if it was dangerous you would label it as such? Like a big red cross or warning label or something? I shrugged; I'd already been charged by a Loch Ness monster. I could deal. I placed a finger on each switch, the smooth silver cold under my touch, and flipped them both up. The same loud buzzing filled the air; this time I had the good sense to cover my ears before it got too loud.

After a few seconds, I heard a click as a door lock disengaged. Looking to my right, I saw that the plywood door was now swinging back and forth on its hinges. Giving myself a self-five, and glad that no one else was around to see it, I made my way to the door, pausing a couple of seconds to see if the alarm for the electricity was going to sound. It didn't. Hoping I wasn't about to become bacon bits, I pushed the door away from me and walked through. The inside of this room was even muggier, the lack of windows and ventilation creating a choking atmosphere. I sucked in a couple of deep breaths, trying to get some kind of oxygen into my system and glanced around. This room looked more like the one from the industrial estate, a large metal table taking up most of the middle of the room. Thankfully this one was not stained a rust colour. I let out the breath I didn't realise I'd been holding. A couple of microscopes were set up along the far wall, along with some test tubes and Petri dishes. The only other thing in the room was a computer, the first I'd actually seen. I guess computers made it easy to track their movements and, for what appeared to be a secret company, that wasn't high on the priority list. Booting it up, I tapped my fingers against the keyboard as I waited for the screen to load. The blue screen suddenly sprang to life, asking me for a password.

Um. 1234?

I looked around the room, hoping that maybe something would jump out at me. When it didn't, I rested my head on my hands, trying to come up with some options.

GAI2017

A large error messages binged up in front of me. It was worth a shot.

RickLaws

Nope. Another error message. As I tried to come up with another attempt, a thought occurred to me. If this was the only computer in the building, it was probably used by pretty much every member of staff. I doubted they would all be able to remember the password perfectly, which meant they had probably written it down. I picked up the keyboard, smiling when a yellow Post-It note fluttered onto the desk. Turning it over, I started typing,

BLU201ACAR2017

Not as complicated as I had been expecting. A green tick appeared on the screen in front of me and the system began logging in. Soon enough, a grey home screen appeared with the GAI logo emblazoned across it. They weren't very imaginative. It was GAI in big letters, the G in grey, the A in red and the I in teal. I clicked on the file explorer and cringed as the fan immediately roared to life like a plane taking off; the computer was slow, lagging and I wondered how old this thing actually was. Eventually the file explorer opened up, revealing a whole host of folders, most with the same codes on as the cage switches. I opened the one named OTT103ACAR. I wanted to know more about Pip. The only thing in there was a single document; loading that up, I was confronted with what seemed to be a profile.

Name: OTT103ACAR

Species: Otter hybrid. Otter base genome. Also used nursing shark DNA for gills and artic fox DNA for survival in harsh climates.

Traits: Extremely friendly (not viable for further use). Intelligent. Advanced skills of communication; responds to stimuli (human) and evolved vocal responses. Echolocation.

Appearance: Otter base with concealed gills (able to retract completely under fur) and thicker, double-layered fur with grey/white mottling.

Additional Notes: Able to cope in fresh and marine water. 1.5 – 2km an hour swimming speed. 10-40 second dives.

Alongside the fact sheet were some images, I presumed, taken throughout the growth. The first showed Pip barely a day old, in a glass cage. The next was dated a week later but he had grown to about half his adult size and had his eyes open. The third was taken two weeks after that and showed Pip as he was now. I looked between the pictures in astonishment. That must be the accelerated growth hormone my brother had been talking about. The ability to go from new-born to fully grown in a month was incredible, and definitely not natural. I closed down the document, not wanting to read any more. One of the files was marked BLU203ACAR and, without even thinking about it, I had opened that one too. Another profile appeared.

Name: BLU203ACAR/ 'Nessie'

Species: Blue shark base genome. Thresher shark tail. Conger Eel head and neck. Coelacanth for added fins. Common octopus to change shape and colour. Sea mouse for iridescent setae.

Traits: Predatory nature. Strong and fast swimmer. Can change colour and shape to a degree. Sea mouse genes reflect the colour of the water for camouflage.

Appearance: Large, streamlined body. Three pairs of pectoral fins. Whip-like tail. Long neck and rounded head.

Notes: This run was closest to the plesiosaur/ Pistosaurus in appearance. Becoming increasingly adept at using setae for crypsis. Conditioning training has progressed suitably using

fish as response to stimulus. Acclimatised to conditions of the Loch after a number of hours.

The same trio of images accompanied the profile. The first was labelled 'New-born', although I don't think any of these animals were 'born'. In it, 'Nessie' was about as large as my torso, curled in a small tank, eyes closed. The next image was labelled 'Juvenile', showing 'Nessie' about the size of a bottlenose dolphin. The final image was taken from the glass window, showing 'Nessie' feeding by the glass, labelled 'Adult'. There were no dates on these ones but going by the progression in Eli's journal, it hadn't taken long for 'Nessie' to reach the adult stage of development. I clicked the x in the top right-hand corner, going back to the main files. I opened another one or two, again all of them containing the same profile for different creatures. Not that I'd seen anymore living creatures here.

A couple of the descriptions caught my eye, sending a shiver down my spine. Under the file marked PAN308DCAR was the image of a snarling panther. As far as I could see nothing was different about it but as I read further, it became clear that they had modified the animal to be able to hunt more effectively than it already did. Similar to BLU203ACAR, they had added common octopus and sea mouse genes which would help it camouflage. I shook that terrifying image out of my head and kept scrolling down until I came to a file simply entitled 'Stage 3'. It was the only one not containing a creature code. I double-clicked, waiting for the document to open up. It seemed to take an age, the mouse spinning as it loaded. Eventually, a white page appeared in front of me. In the centre it had 'Stage 3' underlined. I scrolled down and reams of text suddenly appeared; scanning the text quickly, my eyes settling on one paragraph as I caught sight of Eli's name.

Successful completion of Stage 2 (the 'Nessie' Project) has allowed for commencement of Stage 3. The initial stages will focus predominantly on the release of the 'Nessie' Project into the designated release sites. Following this, our teams will continue to monitor the released subjects via tracking chips. The process has already begun to buy property near the release sites in order to build docking stations. We expect this to be completed within the month. Therefore, we are now looking to relocate the current team to the newest project site, where our lead scientist Elliott Farrow will begin research. We have prioritised the 'Lycan' Project. Our research shows that the best site for the newest lab is just outside Freiburg. Project commencement will begin once we have successfully transferred all assets to the new site and released subjects from the 'Nessie' Project.

Freiburg.

At least I had a name. I had no idea where it was, but I had access to the internet, so it wasn't going to take me long. A few minutes of searching told me that it was a town in the Black Forest in Germany. I had no idea how far outside Freiburg they were planning to set up, but I had somewhere to start. Elation ran through me and I backed away from the computer, grinning, quickly turning it off and exiting out into the control room. Everything seemed the same as when I had gone into the room. I glanced over towards the stairs and the door, but I couldn't see Pip. If he had come down, I was sure he would have found me, so I shrugged, telling myself he had probably curled up somewhere in the lab. I wasn't sure if he was going to stick with me once we got outside. Part of me hoped he did, but I wasn't going to force him to. I'd be no better than them.

As far as this crazy nightmare has gone, this was pretty easy.

As I stepped out of the control room and pulled the door shut behind me, I was struck with a strange feeling. I froze, noting the tingling that was arching across my shoulders and my spine. Slowly, I pivoted on my heel, eyes scanning for whatever could have caused the sensation. It wasn't so much something in the air, but this feeling of being watched again. As I scanned the far end of the room, I realised the air was colder than it had been when I'd entered the plywood box. At the left-hand side of the room, between the two walls of cages, I could see movement in the plants and the whiteboards. Carefully, I made my way towards them. As I reached eye level, I saw that there had been a door in between the cages, a door which was now open.

Door 1 or 2 I'm guessing.

From the damp, earthy smell, it seemed like it led outside. Nothing else was moving, but I still couldn't shake this sensation of being watched. I spun on my heel, scanning the cages on the right-hand side of the door. I hadn't looked at these cages earlier, so realistically I wouldn't know if anything was wrong, but I checked anyway. Halfway down the cages, something had flopped through the bars; it looked like a paw but chunks of it were missing. As I went to move closer, it moved, and I stilled. The paw seemed to float up into the air and then, in a flash of white, another chunk of flesh was missing. I let out a small sound, caught somewhere between a squeak and a sob.

Tell me it's not invisible. Please.

As the sound left my mouth, the paw dropped down to the floor. A low rumble snaked across the air towards me, curling around my feet. It was only when I really focused that I realised a pair of gold eyes were staring at me. The air around them seemed to move weirdly; the low rumble increased to a growl and the concrete and bars seemed to *move* to form the shape of a creature. It looked like a big cat of some kind.

Like a panther maybe?

My stomach dropped. The bars seemed to shimmer, the colour changing from a silvery grey into a deep black and within seconds I was staring at a large, very muscled, very angry panther.

Surely this is taking camouflage to a new extreme? How did this thing even get out? I didn't open any of the cage doors. Unless...

I glanced back to the open door that I had assumed led outside,

Maybe it didn't get out. Maybe I let it in.

Before I had much time to consider that fact, the panther began to get up from its sitting position.

Okay. Time to move.

I flicked my eyes to the side trying to find somewhere I could hide. My best bet would be Pips cage.

Pip!

My stomach sunk even further. The door to the main lab was open. As was the door to the cave. I was beginning to understand why they had the ability to lock every single door in this place from both sides. I guess, when you're playing with predatory super animals, it's better to be safe than sorry. If this thing got out, who knows how many people it would kill. No one would be able to catch it.

Why the fuck did they make it?

I needed to get to the door to the main lab before it did. Now, I was fast, but not outrun a supernatural panther fast. I needed some way to distract it, so I could at least make it out of this room and hopefully stop it from getting any further. I looked back at the panther as it stared at me, teeth covered in blood.

Food.

I was sure I looked incredibly tasty, but if I could give it something bigger and easier, hopefully it would go for that. Maybe if I could get to the control room, open the door to the wolf-polar hybrid's cage and deactivate the electric shield the panther would go in there. It was worth a shot. I didn't think the plywood room would take much of a beating, but it might give me enough time to get the doors open. Plus, it would probably be too distracted trying to get to me to notice the open door. Decision made, I took a split second to figure out how long I had to get to the control room before it caught me. Seconds. The fact that I was on the right side of the room was a bonus, but I'd shut the door behind me, so I'd lose any extra time there. The low growl came from its mouth again.

Right. Go!

Darting to the right, I took off at a dead sprint to the control room. I could hear the click of its nails on the stone as it scrambled after me. As soon as I was close enough to the door, my hand was out, reaching for the handle. I yanked it open and shimmied inside, just as the panther slammed into the plywood. The entire box shook. I hurried over to the control room, flinching every time the panther flung itself at the door. It began to scratch the wood, its claws making an awful sound as it chipped away at the door. I scanned the codes looking for the one that started with POL. I found it and flipped the switch. The familiar buzzing filled the room; as it started, the attack on the door momentarily stopped. I leant close to the window to see the panther stop and fall back, head cocked as it listened to the sound. My movement towards the window caught its attention and it launched itself at the plexiglass, hitting it with a *thwomp.*

My heart thudded in my chest, breath coming in short, sharp bursts. From this close I could see the sinew and muscle hanging between its teeth from whatever poor creature it had started to devour. Its black fur was dampened with blood, turning the already dark colour into a terrifying cabernet. The buzzing stopped and I watched with bated breath as the door clicked open, slowly pulling back. The sound of the door, the tinny metal whirring, attracted the attention of the panther as well and it dropped back down onto its haunches, spinning to stalk towards the door. Like Pip though, it didn't step through. Instead it scented the air, eyes focussed on the carcass of the creature inside. The pause seemed to stretch on for hours, this weighted silence shattered only by my harsh breathing. Then, the alarm rang out across the room and the blue electric fizzed across the doorway. I couldn't even cover my ears, my hands frozen to my side. The panther stalked back and forth in front of the door.

It's working!

As soon as the electricity died away, it leapt into the cage, tearing a huge chunk out of the carcass's shoulder. Leaning back to the switchboard, I flipped the switch back up, hoping that it would do the opposite and close the door. There was a short, sharp buzz and the open door disengaged from the wall, slowly, achingly slowly moving back across. I took my opportunity to move out of the control room, the panther still tearing chunks off of the carcass. Blood dripped from its open jaw and I forced myself to look away.

Quietly, I edged around the side of the plywood box, the door almost closed. It hadn't seemed to notice. As soon as I was clear of the box, I set off in a sprint, eyes focused on the stairs. I heard a roar behind me, my footsteps alerting the creature to the closing door and the resulting crash of metal. I didn't look behind me. But I could imagine what had happened as I made my feet move faster across the uneven stone surface. There was a screeching sound, like metal being forced back, accompanied by another roar. I reached the steps and bolted up them, the rickety wood swaying from side to side. Launching myself from the last step, I landed in the lab, turning and kicking the stairs as hard as I could. Below I could see the panther forcing its way out of the cage. As I repeatedly kicked the stairs, the wood cracking under the force, it wriggled its way through and started racing towards me and the open door. One last kick sent the stairs tumbling to the side. I pressed the button on the control pad, the door sliding shut smoothly, and a lot faster than the animal cages. As the door clicked into place, there was another roar from behind the door, then a thud. I watched the door nervously, hoping it would hold.

Silence.

With a sigh of relief, I sank to the floor. There was a squeak behind me, and I turned to see Pip crawl out from underneath one of the tables, galloping over and launching himself into my lap. I hugged him close to my chest,

"It's okay. You're okay. You're okay." I murmured although I'm pretty sure we both knew that I was partially talking to myself and my still racing heart. Another roar sounded from below, making us both jump. Then the alarm sounded, and I heard a fizzing sound, followed by a pained scream. The smell of burned flesh rose up through the edge of the door and I wrinkled my nose.

I mean, I can't say I'm upset about it. I think we're all better off without that creature roaming free.

I leant my head back and closed my eyes already ready for this adventure to end.

"Guess what Pip? We're going to Germany!" I tried to sound excited, but I could feel my eyes closing.

I guess a quick nap won't hurt.

I didn't have much of a choice. Within seconds I'd given in to sleep, Pip still curled in my lap.

Chapter 10

I woke with a start, limbs jerking as I looked around. Slowly, the reality of where I was coming back to me and I relaxed back against the cold stone wall. Pip wasn't in my lap, but had curled up next to me instead, nose tucked under his tail, making tiny snuffling noises. I smiled softly, concerned with how attached I'd grown to him after only a few hours. Stretching, I groaned, feeling the ache in my muscles; I was pretty sure I was going to have a lot of bruises under my clothes. The dryness of my throat caught up with me and I licked my lips to try and get some hydration. I had a bottle of water in my backpack, but it was over the other side of the room and nothing in me wanted to get up right now.

It was only when I shifted and realised I also needed to pee that I huffed, bracing my hands on the floor to get up. Pip blinked at me from under his tail, but didn't move, obviously satisfied I wasn't about to run off. I hadn't noticed any toilets in here but needs must. I darted back into the cave to do what I needed to do then grabbed my water bottle from my bag, taking long gulps to try and soothe my dry throat. I needed to get some more food and drink before jetting off to Germany. It would probably have to be once I got to the airport.

Somewhere I really need to start going to, otherwise I'll never get to Germany.

I shoved Eli's notebook in my backpack and went back over to the glass window in the wall, doing another check for Nessie. I couldn't see her, and even though she terrified me, I wasn't going to leave her without some more food. I pressed the fish button as many times as I could, watching the jets of water repeatedly propel bundles of fish out into the murky water. Eventually it couldn't eject any more fish, just sending bubbles instead. Satisfied, I found the button I'd used to open the glass and pressed it again. Like most of the buttons here, it did the opposite of what I'd originally pressed it for and closed the wall. It was even stranger watching two large pieces of what looked like stone slide across in front of this window into an underwater world now than it had been when I'd arrived… I looked at my phone clock… nearly 18 hours ago.

Damnit. I slept for longer than I thought. I really need to get a move on.

The wall sealed itself back together with a satisfying *click;* turning away, I looked around the lab to see if there were any other doors I needed to shut. I really didn't want to be responsible for letting any of their creatures out into the world. Nothing else jumped out at me, the only other door I'd opened already shut after my run-in with the invisible panther.

I shook my head as I caught myself.

Invisible panther. No one would believe that.

Pip had uncurled from the floor, padding around after me as I checked the doors and storage containers. I'd put everything back as it was, not that it really mattered since they'd abandoned the place. I cast a glance at his fluffy face as he followed me, unsure as to how I was going to take him with me.

He might not want to come.

I let that sink in. He might not want to. As soon as we got out of the lab, he could run off into the forest and never look back. I really hoped he didn't, but it was a real possibility. Casting one last look around the lab, I walked out of the main door into the cave, finding the concealed button and shutting the door so it no longer looked amiss. Outside, it was early morning, the dewy atmosphere trickling into the cave. I could see the soft rosy light of the sunrise through the canopy of trees. Everything seemed to have calmed down since the storm, not even a hint of the wind and rain remaining. Pip stayed glued to my heel, trotting along, every so often letting out squeaks as he paused to observe something new. I laughed watching him; he'd never been out of that cage. This was all completely new to him and he seemed to be revelling in everything he came across.

I set off back towards the Loch, since that was the last place where I'd had any sense of direction. We wandered back under the tree-lined grassy path, my boots leaving soft imprints in the bright green road. My mind wandered as I remembered the metal circlet I'd found near one of the trees, the circlet I still had in my backpack. I'd completely forgotten about it, the lab distracting me, but now that I knew where it had likely come from, it also dawned on me what it had probably been used for. Something that size and thickness looked like it could have been a collar of some kind. Eli had mentioned finding a way to control Nessie, and probably some of the other animals, and I wondered if that collar had been one attempt at a solution. If it emitted a sound like the one that had pulled Nessie over to the glass, it could probably stop any one of those creatures I'd seen in its tracks.

That would have been nice to have whilst facing that panther.

I'd have to get rid of it before I got to the airport, there was no way I could explain that to security. But, if possible, I wanted to leave it somewhere concealed, since I didn't know exactly what it could do. Eventually, the pathway I'd been following disappeared, the trees climbing a large slope that lead into more forest. My ankle let out a twinge as I remembered rolling down that slope in the pouring rain. Luckily, it seemed like I hadn't done any permanent damage to my ankle. Just bruising to add to my collection. Pip slowed to a halt beside me as I considered how to get back up the slope. The ground was not as boggy, but there were definite patches of mud and, at a steep incline, I had next to no chance of getting up to the path.

Pip looked from me to the slope, starting his chattering noise again. Before I had chance to bend down, he skittered off, sniffing at the slope before launching himself onto a small outcrop. He did this again, jumping up the slope on small pouches of rock and sod. When he got to the top, he looked back down at me and chattered again. I grinned, moving to the first patch he'd jumped on to.

This is great. I'm taking climbing advice from an otter.

I placed one foot on the clump of dirt, jumping up and balancing as I sized up the next step. Next to the second rock was a low hanging tree so I stretched my arms out and grabbed the closest branch, using it to hop over. Slowly, I made my way up the same path as Pip, the outcroppings of rock much sturdier than the rest of the slope. When I heaved myself up to the top, he let out a series of squeaks, bouncing around in front of me. I gave him a quick stroke, swiping the hair back from my face as I looked around. I'd come from the right when I'd been leaving the Loch so I set back off in that direction, careful to stay as close to the middle of the path as I could. A few times, I heard something rustle in the bushes behind me, but Pip paid it no attention, so I told myself it was probably a bird.

We reached the edge of the Loch within fifteen minutes, the early morning light dousing everything with a golden shine. Even the water seemed to sparkle, a complete change from the dull, rain pocked expanse I'd left yesterday. I sat down on one of the rocks surrounding the Loch, shimmying my bag from my shoulders and letting it slide into the gap between two of the large boulders. Pip scurried around, darting into bushes and to the edge of the water, looking back at me with excited eyes.

"Go on then." I rolled my eyes, pretty sure he wouldn't understand me, but surprisingly, he seemed to nod, launching himself into the Loch. I had a momentary burst of panic as I remembered that the literal Loch Ness Monster was in there but reminded myself I'd left her lots of fish, so hopefully she wouldn't be hungry. Or vengeful. I rolled my shoulders, reminding myself of the route back to the main road, and to the next step of my journey. Maybe I could get an animal crate and pretend Pip was a very fluffy dog. Or a ferret. The sun was higher in the sky now, beaming down through a small smattering of candyfloss clouds and I turned my face towards it, enjoying the warmth. Out in the Loch, Pip's head broke the surface for a few seconds before he dove back under, tail flicking above the surface. His fur had completely slicked down, making him look a lot smaller. I grabbed the handle of my backpack, unzipping it and pulling out the collar.

In the sunlight, the shiny metal was almost blinding, the thick band easily the size of that panther's neck. If there was something electric in this collar, I didn't know how to turn it on. As far as I could see there was no button or hidden latch, like the kind GAI seemed so fond of. Hopefully the bottom of the Loch would be concealed enough to keep it away from anything it could harm. I wasn't sure whether it would work on Nessie, given that she hadn't been wearing one, and the bottom of a Loch was better than the middle of a forest.

I stood up, my thighs crying in protest and hobbled my way across the collection of pebbles to the Loch. Pip reappeared again, closer to the shore, squeaking at me. I wanted him out of the water before I threw this in, in case it reacted in any way. I jerked my head to the side, motioning to the large boulders near where I'd thrown my backpack. He squeaked once and dove back under, moving too fast for me to even track him. I turned the collar over in my hands again, wanting to wait until I saw him leave the water. At the very underneath of the collar was a code, etched into the metal. I squinted at it, trying to make out the letters.

"It's the identifying code." I jumped as an all-too-familiar voice snaked its way over my shoulders. Spinning round, I took a step back, water licking the sole of my boot. Caden was stood a few metres behind me, casually grinning with his arms crossed. I opened my mouth to say something, but nothing came out. I'd known he would come to find me, but I guess I had been hoping something else would find him first. He took a couple of sauntering steps towards me, the same cocky smirk on his face; now, it didn't reach his eyes. They were hard as flint, the grey still dark even in the morning light.

He stopped a few strides away, eyes flicking up and down the length of my body. I returned the gesture; it was only as I scanned back up that I noticed the dried blood on the arm of his top, a semi-circle of pin points, almost like a bite, marring the edge of a thick-lined tattoo. He saw me looking and moved his arm, mouth losing the smirk. "Would you like me to show you how that collar works?" His voice was cold, no hint of the joking guy I'd actually liked. I guess I had tied him up and left him unconscious in a warehouse, so I could understand that. Without giving me a chance to respond, he reached into his pocket and pulled out a small black piece of plastic. It almost looked like a phone, but a quarter of the size. "The great thing about these is that they developed them to work across numerous different devices. Anyone with the access codes could use them. And, lucky for you, I have the access codes. So, you get your own personal demonstration." I found my voice, finally.

"I don't think I want one thanks." I turned back towards the Loch, moving my arm back to throw it into the water, hoping Pip was out and staying out of the way. Caden chuckled behind me,

"Nu-uh, I don't think so *babe*." I heard a *click* behind me and a split second later the collar began to emit the same ear-splitting screech that I'd heard through the glass window, except this time there was no glass and no way for me to get away. I let out a strangled sound, dropping to the ground and covered my ears. The collar fell into the shallow water next to me, sinking into the stones. As I pressed my palms to my face, something warm trickled out of my ears onto my skin. Pulling away one hand, I blanched when I saw it was blood. The ringing from the collar increased, tearing through my eardrums and sending my head into a spin. I couldn't open my eyes, my balance completely off. I doubled over on the ground, my head almost touching the stones and *screamed.* I kept screaming until I ran out of breath, the screams petering into dry sobs that choked up my throat. I couldn't stop.

The ringing got even higher. I could feel the heat pounding in my head; my stomach rolled and churned and I fell to my side, desperately trying to escape the sound. Then, with no warning, it simply vanished. I was left gasping on my side, black spots across my vision as I tried to right myself. Caden's feet appeared in front of me, and even with the damage to my ear drums I could hear him laughing. He knelt down so his face was in my line of vision, pulling my chin to the side so I was forced to look at him. The world had reduced to a pinpoint again and the only thing I could see was his face. I tried to get my throat to work, to say *something,* anything, but I didn't seem to have any control over my body now. The gently lapping waves hit my back, the cold sending small shockwaves through me, over and over. Caden's lean fingers gripped my jaw until my teeth hurt. He started talking, the sound just filtering through the static that was buzzing through my whole body,

"It's so *interesting* isn't it? The effect it has on humans. When they designed them, they had only had the subjects in mind, but I've found that they can be just as beneficial when dealing with *irritating girls*." He held up the little black device in his other hand, turning it back and forth between his fingers, "Not quite enough to kill you, but enough to render you incapable of fighting back. Exactly how I like them. You see, *Ari,* I'd been hoping something else would take care of you. First, you almost got electrocuted trying to be a hero but that little rat you let out warned you. Then you pressed the call button and almost ended up drowning under the weight of the water that would have filled the lab if good ole Nessie had broken through. But somehow you survived. So, I gave a little helping hand, directing one of the subjects your way when you stupidly opened the outdoor pen doors and yet you managed to not only escape, but make fried cat fritters."

He sent the panther in. The bastard.

"You're probably thinking, why didn't I just come in and kill you? Well, I happened to enjoy watching you struggle to succeed again and again. In case you didn't realise, the whole lab has cameras. Another thing I can access with this nifty little device. And, despite what you may believe, I'm not a bad guy. I wasn't going to actually kill you; I just thought I'd let something else take care of the annoying issue you'd become. But, as it turns out, it was not to be. There is no way I can let you get to Germany, so I've had to take matters into my own hands. Luckily for me, you came back to the Loch and you still had the collar in your backpack. It was like a perfectly laid out plan, just waiting for me to execute it. Or… execute you I guess." He paused, smiling down at me. This wasn't the smirk or the cocky smile, but a completely malicious, evil grin. It certainly wasn't human. I made a weak attempt to move whilst he was pausing, something which only made him chuckle.

"You won't be able to move for another minute or so. Even then you'll be so incapable of controlling your own limbs, you wouldn't be able to walk, let alone swim." *Swim?* I closed my eyes as I realised his plan, hoping they didn't show the fear that had galloped its way to my chest. Putting his device back in his pocket, Caden slipped both his arms under my prone body, scooping me up with ease. My head lolled back even as I tried to fight it. I had no control. He began walking. I could see, with my head flopping back, the water level rising as he waded further and further into the Loch. When the water was touching my legs and feet, he stopped, moving his hand to lift my head up so I was looking at him.

"I'll tell Eli you send your love." He murmured, mouth flush to my ear, before throwing me out into the lake. I gasped for as much air as I could before I fell like a dead weight, hitting the water with a resounding splash. Holding the largest breath I could, I closed my eyes as I went under, the frigid water immediately stiffening my limbs. I wanted to move, to panic, but I was trapped inside my own body, sinking lower and lower. The dappled sunlight faded, the grey of the deeper water taking over. As I sank, screaming internally at my own limbs to respond, I kept frantically trying to move any part of my body, concentrating on my fingers and toes. Anything to get them to move. I knew that, even though I was a good swimmer, even though I could hold my breath for about a minute and a half, the cold of the water and the increasing depth was eating away at any chance of survival I had.

Out of the corner of my eye, something flashed past. My already racing brain came to the conclusion all to quickly; Nessie. A shadow passed next to me, so large that it couldn't be anything else, her powerful swimming moving the water around me, so I seemed to float. The next second, her neck snaked round, head looming towards me, sharp rows of teeth aiming straight towards my face. I closed my eyes, waiting for the impact. There was a sudden *whoosh* of water next to me and I opened my eyes to see a small, mottled white shape blur past, attacking Nessie's face. Her head pulled around, blood streaming from one eye. She snapped at the shape, but it darted out of the way, tail flicking,

Pip!

The momentary distraction was enough. I felt one of my hands respond, the slow twitch of fingers and, as Pip darted in and out of Nessie's snapping jaws, the rest of my limbs began to work. I kicked with my legs, weakly at first, but enough to stop the slow descent into the Loch. There was blood in the water around me; some of it from Nessie's eye, some of it still leaking from my ears. As the blood floated towards the gigantic creature, her head flipped round again, slitted pupils narrowing on me. Her body curved, the pectoral fins creating a huge current under the water, buffeting me. I knew the air in my lungs was running out, could feel the need to gasp working its way through my system.

As Nessie raced back towards me, I gave a huge kick with my legs, just enough to move me out of her bite. I kicked down with one foot, hitting her on the top of the head, sending her swimming off a little way to circle back. There was a splash above me as Pip dove back down, his eyes focused on Nessie. I began swimming up, arms frantically pulling the water around my body, the small glimpses of sunlight beginning to filter back through. As I moved higher and higher, I could feel the current being created below me. I glanced down through the stinging water to see Nessie flip around in an arc, diving after Pip, who darted in and out of her fins. My eyes widened as I realised her tail was heading directly for me.

I pulled my legs up, tucking them to my body as the end of her tail whipped across the water. There was a slash of red-hot pain in my leg and I looked to see more blood drifting into the grey water, a startling scarlet ribbon. I couldn't see how deep the cut was, but I wouldn't stand a chance if I kept bleeding like this. Pip was distracting Nessie but sooner or later, he would get tired. With renewed determination, I flung my arms up and swam with broad strokes, heartbeat pumping in my ears. The second my hand breached the surface of the water, cool air surrounded me, a welcome shock. I gave another kick and burst up through the surface of the water, gasping in gulps of air. Then I started swimming to the shore. We had ended up nearly in the centre of the Loch, the wide bulging shape meaning I was at least a minute's swim from the shallow, stony shore. Adrenalin raced through me; I had no idea if Nessie was about to surge up and drag me back down. I just kept swimming,

Left arm, right arm, breathe, left arm, right arm, breathe.

I repeated the mantra to myself, taken back to my school swimming lessons, the PE teacher shouting at us from the edge of the pool. It was nothing like this, but somehow it helped. After an agonisingly slow crawl, I could see the shallow water and the stones, slicked with spray and shining in the sunlight. As soon as my legs hit the stones, most of the fight went out of me. I dragged myself up onto the shore, far enough away that the water couldn't touch me and collapsed, eyes still on the Loch. From here, the water almost seemed calm, the occasional ripple belaying what was going on underneath the surface. Frantically I searched for Pip, any indication that he was alive.

Nothing.

I could feel the tears welling up in my eyes, trickling down my face to puddle on the stones beneath me. I closed my eyes, completely exhausted. The forest was alive around me, birds singing from the trees, leaves rustling, so I didn't hear the small splash from the Loch, my hearing still recovering from Caden's little toy. But I felt the cold nose nudging my face. I opened my eyes to see Pip, bedraggled but very much alive. He was watching me with wide eyes, his tiny nose wiggling. As soon as I moved, lifting my head off the stones, he exploded in a rush of action, wiggling towards me, letting out a series of excited yelps. I coughed a laugh, some of the Loch water still caught in my throat. Still too tired to do anything, I scanned over him with my eyes. He seemed okay, although there was a small patch of blood on his side. With the amount of blood in the water though, that might not even be his.

My mind went to the cut on my leg. I couldn't feel my leg, the water so cold that it had numbed any of the pain, but it hadn't looked good even underwater. I let myself lay still for a couple more minutes, hoping I wasn't bleeding out on the stones, but I soon felt my limbs begin to shiver. Heaving myself up into a sitting position, I took deep breaths, trying to dissipate the light-headedness. My limbs didn't even feel attached to my own body, the same kind of sensation as you get just before pins and needles. I concentrated on moving my right leg round, the one with the cut. I winced as it came into view. The cut was deep and long, the tail having sliced through my jeans and down half my shin. It was still weeping blood, a slow trickle that pooled at the top of my boot.

This is not good.

I might have been stating the obvious to myself, but it was that or go into a full meltdown. I had a first aid kit in my bag…

My bag!

Pushing myself onto my hands and knees, I began the slow crawl over to the rocks, hoping Caden hadn't got to my backpack. Pip scurried beside me, his thick fur obviously preventing the cold that was currently sweeping my entire body. When I reached one of the rocks I'd placed my bag between, I scrabbled to get purchase on the smooth surface, hauling myself up. I let all of my weight rest on the rock, leaning over. I could see the handle of my backpack sticking up between the rocks, my face breaking into a relieved smile. There may have also been a few tears but the Loch water still dropping from my hair quickly swallowed them up. Leaning even further over, I stretched out one of my arms and grabbed the handle, tugging until I felt it move itself free of the rocks and slide.

Sinking down onto the stones at the other side of the rock, I dove into the bag, pulling out everything I could reach. The first aid kit was at the very bottom. I pulled it out with shaking fingers, setting it to one side before I moved everything else back into my backpack, which I placed beside me. I didn't have anything to stitch it up, but I did have dressings and gauze, enough to see me until I could get to a hospital. I tore away the section of my jeans that had been shredded, then grabbed some antiseptic wipes and the last bit of water from my water bottle. I upended the bottle into the gash, flushing out small pieces of stone that clung to the edges of the wound then ripped open one wipe and pressed it against my leg, gritting my teeth at the wave of pain that followed. After I'd used the first one, I opened the second, folding it over and placing it as far into the wound as I could, biting my lip to hold in the scream. I pulled that one out, bloody, and discarded it with the rest of the rubbish before taking the dressing and placing it over my leg. The gauze ripped open easily in my teeth, fluttering out. I grabbed it before it hit the stones, applying pressure to the dressing with one hand and wrapping the gauze with another. When my leg resembled something out of a Halloween store decoration pile, I tied off the gauze and sat back against the rock. Hopefully that would hold. Pip nudged my hand, and I petted him, running my hands over his side. I couldn't feel a deep wound so I hoped if there was a cut it would heal fairly quickly.

Packing the remains of my first aid kit back into my bag, I closed my eyes to consider my next move. I didn't know how far ahead Caden was. Hopefully enough that he wouldn't be hanging around when I finally made it to the village. A trip to the hospital was going to delay me by a few hours but it should give Caden enough of a head start that I wasn't going to run into him. It would happen eventually, but I'd rather have a few hours to recover before the showdown. Even better, he could disappear back into the corporate clutches of GAI and I could get Eli out without ever having to see him again.

"It might be wishful thinking Pip, but he's an arsehole and I really don't want to have to see his face ever again." I murmured. Pip squeaked in agreement. I mean, I'm assuming it was agreement. I don't speak otter. I gave myself a few more minutes to recover then scrambled up, wincing as the various injuries made themselves very apparent. I moved my backpack onto my shoulder and began to hobble back towards the trail, my mind already in Germany with Eli.

Chapter 11

I glanced down at the new pair of jeans covering the bandage on my leg. There was a small lump in the fabric, though the hospital had done a much better job at bandaging the wound than I had. Walking through the town on my way to the nearest hospital, I'd attracted quite a few stares. It probably hadn't helped to have Pip trotting along beside me. I'd left him outside when I'd reached the hospital, depositing him behind some bushes with a stern command to sit and stay. He'd plonked his butt on the grass with a disgruntled chitter but remained where he was. Luckily for me the A&E department had been almost empty, the only person before me was a child with a broken arm that he kept proudly announcing to the room.

I did my best, as I hobbled to see the nurse, to keep any wincing from my face, but as soon as she sat me down and unwound the bandage, I couldn't help a small squeak. The air hitting the open wound was a lot more painful than I had expected. She asked me how it had happened. I told her I'd fallen whilst hiking and gashed my leg on a sharp rock edge. She gave me a dubious look but didn't ask anymore questions, instead flushing the wound with some antiseptic much stronger than the wipes I'd had in my first aid kid. I know because I had to bite the inside of my mouth to keep from screaming. Then she stitched me up. I'd never had anything stitched before, and I hope never to have to again; it was not pleasant. I may have also told her I was crying from hay fever. She had the decency not to call me out on that one. When she was done, she wound a bandage around my shin and handed me some cream to apply to the wound, with a concerned look in her eyes. I thanked her, fervently hoping I wouldn't be back.

Pip was still sitting outside when I came out; he jumped at me with far too much enthusiasm, attracting concerned glances from a lot of bystanders. Given that my jeans had still been a shredded mess thanks to my DIY surgery, I figured I would need some new jeans before I would be allowed on a plane. And possibly an animal crate. Weirdly, I could find both in the same store in the town centre; an outdoors/pet store. It also had a café. It was pretty busy, so they'd clearly cornered a good market. Inside, I made a beeline for the pet section, very aware that Pip was following me like a dog, but that he looked like a wild animal (which I guess he was). They had a multitude of crates and travel cases, along with blankets and even travel sickness pills for animals. Pip glanced at the crate I picked up with trepidation but didn't seem to want to leave me to avoid travelling in it. I also grabbed a harness and leash. He *really* wasn't happy with that one but eventually, I managed to strap him in, telling the store assistant that he was a special breed of ferret. It's funny what people will accept when they don't know what else to say. Before I went to buy some new jeans to cover my whopping great bandage, I picked up a variety of treats. I realised I had no idea what Pip could and would eat and when he had last eaten.

The clothing section was much the same as any outdoorsy type store. Rows and rows of every waterproof jacket you could ever possibly need (and a lot that you probably didn't) followed by a single rack of clothing for the rest of your body. The jeans were easy enough to find; there was only one pair in my size, so that made my decision easier. Since I had no idea what was waiting for me in Germany, or how long it would be before I got to another store like this, I dipped into my emergency cash to buy a couple of layers of extra clothing, some socks and a new pair of boots. Then I asked the cashier if I could pay for the clothes and change into them straight away. He glanced down at my missing shin fabric and nodded, pointing me in the direction of the changing room. I could have used a card, but I didn't know how much it was going to cost to get to Germany.

As I walked out of the store in my new clothes, with Pip scurrying along next to me, it occurred that maybe I should tell someone I was heading to a different continent. Pulling my phone out from my backpack (I was so glad I'd decided to leave it in there instead of my pocket. I wasn't sure it would have survived my dip in the Loch.) I sent a quick message to Jake and Becca. I was sure Jake had filled Becca in by now about my impromptu trip to Scotland, and at least if I went missing, they would have a vague idea of where I was. Given that I didn't even have an exact idea of where I was heading, I couldn't tell them more than Freiburg. Almost immediately my phone buzzed, texts from the both of them coming in simultaneously.

Please don't do anything stupid xxx

Try not to do anything more stupid than you've already done J x

I grinned; they didn't know half of the stupid shit I'd done. It was a good thing they didn't or they'd both be on the next plane up here to detain me. Reassuring them that I was fine, I put my phone back in my pocket and made my way back to my hotel to grab the rest of my stuff and drive back to Inverness airport.

***

Once there, my suspicions that getting to Freiburg wouldn't be overly straightforward were confirmed. There were no direct flights from Inverness to the nearest airport to Freiburg, which was Frankfurt. As I stood at the help desk, Pip snuffling around in the crate at my feet, I could feel the despair start to set in. Caden had a good 6-hour head start on me, which was great in terms of not running into the guy who'd tried to kill me, but not great for getting to Eli before they decided it wasn't safe and moved again. All in all, it would take around five hours to get to Frankfurt and another two on a train to Freiburg. That was, until the woman at the helpdesk informed me that Pip wouldn't be able to travel for at least 24 hours. I stared at her.

"Why not?" It was never going to be as straightforward as two planes and a train.

"They need 24 hours notice in the receiving airport, as well as copies of your pet's passport and recent veterinary certificate of health. You do have those, don't you?"

Nope. That would require Pip to actually be a ferret. Any vet would be able to see he isn't and then we would open up a line of questioning I don't really want to answer.

I nodded enthusiastically.

"I do. I've packed them in my suitcase though,

so I'll need to go and find them." I gave her a toothy grin and moved away from the helpdesk, hoping she couldn't see the worry come over my face. Sitting down on a row of seats, I lifted Pips crate onto my lap. He snuffled at my hand through the grate.

"What are we gonna do buddy? I can't leave you here, but I have to go to Germany." I chewed my lip as Pip tilted his head, watching me. Could I call Jake? He'd be on the next train up here to take Pip back with him. I looked back at the almond eyes that were studying me through the bars and shook my head. I couldn't take him from one cage only to hand him off to a strange person in another. I'd just have to find another way to Germany. I started searching alternative routes.

"Looks like you and me are going on a lot of trains." Already the thought was exhausting. The journey would take nearly a full day. I scanned over the route and sighed. It was this or leave Pip behind. There was no way I was doing that after he saved my life. I knew what Jake or Becca or even Eli would say, but for the first time in my life, I didn't care. Adding the train tickets to my basket, I hoped I'd still get to Freiburg in enough time. My first train left from Inverness station in just over two hours. I glanced around, peeking through the throngs of passengers around me, trying to find something that would get me to the station. A shuttle bus sign at the far end of the airport jumped out at me, offering transfers to and from the station. Feeling a little bit of hope come back, I jumped up grabbing my suitcase and Pips case. The sudden movement made a lot of the people walking around me pause; every single one of them immediately looked at Pips case. I wasn't sure on the restrictions on trains, but I was willing to bet somewhere along the line, I would need to prove that Pip wasn't a wild animal. Which I couldn't do. Instead of heading to the shuttle bus, I made my way to a luggage store, finding a large backpack with some vented fabric on the top.

Perfect for a small otter to hide in.

Buying it, I locked myself in the disabled toilet, letting Pip out of the crate.

"Right buddy. We need to keep you hidden. So, what we're gonna do is put you in here" I held up the backpack which Pip sniffed curiously, "and you're gonna stay quiet. There's ventilation, so you'll be able to breathe, and I'll sneak you food and drink. Sound good?" Pip chittered, which I took as a yes. Transferring some of my worn clothes from my suitcase to the backpack I made him a bed and hoisted him in. He immediately curled up, blinking up at me as I folded the top of the backpack over and clipped it into place. Then I placed my smaller backpack in my suitcase and hid the animal crate by the door of the toilet. Carefully, I lifted the bag up onto my back, trying not to jostle it too much.

"You okay in there?" There was an answering squeak. I let out the breath I'd been holding and settled the backpack into the middle of my back. Taking hold of my suitcase handle, I edged my way out of the disabled toilet and back into the airport. The guy holding the shuttle bus sign was still there. I made my way over as smoothly as I could, most of the crowds moving out of the way of my suitcase, which I wheeled in front of me. My leg still ached with every step, but the cream had numbed most of the pain, so I hopefully didn't look too suspicious as I approached the driver. Within a few minutes I was sat on the shuttle bus, Pip's backpack held gingerly on my seat as we set off to Inverness station.

I really hope this works.

***

Inverness – Edinburgh: 3 ½ hours.

The coach around me was mostly quiet, only one business man tapping away on his laptop about a quarter of the way down. I chose a pair of seats near the doors, mostly hidden from view of the rest of the passengers and shoved my suitcase in the footwell of the seat by the window. Then I carefully removed my backpack and placed it on the seat by the window before sliding into the aisle seat. Pip had barely made a sound since I'd put him into the bag in Inverness airport. I hoped it was because he knew he needed to stay quiet, but a larger-than-I-would-like part of me was freaking out that he hadn't had enough oxygen, so when I unclipped the top flap to see two bright eyes staring back at me, a weight lifted off my shoulders. Giving him a quick pet, I placed a small tub of water and some food in the bottom of the bag. I could hear him gently lapping at the water, every so often pausing to crunch some of the treats I'd given him. The train pulled away from the station, jolting me forward. I'd forgotten how lethargic trains felt before they got going, the agonising slow build-up. I rested my head back against the seat, keeping one eye on my backpack. I was going to have to sleep more than a couple of hours at some point. I checked my train tickets, noticing an overnight gap in Gare Du Nord. I was sure there would be a hotel near the station somewhere that I could sleep in for a few hours until my next train in the early morning. I was hoping for the sake of my bank account that I wasn't going to have many more hotels to pay for. I was getting dangerously close to my overdraft. As I retrieved the empty water tub from Pip, it dawned on me that he was going to have to use the bathroom at some point.

He can hardly go in the train toilet.

Hopefully, he would be okay until we got to Edinburgh, then I could find somewhere to let him out. I shook my head as the idiocy of transporting a genetically modified otter in a *backpack* really hit home. At the airport I'd been working on a few hours sleep and adrenaline. Now the adrenaline had passed, I was running on fumes and cynicism. I silently cursed myself. If we made it to Freiburg without being caught, it would be a miracle and, given my recent run in with the Loch Ness Monster, I wasn't having much luck in that department. Pulling out a pen and paper from the front pocket of the backpack, I started figuring out my plan for when I actually got to Freiburg. Positive thinking and all that. Given what I'd seen in the area surrounding Freiburg on the satellite images, and the apparent preference of GAI to build underground labs in forests, I had a lot of ground to cover. I mean, it was the *Black Forest.* HQ of Brothers Grimm. Famously frightening and incredibly vast. I started noting down possible routes, using Freiburg as a base. There was no way I was bringing Pip with me; he would have to stay in the hotel. The train picked up its pace, the jolting easing into a swaying motion instead. I placed one hand in the backpack, stroking Pip's soft fur whilst I continued to scour the satellite map for any possible place GAI could be hiding.

***

Edinburgh – London Kings Cross: 4hrs 15 mins

I looked up from my notebook as the doors

opened behind me. A young couple walked in, their hands interlocked even in the narrow alleyway of the train carriage. They didn't pay me any attention, just walked down to the middle of the coach and slid into a block of 4 seats. I'd been lucky with the journeys so far. In between my train from Inverness and this one I'd had just enough time to dart to an outdoor area of the station and let Pip out to do his business before grabbing some more water and jumping on this train. The carriage I'd picked had been empty when I'd got on, save for a member of the crew who simply smiled at me as I chose a seat. Since then, a few people had trickled in, picking seats far enough away from me that, if I wasn't so relieved, I would have started to take offense. Pip had been so well-behaved; anyone would think he was actually a domestic pet. The second I'd let him out at Edinburgh station he'd hastily done what he needed to do and darted back over to me, ready to go back in the backpack. It seemed like he'd made himself pretty comfortable. As I glanced in the bag, I could see that most of his body was hidden under one of my jumpers, his nose tucked under his paws as he slept. I didn't know if it was the motion of the trains or the warmth of the backpack, but he seemed perfectly content. Every so often, I fed him another couple of treats, the bag slowly dwindling. I'd have to find some actual food for him soon. Clipping the lid onto the bag, I wrapped the straps around my arm and let my head fall backwards against the seat. I could feel my eyes closing, getting dangerously close to falling asleep. I set an alarm for half an hour before we arrived in Kings Cross, hoping that the carriage wouldn't fill up anymore and let my eyes drift closed.

"You're such a sap Ari." I raised my head as Eli walked over to me, eyebrows raised. I was feeding a squirrel some peanuts out of my hand, laughing every time his paw touched my palm.

"Why? Because I'm doing something nice?" I sprinkled some more peanuts in my hand, grinning as the little creature's eyes widened and he began grabbing as many as he could hold. Eli shook his head, watching.

"He can fend for himself. He's a wild animal Ari. Not meant for you to play with." There was an undercurrent of something in his voice, but I couldn't figure out what it was. I turned back to the squirrel, loving the way his fluffy tail flicked to the side every now and then.

"It's making him happy Eli. It's hardly a crime." I kept my eyes on the animal in front of me until I heard Eli sigh and walk away, his feet crunching across the grass. We agreed on most things, but we always seemed to come to blows when it came to animals. He saw them from a strictly biological point of view; he wanted to know why they acted the way they did. I wanted to help them. I finished the

bag of peanuts, emptying the last few crumbs into my hand. When he was finished, the squirrel put both his paws in my palm, blinking up at me, his nose twitching. I laughed and shook my head.

"Sorry buddy, they're all gone." He seemed to consider me for a few more seconds then scampered away. I stood up, brushing leaves off my knees and turned back towards the house. Eli was stood at the kitchen window, frowning at me. I ignored him.

I woke from the dream as the train stuttered to a stop in a station. The carriage was a little busier now, a low hum of voices drifting across the seats. Immediately, I opened the backpack, suddenly afraid Pip wouldn't be there. He was. He pulled his nose from under my jumper and blinked, disgruntled. I suppressed a smile at how human he seemed sometimes. It was just like the squirrel, in a way. I checked my phone, turning off the alarm that was about to sound. A couple of hours of sleep was better than nothing.

***

St Pancras International – Gare Du Nord: 3hrs 15 mins.

Up until this point, I'd managed to avoid most of the people by picking the most deserted carriage; because of the time of day, they'd not been very busy. But I didn't have that option on the Eurostar. I'd also forgotten that I would have to go through security. In line for the bag scanner,

I chewed my bottom lip, eyes darting. If I put my backpack through the scanner, Pip would be discovered in an instant. I needed a distraction. The security line was quite busy, so I was willing to bet that they would already be stressed. I just needed to add to the mix. As I neared the front of the queue, I made sure to increase my limp on my injured leg. Then, as I was motioned forward to put my stuff in a tray, I stumbled forward, crying out. Immediately, the attendant ran towards me.

"Ma'am? Ma'am are you okay?!" He crouched down in front of me. Since my leg really did hurt after hitting the floor, a few tears came easily. I gasped a couple of sobs for good effort,

"N-no I can't walk, my leg..." I trailed off, glancing at my leg. He looked too, so I continued, "I have a recently stitched wound and I think it may have just split open." His face went a little white as his head whipped around, looking for another member of staff. "Can you- could you take me to a seat?" I wheezed, wincing for effect. He nodded, helping me up. "Oh! My suitcase." I glanced over to where I had abandoned it.

"It's okay. We can have someone take that through security for you. If you'd just come this way..." he took my elbow and began to lead me to a seating area, away from the main area. I could see the route through security from here, a separate section that wasn't in use today. As I lowered myself onto the seat he stepped back,

"I'm going to get one of our members of staff who can help you. Just stay here." He hurried off, talking quickly into his radio. As he disappeared, I opened my backpack, pulling Pip out. I had no idea if this would work, but I had no other option at this point. He'd understood me before. I placed him on the floor, hoping the member of staff didn't come back.

"Run through there" I pointed to the empty security area, "And wait." Pip looked over to the area and back at me.

Please understand me. I don't know how you've done it before, but I really need you to do it now.

After a couple of seconds, he squeaked and darted under the chairs, just in time for two members of staff to round the corner. The guy who'd helped me over here was talking to an older female staff member who was holding a first aid kit. They both smiled as they stopped in front of me.

"I hear you're having some issues with a wound on your leg?" her voice was kind, matching her smile and I felt bad for deceiving them. I nodded, wincing as she knelt down and felt my leg. As she rolled the leg of my jeans up, I took a deep breath and screamed. They both immediately crowded around me. From the corner of my eye I saw Pips fluffy tail disappear into the empty security area. A smile flickered across my face. The medic unwound the bandage on my leg, eyes widening as she took in the weeping wound. "That looks… pretty dramatic." She finished, gingerly prodding the area. Some blood trickled out around the stitches. "I'll give you something to numb the pain honey." I nodded. The guy had turned away, his face incredibly pale. Soon enough I was rebandaged and helped through security, my backpack flying through with no issues. As soon as I was through, I veered to the right, finding the exit from the separate security area and slumping down by it. I pushed my backpack onto its side, making sure the flap was open and pretended to be engrossed in my phone. Less than a minute later, Pip scurried into the backpack. I left the bag open for a few more moments, making sure I didn't make eye contact with the security guard who wandered past. Once he'd gone, I lifted my bag back up and closed the top, whispering to Pip through the ventilation,

"Well done, buddy."

Now to hope the whole plan didn't fall to pieces at the other end.

***

Gare de l'Est – Karlsruhe Hbf: 2hrs 30 mins

I felt human for the first time in days. After the Eurostar had arrived in Gare Du Nord, luckily with no one sat next to me, I found a cheap hotel for the night. I'd bought some water and food and shoved the 'Do Not Disturb' sign on the door. As soon as it was locked, I'd let Pip out. He jumped onto my lap, nudging my hand to get me to stroke his head. After that he'd scampered around the room, darting under the bed and back out. I sat in the middle, grinning as he jumped over my legs. He didn't seem any worse for wear after our escapades. I, on the other hand, was exhausted. I fed him some tinned fish, wrinkling my nose at the smell, and gave him a bowl of water before climbing into the bed, asleep almost before my head hit the pillow.

When I'd managed to get my eyes open some six hours later, I found Pip curled up at the end of the bed, head resting on my feet. He jumped up as soon as I did, chattering non-stop. My mind drifted back to St Pancras, and countless times before that, where he'd seemed to understand me perfectly. In his notes back in Kincraig, I'd read that he had evolved advanced communication skills, but they hadn't written anything else down. Curious, I sat down in front of him, waiting until he was calm, watching me closely.

"Pip." His head tilted, "Go to the backpack." He turned and walked over to where the backpack was laying, strewn on its side. "Go into the backpack." Immediately he disappeared inside it. I watched in amazement. I didn't know whether it was the genetic modifications or the training my brother had been doing with him, but he understood everything I was saying. I called him back out and he hurried over to me, jumping into my lap. We stayed like that until I realised we had a train to catch in half an hour and it was still a ten-minute walk to the new station. I powered to the station, glad my leg was still pleasantly numb and, for possibly the first time in my life, found the platform with time to spare.

The train itself was smaller than the previous ones, with spacious seats. I'd grabbed the first pair I'd seen, nerves beginning to curl in my stomach as I realised I would be in Freiburg *today.* Maybe even find Eli today.

***

Karlsruhe Hbf – Freiburg: 1hr

The final train before Freiburg.

I sat down, barely able to stay still. All of the seats in this train seemed to be blocks of four. I picked the one furthest away from the doors, hoping no one would sit this far down the carriage. Unfortunately, about half way through the journey, a pair of trainers appeared next to me. I looked up to see a middle-aged man in a suit with bushy eyebrows staring at me. He motioned to the seat across from me and I nodded; I couldn't really say no. I tried to close the flap of the bag, clicking the buckle into place without really looking. He placed his shoulder bag on the window seat and folded himself into the chair, his feet almost touching mine. I tucked my knees in, praying that Pip would stay quiet, like he'd done for most of the journey. As the train pulled away from the station, the clicking noise of the tracks disguising most of the background noise in the carriages, I relaxed my shoulders. I only had half an hour to go. After avoiding security and sneaking an otter around stations in four different countries, I couldn't let this all go to pot now.

The train moved along smoothly for the next 15 minutes. I pulled my notebook out, doodling in the margins of one of the pages. I could see the man look up every now and then to study me, but he never said anything. As we were approaching the final station before my stop, I began to put everything away, securing the various pockets. The train pulled into the penultimate station, but instead of the smooth glide to a stop that had accompanied every previous station, it juddered, sending my backpack flying forwards. I flung my hands out to stop it, feeling Pip scrabble against the sides as the sharp motion threw him about. As he was forced back against the seat, he let out a quiet squeak. I froze, holding my breath. The man looked at me, one eyebrow raised in confusion. His hands were on his own bag, saving it from falling to the floor. I shrugged, trying to look nonchalant. Pip stayed silent now, the train at a standstill. After a couple of seconds of heavy scrutiny, the man looked away. I removed my hands from around my backpack, letting it settle back into the seat, but I couldn't relax. For the last ten minutes of the journey, I was on edge. I could see his eyes flick to the backpack every minute or so, eyebrows furrowed as he studied it. As soon as the train announced *Freiburg* I stood up, carefully manoeuvring my backpack onto my back and grabbing my suitcase, beginning the walk down the train to the doors. When I'd reached them, I looked back. He hadn't moved, but he was still watching me. I turned away, my hand clenched around the handle of my suitcase. As soon as the doors opened, I jumped off the train, not looking back until I walked out of the station and into the afternoon sun. Then, and only then, did I let myself smile.

I'd made it. I was here and I was one step closer to finding Eli.

Part Three
Germany

Chapter 12

I left the hotel room with a backwards glance at Pip who was curled up on one of the single beds; I'd told him to stay quiet and stay put and in response he'd gone to sleep, which I guess fulfilled both of those criteria. The hallway was deserted, the drab carpeting softening the impact of my boots as I clomped along. I'd managed to snag a quick nap before heading back out since I didn't know how long it was going to be until I got to sleep again. The reception clerk nodded at me on my way out and I smiled a hello. Hopefully they would respect the 'Do Not Disturb' sign, otherwise they were going to get a fluffy surprise.

Once outside, I marvelled again at the town I'd found myself in. The streets underfoot were cobbled, shining with the light mist of rain that was falling. Everywhere I looked I felt like I'd fallen into a fairy tale; the houses painted in baby blues, delicate pinks, sunny yellows and deep reds overlooked by trickling fountains. Spires reached up into the watercolour sky, decorated with grinning gargoyles. Every so often the bubble would be broken by a tram quietly making its way through the old streets, slicing apart the crowds of people. If you looked above the houses and the churches, it seemed as though Freiburg was nestled into a mountain side, the lush green of endless trees circling the town. I couldn't help but wander for the first few minutes, my eyes drawn to each new thing, as I navigated my way down the streets. I stopped by the edge of a canal, leaning over the wrought iron fencing. Around me buildings painted the landscape, ivy climbing and snaking its way across brickwork. It was impossible to equate this beautiful town with GAI. Sighing, I stepped back from the canal, pulling up the map I'd saved on my phone.

The town itself was almost directly in the valley of two mountains on its Eastern side. Initially I'd panicked about where to start my search, since GAI could have gone in any direction from the centre of Freiburg, but once I'd pulled up the satellite imagery, I was almost positive they would have headed out to the East. The North and the West only had small smatterings of trees, bordered by more towns and villages and the South, although it led into mountain and woodland eventually, it was a fair trek from Freiburg itself, so I'd decided to concentrate my search on the Eastern side. There was a major road feeding through the two mountains and a couple of small towns on the edges of the woodland. Deciding I should just get started, I made my way through the streets of Freiburg, passing through the botanical garden until I got to the first trail, Waltersbergweg. I'd been trying to think like an evil company of scientists, and I figured they would want some kind of running water source near the lab, as well as the cover of a lot of trees. Almost parallel to the trail was a creek, Glasbach, the first of many creeks in the area I'd decided to start with.

Securing my backpack onto my shoulder, I set off on the trail. The ground underfoot was soft, the drizzle pervading through the dense canopy of trees. All around me I could hear animals and birds, rustling in leaves and scurrying in the undergrowth. Every so often, I would stop, and the noise seemed to stop with me. The forest itself was huge, the sunlight filtering through to leaves of the trees in dappled waves, warming the air around me. I could barely see through the foliage, keeping my eyes fixed on the trail instead. When the tree cover broke, every now and then, I could hear the trickle of what I hoped was Glasbach. I didn't really know what I was looking for as I trudged further and further into the Black Forest; some kind of indication that a lot of people had been in one place, I guess. Eventually the trail ran out. Up ahead I could see an indent in the trees, clearly made by hikers who'd decided to go off road. I grabbed my bug spray out of my bag and quickly sprayed myself. The last thing

I wanted was to get bitten. I tucked my jeans into my socks to try and avoid any ticks and set off into the treeline. This impromptu trail was definitely not going to be easy. Leaves and sticks crunched underfoot as I clambered over some fallen tree trunks and shimmied round rocks. The small compass I'd picked up in Scotland was keeping me in a vaguely straight line but, besides the knowledge that I was heading in a vaguely NE direction, I was lost.

How am I ever going to find this lab? It's useless. It could be anywhere, like literally anywhere. I'd have as much luck blindly throwing a rock.

I kicked a small rock, half wondering if I should actually pick it up and throw it. The deeper I got into the forest, the damper it became, the air clinging to me in droplets, my hair stuck to my forehead like a soggy crown. I lost track of how long I'd been walking, just trudging on hoping that somewhere up ahead I would find another trail or people. After what felt like hours, the forest seemed to thin a bit again, opening up so I could breathe without getting pine needles up my nose.

Maybe this means there's another trail coming up.

I ploughed forwards, somehow finding some enthusiasm, even though most of my body was aching. I'd applied a fair amount of numbing cream to my leg before setting out this morning, which meant it was the only part of me that wasn't aching. After a few more minutes of walking, I started to hear voices drifting through the bark of the trees. I picked up the pace, tripping over tree roots and moving low hanging branches out of my way. The crush of trees suddenly opened up completely, a clear path leading to what appeared to be a field. At the very least, I needed to sit down. Sweating, I broke through the tree line and out into the open space, stopping short as I realised that I'd reached some kind of picnic area. A few people looked up as I appeared, but most continued eating, their chattering filling the air of the small space with ease. In the centre of the groups of people was a huge tower that broke through the tops of the trees. It seemed to be made of metal, an internal stairway exposed through the white painted structure. At the top I could see a family, a small child jumping up to point at something in the distance.

That could be a pretty good vantage point.

I found a spot of ground near the tower and collapsed onto the floor in a graceful heap. I would wait until the family were done. Pulling off my bag, I grabbed a bottle of water and a cereal bar, chugging the water until I finally felt like my throat wasn't a bone-dry desert. Then I unwrapped the cereal bar, keeping an eye on the family as they wandered around the top of the tower. After another ten minutes, they began to make their way down. None of the other groups of people made any move to get up, so I stood, dusting the mud off of my jeans and swinging my backpack back onto my shoulders, smiling at the family as they walked past.

The white paint on the banisters was peeling, small pieces flaking into my palm as I started to climb. From the ground, it hadn't seemed like that many stairs but as my thighs cried at me on the second flight, I realised I may have underestimated it. Gritting my teeth, I continued up, hands running along the banisters to pull myself up the next few flights. The blue sky sparkled through the patterns in the ironwork, interspersed with fluffy clouds. By the time I reached the top, I was wondering if I needed to take out a gym membership when I got home. From the top of the tower, you could see for miles; I felt a smile tugging at my lips as I stared out at the patchwork quilt of green tree tops. The groups of people on the ground were doll-sized, their faces still visible, but their chattering blown away on the breeze far below me. Bringing up the map again, I swung around trying to identify anything that would help me. I could see another clearing in the distance, set even deeper in the forest,

Maybe I'm looking at this all wrong. I need to think logically; how would they have got everything in to the lab? There are hardly any roads here, but they

could have transported the equipment in by air. In that case they would need a clearing to land in. That looks like there's a lot of tree cover which means it probably wouldn't be that popular with tourists, just the occasional hiker.

As I talked it out in my head, my confidence grew that I was in the right place. It's pretty easy to convince yourself of something when you're dehydrated and in pain. I made a note of the direction of the clearing and put my phone away, moving back to the staircase. As I was about to step down, a flash of movement from the trees caught my eye; pausing, I looked over the rail as a runner broke through the trees. He slowed as he got to the clearing and, involuntarily, I scurried back, fear pounding through my veins. Without the leather jacket he was almost difficult to recognise, but his grey eyes and long hair, tied into a loose ponytail, were pretty obvious.

I mean, this is a good thing. If Caden is here, that means you're close.

I was babbling inside my own head. I'd been reduced to a tearful, shaking mess and he was literally like thirty feet below me. He could hardly reach me. Funny what someone trying to kill you repeatedly does to a person. I peeked through the metal bars, keeping my body hidden from view as much as I could in a structure with no walls. He glanced around the clearing, jogging on the spot then, after an agonising few seconds, took off across the clearing, going back into the trees in the direction of the clearing I'd spotted.

Follow him.

I hurried down the stairs, not wanting to lose much time. Part of me was screaming at the thought of following my would-be murderer into the forest, but he would probably be heading to the new lab and I needed to find it. I didn't fancy spending a night in the Black Forest hoping I didn't get eaten by a wild animal... or an escaped genetically engineered animal. As it was, the sun was beginning its slow afternoon descent, ready for sunset.

As soon as my feet hit the grass around the tower, I broke into a jog, following the path I'd seen Caden take into the forest. It wasn't as thick as the foliage I'd come through to get to the tower, but I still found myself slowing, hopping over tree roots. There were a lot of leaves underfoot, which didn't bode well for me. I slowed right down to a walk, trying to avoid the loud crunching of the leaves by stepping on the tree roots instead, jumping from one to the other. I couldn't see Caden, but I could see the ident of someone's shoes in the trail in front of me, the twigs and grass flattened. It was slow progress. I stopped every now and then, listening for any movement ahead. As I got closer to the clearing, I tried to walk parallel to the route Caden had took, making sure as much of my body as possible was hidden behind trees whenever I stopped. He would probably be cautious as he approached the entrance.

After twenty minutes of careful walking, I came to the edge of the clearing I'd seen from the tower. It was completely empty, not even the suggestion of a trail leading off from any part of it. From where I stood, I could see another indented line of footprints cutting across the corner of the clearing to head into another patch of trees on the right.

Keeping my eyes on the footprints, I stayed in the treeline, walking towards Caden's re-entry point. I didn't want to step out into the open. If I was as close as I thought I was, I was pretty sure they'd have cameras watching the clearing, in case they needed to dissuade any wayward hikers. As I neared the end of Caden's trail, I dropped down to a crouch. A beam of sunlight had reflected off of something in the trees; as I looked closer, I could see a small orb attached to a knot in one of the tree trunks. Cameras. Even though I knew they would probably have them, since Caden had tapped into the ones in the old lab, disappointment still curled in my belly. It had hardly been easy up until this point, but it had just got a whole lot more difficult. I had no idea how to disable cameras. The only evasion techniques I knew came from watching movies, so I doubted they would be that effective. A bird passed in front of the camera and it turned, tracking the movement.

They're motion-activated.

I just needed something in motion that wasn't me to keep the camera looking the other way. I looked around, trying to find something I could use, but given that trees were generally inanimate, I didn't really have a whole lot of options. As I was debating going back to the town and bringing back something I could use, a rustling to my right made me pause. I crouched lower in the undergrowth, my mind spiralling,

What if its Caden? What if this is a trap? I might be about to get shot or tied up in a net or…

My panicked thinking trailed off as a pair of large brown eyes appeared through the leaves. A cautious step forward revealed chestnut fur and a large, twitching nose.

It's just a deer.

The deer stepped even further forward, head flicking from side to side, its ears twisting as it listened. I kept myself as quiet as possible, not wanting to risk spooking it and drawing the camera this way.

What if it could draw the camera the other way?

As the deer stepped in front of me, it paused, bending down to chomp a mouthful of the lush grass, before carrying on its nervous wandering.

Once it was a few feet away from me, nearly in the line of the camera, I grabbed a twig from beside me, sizing up the distance.

I really hope this works.

I gently threw the twig to land just to the left of the deer, away from the clearing and towards the camera. As I'd hoped, the deer spooked, flying forwards and crashing through the undergrowth. The camera twisted, tracking its path and as soon as I was out of its range, I shot forward, darting to the cover of the trees behind the camera. Pressed up against a tree trunk, I took a few deep breaths, waiting for an army of GAI workers to come out and detain me. When they didn't, I let myself relax slightly. Once I'd checked the surrounding area for any more cameras, I took a couple of steps forward. If the camera was used to keep an eye on the people passing through, it was also probably used to let the right people in. To the left of the tree that the camera was sat in was a slight gap in the foliage. Not enough that it would be noticeable to anyone passing by, but from here I could see the faint trail. It seemed to disappear between two large tree trunks.

I'm willing to bet that the entrance is somewhere in there.

I approached cautiously, keeping an eye out for any possible trip wires or triggers. A lot of GAI's ability to stay hidden seemed to rely on the fact that, to the public, they no longer existed, so why should anyone be looking for them? It was defensive rather than offensive. Even in the deserted lab, it hadn't been that difficult to get in. Luckily for me, that complacency was working to my advantage. They'd left Caden to deal with me and didn't expect anyone else to be a problem. I was really looking forward to surprising them. As I reached the tree trunks, I noticed that beyond them, the air seemed to warp slightly, like a thin veil over an image.

Bingo.

Moving closer, I could see it was actually that. There was some kind of fabric backdrop, covered in hanging branches and vines. More than likely, the entrance Caden had used was behind the overgrowing foliage. I went to walk towards it then stopped.

I can hardly walk in the front door. If I want to find out if Eli is even in there, I probably don't want to be caught within the first few seconds.

I considered the tree trunks again. If it was the same as the other lab, it was going to be underground. Underground meant that they still had to have a fire escape and be able to circulate air somehow, probably with covered vents, or another entrance, like the door I'd opened in the Zoo Room.

Looks like we're sneaking in.

I walked to the right of the tree trunk, and the copse of trees behind it that I assumed hid the rest of the door, and started walking in a straight line, hoping that I would come across another indication of the lab. After the thick copse, the trees thinned out again, a smattering sparsely covering the ground, small ferns dotted in between, brushing against my legs as I crept past. I had no idea how thick the ground covering was between my feet and the lab. I certainly didn't want to blow everything because someone heard my footsteps on the ceiling. I'd walked for a couple of minutes before I paused, a small breeze blowing around my ankles.

Crouching down, I brushed aside the twigs and leaves, surprised when the dirt also brushed aside. After a few seconds of brushing, something silver glinted under my palm. Pushing away the last of the dirt, I was greeted with a vent. Cold air blasted out of it, with an undercurrent of something clinical. A grin spread across my face. It was quite a large vent, about a metre across, more than enough for me to slip into. I didn't know where it would come out, but hopefully I would be able to get to an empty room. I had a brief mental image of every time this had gone wrong in films, but I wasn't sure I had much of a choice. Finding the edge of the vent, I eased it up, the metal creaking slightly under the pressure. As soon as I had the vent up, I placed it down to the side, close enough that once I was in, I would be able pull it back over. I leant into the vent, peering around. It was pretty dark and further down the vent I could hear the clicking and whirring of machines. I was going to be blind until I reached an opening.

You'll be okay.

Sitting on the edge of the opening, I dangled my legs into the vent and took a few breaths. My backpack was resting on the ground next to me. In one smooth movement, I lowered myself down into the vent, waiting until I felt metal beneath my feet before I let go of the sides. Grabbing my backpack, I dropped it down to the floor, wincing as the metal echoed. The forest was still completely silent, barely a breeze rustling the leaves. It felt eerie. With a decisive jolt, I pulled the vent lid back over the top, crouching in the filtered overhead light. Slipping the backpack straps over my arms, I started crawling in the direction of the machines, hoping that led to the main areas of the lab. The vents seemed to be made of a thick metal, luckily for me, although there was barely enough room for my movements. The cold air that wafted through the vents blew my hair around my face.

After a few minutes of crawling, the tunnel started to lighten, and the whirring of machines got louder. I resisted the urge to speed up, my nerves replaced with excitement. Or possibly indigestion. Either way, I wanted to get into the lab and actually get what I came for. I could see an opening ahead; as I approached it, above the whirring of machines, there were voices, murmuring. Crawling up to the edge, I laid flat on my stomach, careful to make no noise, and peered over the edge. The room below was full of equipment, multiple machines whirring and spinning, lights flashing. Every so often one of them let out a beep. The murmuring voices I'd heard were attached to people as two men in lab coats came into view. The shorter one moved to the machine closest to me, his short black hair the only thing I could see from this position. I could almost hear what they were saying but some of it was lost to the machines,

"...arc...come loo...this." The other scientist came over, his hair shaved close to his head, a salt and pepper grey. He leant over the machine, taller than the first scientist, and from this angle I could actually see some of his face. He had a smattering of facial hair, over his lip and on his chin, a light grey and kind but piercing eyes.

He's making monsters. That's not kind.

He pushed the sleeve of his lab coat up to reach for a vial, revealing toned arms.

I don't think I fancy my chances.

"What was...previous...readin...om?" He murmured, checking the clipboard nearest to the machine. As he turned to face the first scientist, I caught a glimpse of his name badge.

Marc.

Marc waited for the response, head tilted as he considered whatever was on the clipboard. The first scientist pointed to something on the paper,

"Much lower...cell counts off..." He spun around to reach for the table behind him and I caught his name badge as well.

Tomas.

He was younger than Marc, with a moustache and stubble across his jawline. His eyes flashed around the room, dark and scrutinising.

They seemed to confer about something under their breaths before they pressed some more buttons on the machine almost directly below me. Unless they suddenly left the room, I wasn't going to be able to use this opening. Waiting until they had both turned away, I scurried over the opening, hoping I hadn't caused a shadow. There were more noises coming from further down the tunnel, so I kept going, rounding a sharp corner to come to a sharp halt. Another opening had sprung upon me, tucked directly after the corner. I couldn't hear any voices, but I still laid down, eyes peeking over the edge of the grate. The room below me seemed to be some kind of storage room, full of containers and boxes piled on top of each other. Directly below the grate was a large metal filing cabinet. I sized up the gap between the grate and the top of the cabinet.

I can make that.

Tilting my head, I tried to take in the rest of the room. As far as I could see, there wasn't anyone in the room. The only light on was a small overhead bulb that barely lit up the space. Making a decision, I started pulling up the grate. This one, unlike the one that led outside, was screwed in placed. Shrugging off my backpack, the smooth fabric making a *whooshing* sound across the side of the vent, I rummaged until I found a 5p coin. The edge of the coin fit perfectly inside the screw, meaning I could slowly unscrew each corner. I kept one eye on the room below in case anyone came in, but it remained quiet. The noises I could hear from the first room carried on down the tunnel. Slowly, the screws came out of the corners of the vent that I moved aside, wincing as the metal scraped against the edge of the tunnel. No one came running. Breathing a small smile, I sat on the edge of the vent, dangling my legs into the room. The metal filing cabinet was just out of reach but lowering myself down with my arms meant I could place my feet securely on the smooth surface. As soon as I felt the filing cabinet, I looped one hand around my backpack and dropped down into a crouch. Taking in the rest of the room, I was relieved to find that there hadn't been anyone else in there. Even better, there were no windows, which meant anyone walking by wouldn't see me subtly infiltrating their top-secret building.

Now...how to get down.

Just because there were no windows, it didn't mean I wanted to risk making a load of noise. I knew for a fact that there were at least two people nearby. Next to the filing cabinet was a desk, probably about a metre and a half away. Shimmying down the edge of the filing cabinet, I made it to the desk, with another quick jump to the floor. As I stood up from the jump, I couldn't help grinning properly now.

I'm in.

It was such a great feeling, the impossible task that I'd set myself now just that little bit easier. I had a quick look around the room, taking in the stacks of papers. I'd had enough of stacks of papers. The only issue with the room having no windows meant that there was no way to tell what was outside. I could open the door into the face of Caden for all I knew. Creeping over to the door, I slowly turned the handle and cracked the door open. Luckily it seemed to open into another hallway, dimly lit. I risked opening the door a bit further, poking my head out slightly. The hallway extended both ways; one side disappeared around the corner, the other stretching into flickering darkness. There were a few more doors lining the opposite side of the hallway, but no sign of any other people. As I was about to step out of the door, I heard footsteps echoing from around the corner.

Shit.

I backed into the room, hurrying over to a small space behind the storage containers that I'd spotted from my bird's eye view. The footsteps continued, stopping in front of the door. I closed my eyes against it, terrified that my victory was about to be stripped away. The door opened. I pressed myself to the floor, hardly daring to breathe. Black boots made their way to the desk, pulling out a stool and sitting down.

Don't look up. Please don't look up.

I was stuck. There was a shuffling of papers, followed by a cough. I let out a shallow breath, willing them to leave. The chair suddenly scraped back and there was a loud thunk, as something hit the floor. I opened one eye, my next breath freezing in my throat. On the floor by the desk was a leather bound, dark brown notebook, tightly bound with cord. The next second, the owner of the black boots leant down, sunlight dappled hair catching the light. I closed my mouth against the small sound that worked its way up my throat. Strong hands picked up the notebook and, as they moved back up, I caught a glimpse of sea-green eyes.

My entire body had frozen, the brother that I hadn't seen in three years suddenly *right there* in front of me. He stood back up, the image ripped away from me as I blinked, unable to believe that I'd actually seen him. A little part of me was so scared he was dead. But he wasn't. He was right here. I started to sit up, ready to run over to him, already bursting with excitement but as I straightened up behind the storage container, I heard the door open again. Another set of footsteps plodded across the room. I slid back down the wall, shaking, as I tried to stay quiet even though there was a sob working its way up my throat.

"Hey, Eli." Of course, it had to be Caden. His voice, even with that soft American twang, sent chills across my body, that same fear pounding through my veins again. The kind of all-consuming fear that set every nerve ending on fire, that robbed the breath from my lungs and put a chokehold around my throat. I could feel myself falling down into a hole, the grey haze closing in. He was *right there.* I took a shaking breath, hoping they couldn't hear me. To my ears it sounded like I was screaming with every intake of breath. As the wave of fear peaked, crashing back over me, the soft response held it back.

"What do you want, Caden?" There was venom

in his voice, but it was still my Eli. My brother. The fear retreated. Eli was here. I was okay.

"You're needed in Lab 2." This time Caden's voice didn't have as much of a hold over me. It tickled at the barriers of my mind, almost breaking through, but it was kept at bay. There was a sigh, then the chair scraped back across the floor.

"Fine." Despite everything, I smiled. Two sets of footsteps walked back across the room and the door shut with a loud *click.* Even though Eli was leaving, he was here, and he was alive.

I could save him.

Chapter 13

I held my breath until I was sure they had left. The silence seemed to stretch around me, the small space I was crouched in echoing. My breathing was ragged, the shock of seeing Eli after so many years catching up to me in a rush. It was better than I'd hoped for. He was *alive* and still… well… *Eli*. I could feel the tears coming on. Sitting back, I blinked them away. I didn't have time for this. Now that I knew Eli was okay, I had to get him out of here, which meant I had to find him, again. After a few more seconds of listening for any footsteps, I stood up and shimmied out from behind the storage container. The room looked the same as it did before Eli had even come in; hopefully Caden hadn't noticed the open vent. Chewing my lip, I wondered if I should put the vent cover back over in case anyone else came into the room. Clambering up onto the desk, I put a foot on one of the boxes and scrambled up onto the filing cabinet. It was not as easy as the descent. Reaching one hand up into the vent, I felt around for the cover; I wasn't very stable stood on the cabinet, but I didn't have much choice other than to stretch up onto my tiptoes, both hands in the vent.

Let's hope this isn't my route out. I don't think I've got the upper body strength to get back in there.

Eventually, I grasped hold of the edge of the vent cover, the sharp metal digging into my fingers. Slowly, I slid it over, wincing as it made a scraping sound against the bottom of the vent. I tried to lift it from the edge I had hold of, but the weight of the cover was a lot more than I could support from the position I was in.

I doubt anyone is listening to the sounds in the vents. It probably sounds like machinery.

That didn't stop my heart from racing as I inched the vent closer; it dropped as it reached the opening, almost landing on my head. Cursing under my breath, I pushed it back up, moving my hands so that they were flat on the grate instead of grasping the edges. Holding my breath, I moved it into place, breathing out when it settled into the opening without any loud crashes or bangs. Pretty successful all things considered. Hopping back down from the filing cabinet, which wobbled precariously under my feet, I slid off the desk and landed on the floor. I brushed some hair out of my face, the wayward waves frizzing up, half from the warmth and half from the stress. Luckily, I hadn't had to look in a mirror since my trek through the Black Forest. Eli might not even recognise me. *I* might not even recognise me. Picking my backpack up from the floor near the desk, I started planning.

Caden had said Eli was needed in Lab 2. Hopefully they put signs on their labs. Which meant, I needed to somehow get to Lab 2 without being seen and then get Eli out of there without either of us being seen. Easy. The sheer impossibility of what I was about to try and do weighed down on my shoulders. Up until this point, it hadn't exactly been plain sailing but, apart from Caden, I hadn't had to plan for other people. It had been me, a genetically modified otter and a Loch Ness Monster which, in my opinion, was still much easier than people. My leg started throbbing, the cream having slowly worn off over the course of the day. Or, maybe, it was just the memory of good old Nessie trying to kill me. I didn't really have the time or the option to unbind and redress my leg here; I was just going to have to deal with the pain. Hitching my bag onto my shoulders, I made my way over to the same position I'd been in before, trying to hear any footsteps outside the door. Again, it sounded quiet. I inched open the door, peeking out, relieved when the hallway came up empty. I quickly slipped out of the room, making sure the door didn't slam behind me. Now this was uncharted territory. A very large part of me would have liked to stay in my nice, small deserted room, waiting for Eli to come back, but that was wasting time. Unlike the rest of the building, which seemed to be made of some kind of reinforced metal, the floor was covered in lino. Probably, I realised with a jolt of discomfort, so they could easily clean up any mess. I had no idea which way Eli and Caden had gone. I knew which way the room I'd seen, with your friendly neighbourhood crazy scientists Marc and Tomas, was. I didn't know if that was the right direction; they had been in some kind of lab though, so it made sense to head that way even if I *really* didn't want to.

I stepped over to the other side of the hallway, relieved that my shoes didn't make too much of a noise on the lino, then hugged the wall as I crept towards the corner. I wasn't really sure what I was going to do if someone appeared. The likelihood was panic. Poking my head around the corner, I grinned to see another empty corridor. It was lined with more doors on the left-hand side, some with windows but the right wall was bare. Hopefully no one decided to go on their break as I was walking. From where I was, I could see tiny signs next to each of the doors. As I slipped around the corner, I squinted at the closest one. This one, I was glad to see, didn't have a window.

Lab 4.

I was pretty sure that was the one I'd seen earlier, so I quickly moved past it, constantly checking behind me. The next door was a few metres down, but it also had a large window. Dropping to my knees, I scurried over until I was under the window. A quick glance in revealed that, luckily, it seemed empty. I could only see half of the room, but when after a few seconds no one had appeared, I was pretty sure it was vacant. That didn't mean I was going to stand up. If I could see myself, I probably would have laughed as I began crawling along the floor, careful to keep out of the view of the window, just in case. The sign next to the door of that one read Lab 3. A small thrill of excitement (or possibly gut-wrenching fear, it was hard to tell now) ran across my skin; that meant that Lab 2 was next, which meant Eli. Lab 2 also had a window, so at least I could see if anyone else was in the room before I charged in like a madwoman. I started crawling towards it, but before I reached the window, I heard a handle creak behind me. Spinning round, I saw the door of Lab 4 begin to open.

Shit. Shit, shit, shit.

I didn't have much time to make a decision. Hoping that I was right about Lab 3, I darted to the door and opened it, slipping inside before the door to Lab 4 had fully swung open. I crouched behind it, panting as voices filled the hallway.

Don't come this way, don't come this way. There isn't anymore to this plan.

The voices faded off, clearly having gone

around the corner I had been hiding behind only minutes earlier. Closing my eyes, I slumped against the closed door of the Lab. After a few seconds the rushing in my ears had subsided to gentle ocean waves and I looked up. The bit of the lab I had seen from the hallway had really only been half of it. Off to my right was a lot more. The first thing I could see, and would really have preferred not to see, was two cages. The same cages as in the previous lab. They were dark, the right half of the lab entirely in shadow, with only a dim idea of the layout coming from the lights on the left-hand side. But even in the low light, the thick metal bars of the cages were unmistakeable. I felt myself recoil, the memory of the panther and the dead experiment still far too fresh in my mind.

I hope Pip's okay.

The thought popped into my head, unbidden. Well, kind of. I was staring at the same cages I'd rescued him from after all. It was now approaching… I checked my phone… nearly eighteen hours since I'd set off from Freiburg. If he'd understood what I'd been telling him then he should be okay, but there was still the little doubt at the back of my mind. Shaking off the thoughts, I crept further into the right- hand side of the lab. I could hardly go anywhere else yet, especially when Marc and Tomas could appear at any moment in the hallway.

Maybe there's another vent through to Lab 2.

I glanced around, wondering if turning the light on would alert anyone outside the room that I was here. I decided against it, even though I was becoming decidedly uncomfortable in badly lit spaces. The rest of the right-hand side of the Lab seemed to be mostly machines that I had no idea what to do with. Or what they were called. You could tell me they created magic fairy dust and I would be none the wiser. Shrugging, I scanned the ceiling for a vent but there didn't seem to be any visible. Resolving instead to wait by the window until I saw Marc and Tomas go back into the neighbouring lab, I turned away from the darkened space, ready to be back in the well-lit, if still creepily clinical, area. It was as I turned that I heard it. It sounded, to begin with, like air blowing through a small gap, that rasping kind of sound. It was only as I paused and listened closer that I realised it wasn't a continuous noise; instead it seemed to be coming in bursts, pausing every few seconds and starting again. Like breathing.

Like...breathing...

Slowly, I turned back to the cages, eyes wide.

Please don't let something be in there. I really don't want to see anymore of their awful experiments.

It kept going, the rasping combined with a rattling, flehm-y noise. I tiptoed over to the nearest cage, squinting through the dark. A pair of almost completely white eyes stared back at me. I resisted the sound that jumped into my throat.

Can I, for once, not find some kind of twisted experiment in one of these cages? Is that too much to ask?

The white eyes continued to stare at me, shuttering off into darkness every now and then as the creature blinked. From the sound of it's breathing, it wasn't doing well. I crept a bit closer, crouching down by the bars. I still had my torch in my bag, so I grabbed it, turning on the beam. I needed new batteries, the light dimmer than before, but it still did the trick. Carefully I directed the beam towards the cage, moving in tiny increments so I didn't startle whatever was in there. That was the last thing I needed. To begin with, I couldn't see anything wrong with it, besides the eyes. From its position on the floor, it looked exactly like a wolf. It had black fur, and a long snout with large canines. Its chest was rising and falling quickly, the black fur reflecting the light from the torch making it look wet. It was only when I moved the beam across the rest of its body that I realised it actually was wet. The liquid was so dark, it almost couldn't be distinguished from the colour of the fur. I could only assume there was some kind of wound on its side, probably caused by one of the scientists.

As I started to get up, I bumped my head on something hanging from the bars. Moving back, I could see it was a whiteboard, again the same as the labs in Scotland. I quickly moved the torch beam onto the whiteboard,

WOL304CCAR

Developed abnormalities – cataracts in eyes. Suggest immediate removal of embryo. Subject can then be terminated.

I looked back at the creature in the cage with pity. The cataracts explained the nearly white eyes. I didn't know how much it could see but it flinched whenever my torch beam landed directly on it. But it was the realisation of why there was blood on its side that hit the hardest. This animal had been pregnant, and they'd taken it after she had developed cataracts. Whatever had been inside her was clearly something important. I shuddered to think what it was. I backed away from the cage; it didn't even look like they were going to 'terminate' it, as the whiteboard had suggested. From the state of the wolf, it looked like they were just going to let it die. Turning off the torch, I moved with determination back towards the window. I was done with this company and these people. I didn't want to have to spend a minute longer than I had to here. They were monsters, much worse than what they were creating. I didn't want to dwell on how much of a hand Eli had had in all of this. From my vantage point at the edge of the window I could see that the hallway was empty; my foray over to the cages meant I had no idea if the scientists had gone back into the lab yet, but I didn't want to stay in this lab any longer. I had a plan.

Step 1: Get next door.

Step 2: Get Eli.

Step 3: *Get the hell out of here.*

I never said it was a good plan. Wrenching the handle a little more forcefully than it needed, I stepped back out into the hallway. It was quiet, but that didn't mean anything. I realised too late that they probably had cameras in at least one of the places I'd been in. Either that meant they were playing with me, or I'd managed to avoid being seen by being in the right place at the right moment. I didn't think that luck was going to stick with me. Pulling the door shut behind me, I made my way along the corridor again, towards Lab 2. As I was within a couple of metres of the door, I heard the footsteps I'd been dreading behind me. There was a moment of silence as I slowed, hoping they just didn't see me.

"Hey!"

Of course, they saw me. I was hardly inconspicuous. Maybe I should have stolen a lab coat. The footsteps picked up behind me, two sets running. I made a break for the door, but before I could reach it, I was tackled from behind, hitting the ground with a *thud.* Rough hands pulled me up and spun me round and I found myself face to face with Marc, the older of the two scientists. He glared down at me, his eyes narrowed, and I felt myself trying to lean back as if, if I leaned back far enough, I'd be able to avoid his gaze or disappear into the cold lino. I'd made a mistake earlier thinking his face looked like it could be kind. That was definitely not the case now. Behind him, I could see Tomas, his mouth set in a hard line as he also glared at me.

"Who are you?" Marc's voice was gruff and deep as he snapped at me. I shook my head instead of giving an answer. I didn't know what to say. I'd managed to make it this far but now I was literally in the hands of the enemy. Again. His grip tightened on my upper arm,

"Who. Are. You?" I avoided his gaze, looking down at the floor. After a few seconds of silence, I found my voice again.

"No one. I'm no one." I could hardly say I was Eli's sister. I had no idea what that would do. Tomas stepped up so he was next to Marc instead of behind him, leaning close enough to my face that I could almost feel the stubble of his facial hair.

"You might as well tell us. You'll be talking one way or another. How did you get in here?" His voice was equally pissed off, but not as deep, giving him less of the evil villain vibe that Marc had going on. It gave me a bit of confidence.

"You have really shit security." I grinned as I said it, but soon wished that I hadn't. It was not well received. Marc's glare deepened. Still maintaining a firm grip on my arm, he turned to mutter to Tomas,

"Go get someone to take her to Rick. If she's broken in, we have no idea how much she knows. Rick will find out." Tomas nodded, starting to spin on his heel but before he could take another step, a voice that was unfortunately well known to me interrupted us.

"There's no need. I'll take her." I tried to stop the involuntary stiffening of my shoulders, but I couldn't. I felt the blood drain from my face. Marc saw it and gave a small smirk to the person I knew was stood behind me.

"Looks like you might do a better job of getting her to talk. She's all yours." With a shove, he pushed me backwards. I stumbled across the lino until I hit a solid object, his hands coming up to steady me, warm against my skin. At one point, I might have blushed at that, but now it just sent ice cold terror racing through my veins. Marc and Tomas nodded at the bastard behind me and disappeared back into their lab. The hallway fell quiet. I couldn't say silent because the fury was radiating off of him in waves so violent, they were almost tangible, and my breathing was pattering out of control. The air held a baited tension, the kind that was waiting for one of us to snap first, for one of us to slip and lose the tentative hold we had on our emotions. I didn't want it to be me. It was only when he dropped his hand, dragging his fingertips down my arm, that I moved. Spinning round, I scrambled backwards, barely able to make myself meet his eyes. I managed. They were pure fury, now the grey of rolling thunderclouds. I couldn't stop my hands from trembling so I gripped them tightly into fists instead.

This is it. He's going to kill you. Himself this time.

I had nothing; no way out, no weapons besides a worn-out torch, nothing to bargain. I could only hope that his desire to kill me was superseded by his ability to follow protocol, which I assumed was taking me to Rick. They hadn't given a second name, but it couldn't be anyone other than the founder of GAI, Rick Laws. As I mused this over in my head, Caden seemed to make a decision. He stepped forwards, his torso towering over me so I was forced to crane my head up to stay looking at his face. His hands gripped my shoulders, nails digging through the fabric into my skin. I winced but didn't say anything. When he spoke, in a low, barely controlled voice, it took me a few seconds to register it. It had hardly been louder than a whisper.

"How… how are you alive?" The air seemed to snap around us, the rage almost physical. I made my feet stand their ground and swallowed around the lump in my throat.

"I guess I got lucky." I whispered too, but I wasn't really in the position to control it. It only seemed to enrage him more. His mouth thinned, almost disappearing and his fingers dug into my skin even harder.

If I somehow get out of this, I'm going to be a patchwork quilt of bruises.

"Got…got lucky?! I incapacitated you and threw you in a lake with the Loch Ness monster! You should be tiny pieces of fish chow and yet here you are, in *Freiburg,* walking around like nothing happened. Why won't you just give up?!" My confidence grew slightly. He hadn't tried to kill me outright. Something in the carefully contained anger of his body told me he couldn't, not yet, not now I was here. So, I managed to splutter out the question that had been on my mind since I'd overheard him, all the way back in his dorm.

"Why do you hate me?" The fire burning in his eyes seemed to douse itself for a second as he blinked at me, trying to take in the question.

"What?" It was muttered between clenched teeth but, it wasn't another death threat, so that was improvement.

"Why do you hate me? Like, you hate me this

much and I don't see why?" It felt good to ask the question, even if it was to a person who could quite easily kill me. He froze for a second, eyes going distant, then refocussed on me, all the rage sparking again,

"Why do I hate you? You *tied me up, drugged me* and *left me for dead.*" He gestured with one hand, dropping it momentarily from my arm.

"I mean, actually, I left you cereal bars." I think I was high on adrenaline. I could hear the words coming out of my mouth and I couldn't stop them. His mouth dropped open and twitched at the edges and for a second, the guy who had broken into a police station with me fluttered back, before he was replaced with the monster underneath. "But, before that. I heard you on the phone. You seemed so disgusted by me. What did I do?" Part of me was still a little girl confused and hurt by a boy. She wanted answers. I wanted her to shut the hell up.

"You... you kept me in that hell hole for *3 fucking years.* I couldn't leave. I was assigned to stay there until you gave up whatever search you were on. Yeah, we knew about it." He added, seeing my shocked face, "You're not as great at this sleuthing thing as you think you are. I mean, were you so blinded by the need to get to your brother that you actually believed I could break into a police station evidence room? God, you idiot. That was a set up and I can't believe you fell for it. Well, actually, I can. Then, not only did you keep me there for three years, you actually managed to have a break through and find some information out. So, what did you do? You walked straight into my hands. Then, I couldn't leave until I'd convinced you there were no leads. But you just didn't give up. You just keep coming back. I mean... a LOCH NESS MONSTER and yet, I couldn't kill you." Ouch. I wasn't going to lie, it hurt to know someone hated you that much, and it was for something that wasn't even my fault. I crossed my arms, shrugging off his other hand.

"Look, I'm sorry I kept you in such a *hell hole,* but I hardly knew I was doing it, did I? I don't feel like that warrants throwing someone in a lake as monster chum. I can't imagine you ever dealt well with being dumped. What did you do to them? Grind them in a wood chipper? Is that seriously the whole reason you hate me?" I was in this deep, no point in stopping now. His jaw twitched.

"I didn't- I had to listen to Eli hark on about you for almost an entire year. He wouldn't shut up about his little sister and how great she was. Do you know how irritating that is? God, I even know that your favourite colour is blue. I don't need to know that about you and yet, I do. So, it's hard to like someone when you're all I heard about, on and on for a whole year. Then you go and do all this stupid shit, over and over again and I just had to deal with it. I could have been here, with the team, developing the newest assets but I wasn't. I was with you and your brother. It was nauseating." I stared at him for a few seconds,

"So, what you're saying is you developed a hatred for me that lead to repetitive attempted murder because of a load of stuff I had no control over? Does that seem fair to you?" He seemed taken aback, some of the fire dying from his eyes,

"Why should it be fair? It wasn't fair on me." He snapped.

"Oh, boo hoo, you poor baby. You know I actually liked you right? I thought I could trust you. I did trust you."

"Well that was stupid. What did you actually know about me? Pretty much nothing. It's not my fault you were acting like a silly little girl with a crush." Before I could stop myself, my hand was flying towards his face, connecting with his jaw as a fist. My mouth dropped open as his head snapped to the side.

Well, that's done it. Well done.

He turned back to me, rubbing his jaw. His eyes were flat now. He grabbed my arm, the one that had just punched him clean across the face and yanked me forward,

"This conversation is over. Come on." He dragged me alongside him, not even looking down at me, eyes focussed on the corridor ahead. My shoes squeaked along the lino. I assumed he was taking me to Rick. It would be nice to meet the guy behind all of this, were it not for the sneaking suspicion that Caden wasn't going to let me out of here alive. That kind of put a damper on things. More rooms flashed past, the windows showing yet more scientists with more machines. I hadn't had any idea the organisation was this big when I'd been at the lab in Scotland. There, it had seemed like a small operation. Here, almost every few metres there was another room, another group. I hated to think how many experiments were going on in here, how many scientists believed they were doing something admirable.

Eventually we turned a corner. This corridor, although still the same lino and metal, felt different. It was bare, no doors on either side, no windows. I dragged my feet across the floor, wincing as Caden pulled me forward, fingers digging into already-forming bruises. I started grumbling under my breath, ignoring the daggered looks he sent to me. In the distance I could see the end of the corridor, framing one single door. The closer we got, the more Caden seemed to stiffen up. I guess even psychopaths were scared of someone. The door wasn't marked, imposing itself on the hallway with all the airs and graces of a boss's office. I felt the knot in my stomach tighten as we came to a halt. Caden looked at me sideways, opening his mouth as if he was going to say something but whatever it was floated away into the echoing silence of the hallway. I wasn't sure I wanted to know what it was to be honest; he'd looked almost apologetic, which didn't fill me with confidence for what awaited me on the other side of the door. He sighed, the sound hanging between us, then raised his hand, ready to knock on the door,

"Wait…" my voice sounded tiny in the cavernous space around his, but I needed something, anything to delay this. He paused, hand stopped in mid-air, "I want to know, was there any part of you, any part at all, that actually felt something for me?" Maybe, if he did, he would reconsider. He began to respond then stopped, as if unsure. I saw his gaze harden seconds later.

"No." It was said sharply, clipped. A little part of me slumped; there went my only escape. Before I could say anything else, he raised his hand again and knocked this time, three short, sharp beats. There was a pause then the door seemed to click, pulling itself sideways. He pushed me through. I stumbled into darkness, my eyes trying to adjust. The lights came on, a gradual fade in, dousing the room in bright halogen light. Caden stepped into the room behind me and I jumped as I heard the door swing shut. I couldn't see anyone, but I'd learnt that that meant nothing. Directly in front of us was a desk, cluttered with stacks of paper. I half expected the chair to swing around and present the infamous Rick Laws, complete with evil cat. It didn't and I was kind of glad because I don't think I would have been able to stop myself from snorting. But there was movement. A figure appeared from behind a bookcase to my left. I jumped slightly and tried to cover it up, but I know Caden saw it. The figure walked towards me until his face was completely in the light.

"Ah, Miss Ari. So very nice of you to join us. I've been so wanting to meet you."

Chapter 14

The man in front of me didn't look anything like the picture I'd built up in my head. I'd imagined Rick Laws as a crazy-eyed maniac, unsettling with a psychotic grin. That definitely wasn't this man; he looked, well, normal. Like a businessman that you'd pass on the street. He was tall, much taller than Caden who seemed to shrink in his presence, with short black hair, ebony skin and piercing blue eyes. They were unsettling, yes, but not because he looked psychotic. They seemed to burrow into your skin. I struggled to look away but eventually I cast my gaze to the side, creeping a look at Caden. He was staring straight ahead, not making eye contact, but his hands were clenched and from what I could see he looked a little...scared?

Surely not? He's actually crazy. If he's scared, what the hell is this guy like.

Rick drew my attention back to him by clearing his throat. I met his gaze again, instantly wishing I hadn't. He was smiling at me, a soft smile that seemed completely at war with the intensity of his eyes, arms lightly folded until he was sure he had my attention; then he unfolded his arms, leaning back on the desk behind him.

"I hear you've been causing quite a bit of trouble." He had a voice like velvet. I could see how he convinced so many people to do something illegal. I didn't answer but kept my gaze locked with his. If I had any chance of getting out of here, I definitely couldn't be seen as weak. He chuckled and it rolled over my skin in a gentle wave. I could feel Caden's tension radiating in waves beside me. Rick's eyes flicked to him and something passed over his face, almost like disappointment. "From what Caden here had been telling me, you've somehow managed to outsmart him *more than once.*" His voice dropped and I got the sense that it wasn't a comment directed at me but at Caden. The flinch I saw out of the corner of my eye confirmed it. There was a beat of silence before Rick continued, "What I really want to know my dear is how. I left one of my best to ensure you never found your brother and yet here we are. It's just lucky that Eli has no idea you're even here." His smile was still gentle but there was an undercurrent of steel in his words, as cold as the icy blue of his eyes. "So, tell me, how did you, a pretty unremarkable girl, with no background in survival training or intelligence work find and break in to not one but two of my facilities, not counting our little decoy back in England?" His question hung in the air. I realised, as the silence drew on, that I was going to have to answer this one.

"A little bit of luck, a little bit of help and a whole lot of rage. Also, you have shit security." Even to my own ears I sounded like I was being a smartass. Instantly, his entire demeanour changed. The smile dropped off of his face and his jaw clenched. He pushed off from the desk and stalked towards me until we were nearly touching. I craned my neck up to maintain the eye contact.

"You little shit. You think this is funny?! You could have and may still completely derail everything I've worked towards. And for what? Your brother? I hate to break it to you sweetheart but it's not exactly like your brother was all that worried about you for the past three years. He's been living out his dream. *You* would have held him back." He spat the words at my face. I didn't respond, but it was still a punch in the gut.

No, he was concerned. Remember the notebook? He missed you. He cares about you. He's still Eli. This guy is just trying to get to you.

I couldn't help but wonder why Eli hadn't tried to get back to me though. If he'd been here, been alive for three years and he hadn't even tried to get a message to me. Why? I cast a glance at Caden, and another idea formed in my head.

What if Caden set the notebook as a trap? He was obviously in Scotland when I was but for some reason, he didn't choose to approach me until after I'd found the lab.

His eyes flicked towards me, like he felt my gaze, but they were unreadable.

"I seriously doubt Eli was living out his dream here. It's a hell hole. You think what you're doing is so great, but it's monstrous. It's crazy. Just like you, I guess." I held my breath as my bait registered. If I wanted any information, I needed to get the upper hand. Right now, Rick had it, but from how he'd been reacting it was clear he had a few triggers. In my experience, the best way to get people to reveal anything was to get them angry. They stopped thinking about what they were saying and just reacted. I heard Caden mutter something under his breath, but it was drowned out by the shout from Rick.

"I'm not crazy!" *You most definitely are.* "You're just like everyone else; they never understand what I'm doing here. They think its wrong, but I'm helping humanity. My research will help cure diseases."

"That wasn't what I saw. Mutated hybrid animals killed and left to rot on the floor of an abandoned lab. What use would medicine have for a half-wolf, half-polar-bear hybrid? Or the Loch Ness Monster? Don't kid yourself that you're helping science. You're only helping yourself." Caden hissed something again, this time a bit louder so I could hear.

"Stop." I couldn't. It was too late. All the rage I'd felt, all the hurt and the pain from losing my brother had bottled up over the past three years and now I was looking at the man responsible for it all and I was furious. I didn't care about what he would do. I just wanted to hurt him the way he had hurt me. I didn't see the slap; it was only after my face was wrenched to the side that I registered something had hit me. I turned my head back to Rick, his features contorted into something almost animalistic. I could see now why Caden was scared of him. He was a monster. But I wasn't backing down. I rubbed my jaw, easing the sting of his hand.

"That wasn't a denial." I kept my voice even, measured, making sure I didn't shout or show emotion. Someone full of his own self-worth, who couldn't control his anger right now, would find that infuriating. I was betting it was smarting that I was a small, young and a girl at that and I had, as he had said, jeopardised everything he had worked for.

I'm not done yet.

He was panting, the fury emanating off of him in waves. I stretched up onto my tiptoes so I was closer to his face.

"Don't kid yourself." I whispered. He let out a scream of frustration, every inch of the composed businessman vanishing and spun round to punch a fist into his desk.

"Fine! You think I'm only doing this for myself? You don't even know what I'm doing. I can make the world its own theme park! I'm bringing to life the mythical creatures that everyone wishes they could see. It's going to be incredible." He was talking with a kind of fervour, a gleam in his eyes as he stared at me. I wanted, very much, to take a step back or just run as far away from him as possible.

"No one wants to see that thing you're pretending is the Loch Ness Monster. If that gets near anyone, it will kill them. That's hardly going to be something everyone wishes they could see." I couldn't believe that he thought people would enjoy seeing *that.* How were they going to stop it from slaughtering everyone? Was that the 'control' measures they were talking about in the previous Lab? Rick scoffed at me, turning to pace across in front of his desk.

"You don't *see* it do you? You can't, not yet. But you will. Everyone will thank me." He was murmuring now, "Plus, it will bring me millions." I think he had forgotten I was here; me and Caden. He had a faraway look in his eyes as he traipsed around. That, more than his anger, was terrifying. Suddenly, he stopped pacing, turning back to look at me. His eyes were focused again, any of the cloudiness long forgotten.

"We are not here, Miss Farrow, to discuss me and my plans. We are here to discuss you. You have become a thorn in the side of GAI and the best way to deal with thorns is to remove them." I swallowed as a chill ran down my back. He was back to the businessman now, every inch calm and collected. He ran his hands down the lapels of his suit, smoothing them, leaning back against the desk again. If Caden wasn't clearly terrified of this man, I imagine he would have wished him good luck. I could almost see the thought forming in his head. This meeting was very quickly going south; I needed to somehow make myself valuable.

"If I don't come back, everything I've found out about GAI will be released. Including the locations. The government will be all over you and your company before you can blink. Then what will you do?" I was bluffing. I had everything stored, but I hadn't told anyone about it; even Jake couldn't guess what I needed that well. But they didn't know that. I hadn't told Caden I was storing everything. Looking back now, I was glad I'd kept some of the investigation to myself. I saw his eyebrows raise as they both considered what I'd said. I knew they didn't know whether or not to believe me. I just had to sell it, "You wouldn't want photos of your failed experiments and your documents released onto the internet for *anyone* to see, would you? I have copies of all of it. Even a couple of pictures of your very own Nessie. It will be great publicity up until you're shut down by every organisation under the sun for animal cruelty and illegal activity..." I trailed off, letting my words hang between us. I could see Rick's jaw working, the tendons jumping under his skin as he worked over my words in his head. Unless they had a way to hack my phone, they wouldn't be able to disprove it. It would be whether or not he was worried enough that it might be true. Eventually he huffed and motioned Caden over. Snapping to attention, Caden walked to the desk, shooting me a glance as he went by; I couldn't read it. I looked around the rest of the room as they talked in a hushed whisper. One side seemed to be full of books and from here I could make out the titles on the spines of a few of them.

Genetic Engineering in Mammals.

DNA Sequencing and Modification.

Mythical Creatures: A Complete Field Guide.

Evidently, he wasn't lying about trying to create mythical creatures. I'd seen it, obviously, with Nessie, but he was now clearly trying to create more. I could see how it would work. If you released the actual Loch Ness Monster into Loch Ness and set up an independent company to run boat tours where you could guarantee a sighting, he would be laughing. That sonar they'd been using in Scotland made sense; a way to draw the creature to you and, from above the water, it would be almost silent. I cast my mind back to what I'd seen on the computer talking about Stage 3 and the Lycan Project.

What would Lycan be? It means wolf but wolves aren't mythical...

The wolf in Lab 3 popped into my head, used to carry something that probably wasn't just a wolf. It dawned on me a second later and I mentally slapped myself for taking so long to get to it,

They aren't doing another animal hybrid. They're making a werewolf.

That meant human-animal hybridisation. I wasn't even sure if that was possible. Even the thought itself made me feel slightly nauseated.

He might, in his mind, be doing this for the people, but there was a large part of this, that he had even admitted himself, was about money. The amount he could stand to make from this would be insane. It would set him up as one of the richest, most powerful people in the world, all from behind the scenes.

As my mind was spinning, they continued to have their conversation, the hissing whispers breaking into my thoughts every so often. After what felt like an age, my mind going round and round as I tried to unpack what I'd realised, they stepped apart. Caden marched back to me, spinning round and standing stock still. Rick stood up from leaning against his desk, moving towards me, stopping about a foot away. He crossed his arms, the suit stretching across his biceps. His eyes were scrutinising me, the Arctic blue boring into me. I stayed still, even though the scrutiny made me want to squirm.

"It seems, Miss Farrow, that we have reached an impasse. Caden cannot tell me whether or not you are telling the truth, an oversight on his part." He shot Caden a glare. "I do not wholeheartedly believe that you were smart enough to have the forethought. Eli, it seems, got all the brains. But I don't wish to risk GAI and everything I've built just in case you aren't lying. So well done." He shot me a grin, though it didn't reach his eyes. I couldn't pin him down; he was all over the place. But, and I kept the grin to myself as he said it, I'd done what I wanted. I'd avoided, or at least prolonged, whatever 'removal' he had in mind and that meant, I could still get to Eli. "That means, however, that I need a bargaining chip of my own. One, I think, you'll be more than happy to negotiate with. So, Caden, please go and fetch Miss Farrow's brother and bring him to me. I'm sure she can't wait to see him again."

All the air seemed to go out of my lungs as the

words left his mouth. Caden nodded once, curt, and left the room, leaving me alone with Rick. We stared at each other in silence. He seemed to be holding back a smile as he watched me. Could he see that I was on edge? The thought of seeing Eli, and him seeing me, for the first time properly in three years was incredibly nerve-shredding. I was holding my breath as I registered the footsteps coming towards the door of Rick's office. The *click* of the handle made me jump and I heard Rick chuckle. I turned around as the door swung open. Caden was first through the door; his eyes met mine and he seemed to try and communicate something, but I was already focussed over his shoulder.

Eli's hair was the first thing I saw, the same sunlit blonde as I'd seen hiding behind the storage container. Now I could see him fully, I could see some differences. He was taller, and broader than when I'd last seen him, muscles that hadn't been there three years ago suddenly jumping up from under his shirt. He had stubble across his jawline, a shadow cast across his mouth and somehow the rest of his face seemed sharper. But the main difference was how he carried himself. He walked with a confidence that I hadn't seen from him ever; he'd always hung back, keeping to himself around people he didn't know, but now his eyes were narrowed, and his chin was raised. He hadn't noticed me; his eyes were on Rick. I realised that I was stood almost in shadow. I couldn't get myself to move; my feet were glued to the floor. Whilst he hadn't seen me, I could still pretend that we could go back to how we were. But as soon as he saw me, as soon as I set this timeline into motion, whoever he was now was who I had to accept, and I wasn't sure I was ready for that. I tried to take comfort in the fact that his sea-green eyes, my eyes, were the same. His eyes still looked like him. Not this new, improved version of him. He glared at Rick, no hint of the caution that Caden showed in his posture.

"What do you want Rick?" His voice carried the same venom as when he'd spoken to Caden in the lab and I was reminded again that I didn't know him now. I didn't know what he'd been through. I shook that thought out of my head almost as soon as it entered. It didn't matter, he was still my brother. That was why I had done all of this, why I had come to Germany, fought monsters. He was worth it.

Rick didn't answer him. He simply raised an eyebrow, a movement I knew was directed at me. I took a deep breath, shaking my hands at my side to try and dispel the nerves.

"Hi Eli." My voice was quiet, trembling. His head snapped to the side as I stepped forward, eyes widening and mouth dropping open in shock. The world seemed to balance on a knife's edge.

"Ari?" He seemed afraid to believe it. I nodded, flashing him a small smile. The disbelief slowly morphed into a huge smile, "Ari!" He rushed towards me, sweeping me up in a hug. I returned it, resting my head on his shoulder. The hug almost felt familiar; the muscles threw me off, but as he squeezed me tight, head buried in my hair, I didn't care. It took me a couple of seconds to realise he was murmuring something under his breath,

"You're here. You're actually here." His voice was thick, like he was on the verge of tears and I felt myself tearing up as well. I hated that this reunion was in front of Caden and Rick. I hated it. But, as Eli slowly released me, I realised this was better than I'd been expecting for the past three years. Something inside me, something that had felt empty for so long, was slowly healing. I heard a noise behind me and spun to see Rick walking towards us. Eli was still watching me, his eyes red and puffy, but his gaze flicked to Rick as he placed a hand on my shoulder. The same venom I'd heard in his voice, spread onto his face. I could feel myself shuddering, hating the weight of Rick's palm on my shoulder but I didn't dare move. He'd brought in his bargaining chip and I was listening. But Eli had none of my reservation; surging forward he slapped Rick's hand away from my shoulder, pulling me back until I was at his side. "You don't get to touch her." I'd never heard him talk with so much anger before. I cast him a sideways glance but didn't move away. Rick didn't seem surprised, smiling at Eli indulgently.

"Don't worry Eli, your sister is quite safe for now." He raised his eyebrows at me, and I nodded. I understood his meaning. I'd have to think of my next move soon, but for now, I was safe and so was Eli. Eli, however, didn't seem quite so satisfied. His mouth twisted; everything in his posture was defiant, staring Rick down. He really wasn't afraid of the guy that everyone else feared. They stared at each other for another few seconds, some kind of unspoken battle raging between them. Eventually Rick looked away and Eli smirked.

"Why don't we let these siblings get reacquainted?" Completely suave, Rick carried on as if nothing had happened. No one said anything. After a couple of seconds, he simply turned and ushered Caden out of the door. When the door finally clicked shut, I couldn't think of anything to say. Luckily, Eli seemed to know exactly what to do. He grabbed me into another hug and led me to a couple of chairs at the side of Rick's office.

"How the hell did you find me Ari?" He was beaming at me and I felt myself beam back, the awkwardness I'd briefly felt dissipating into the air. I kept checking myself, unable to believe I was actually talking to Eli again.

"It took a while." I laughed, "The police ruled the investigation pretty much impossible. Our parents hired private investigators but after a year, they couldn't find anything either. They... they seemed to accept that you weren't coming back." I hated how Eli flinched when I said that, "But I wasn't going to give up on you. I mean you're my older brother. I wasn't giving up. So, for the next two years, I started trying to find anything I could. I re read the journal you left constantly, hoping I'd missed something. Then, a few days ago... or I guess a couple of weeks ago now, I keep forgetting how long I've been actually out looking for you, I remembered some strange things that had happened, like that email you hadn't let me see. Do you remember?" he nodded, something flickering in his eyes, "After that, it was easier. I went to your university accommodation looking for Caden. Obviously, I had no idea he was a monumental dick. He claimed to want to help me and we got your journals back from the police evidence. Now I know it was a set up, but I so wanted to trust him, I think because he was a link to you. So, I believed everything he set in front of me; he took me to an abandoned 'GAI building'. I still don't know how much of that was fake. But I found some stuff there that I kept from him. Eventually I decided to tell him everything and he kissed me... he manipulated me," Eli had been quiet, but he jerked as I said that,

"He did what?! That fuc-" I cut him off with a wave of my hand.

"He did it but it's in the past. I let myself believe that too. I feel like an idiot now, seeing all of this, everything he is a part of, that you've been trapped in, but I fell for him a little bit. Anyway, I overheard him on the phone and realised he was working for GAI. So…" I ran a hand through my hair. This would be the first time I was admitting what I'd done to anyone other than myself, "I drugged him, tied him up and left him in that abandoned building." Eli barked a laugh.

"Ari, that's not even half of what he deserves. I know you and I know you're probably feeling bad about it. But you shouldn't." I gave him a small smile. I would still feel bad about it though. I tended to dwell on things. I carried on as Eli chuckled to himself,

"I heard him mention Kincraig and when I questioned him whilst he was sedated, he made a reference to 'lock and key' which I realised meant lochs. So, I went to Scotland and began searching the Lochs. In the middle of a thunderstorm, I stumbled into the cave that led to the entrance of the lab and, it was pure luck, ended up in there." Eli was staring at me, "What?" He shook his head,

"It's just you, listing all of this like it's nothing. You're a pretty cool little sister." I smiled at him but continued with the rest of the story.

"I found your notebook there, the one with your notes to me." He dimpled a grin at me, "I also found a few other...things. Up until that point I had no idea what GAI was really doing. But then I found the room with all the cages and... a dead hybrid. Half-wolf, half-polar-bear." Eli looked away, the same anger from before crossing his face, "I also found Pip."

"Pip?" He stared at me, confused. I grinned, thinking of Pip and how excited he was going to be to meet Eli. Or, reunite I guess. Hopefully I would get out of here, with Eli, and that could happen.

"OTT103ACAR." Recognition dawned, "He's pretty incredible. I rescued him; I could hardly leave him there, he would have died. I want to know more about him when we get out of here, since I know you made him. Then I found Nessie. I may have passed out. But it reminded me of your journal which is when I read the notes. After that, it went quite quickly; I managed to get to the computer in the room of cages, found a document talking about Freiburg and knew where I needed to go next. On the way out, I was attacked by the panther creature. I electrocuted it." Even to myself, as I listed the various things I had been through to get here, I couldn't quite believe that I had done it. I'd almost detached myself from it all, recounting every step like it was someone else's story. Eli was shaking his head in disbelief. "After leaving the lab, with Pip, I had to climb back up to the Loch to find my way back to the road. Caden found me there…" He wasn't going to like this. I hoped Caden wasn't close by. "He'd been watching me. He released the panther to try and kill me. When it didn't, he… he used the collar's sonar to incapacitate me." I could see Eli go still, watching me very carefully, "and he threw me in the Loch." Eli's hand balled into a fist.

"I'm going to kill him." Eli muttered but I carried on. I needed to get this all out, all in one go otherwise I would lose it. Even the memory of being in the Loch was bordering on panic. The feeling of the water crushing me, not even being able to move… "I was drowning, and Nessie was about to attack me when Pip saved me. He attacked Nessie, again and again, until I could move. I got away and climbed out of the lake. Not unscathed. I have a pretty big gash in my shin. But I was alive. So, I got up, got back to the town and got on multiple trains to Freiburg."

"Why trains? Surely a plane would have been easier?" Even angry, Eli was still picking up on the little things.

"It's kind of difficult to get through security and quarantine with a genetically modified otter without a passport. So, I snuck him on the trains. It was fun." I tried to joke, but it was difficult. I hadn't expected telling Eli all of this to affect me so much.

"So, you brought OTT- Pip with you?" Eli's eyebrows were drawn together as he took everything in. I nodded,

"We got to Freiburg. I left Pip in a hotel room with food and water and set off into the forest, because I'd assumed GAI would hide in the woods to stay out of the way. I got to this huge tower in the woodland and as I was at the top of it, trying to scan the surrounding area, Caden came jogging through the trees. He didn't see me. I followed him until I found the entrance to this building and snuck in through a vent and well, I got in. I was in the room when you were at the desk. I was behind that storage container. I was going to reveal myself but Caden came in and I couldn't. I was trying to get to you in Lab 3 when I was caught and brought to Rick and… here we are, I guess." I finished, running out of breath. I let my shoulders drop and looked at my hands. Eli didn't say anything. I peeked up to look at him, only to be confronted with another hug. He wrapped me in his arms, one hand against my hair. When he pulled back, he was crying this time.

"I- Ari- thank you. I don't know how else to say it. But… thank you. You did a lot of crazy shit to get to me, even after all this time. Hands down, you're the best sister. I love you Ari."

Well shit, now I'm crying.

"I love you too Eli. You would have done the same for me." We grinned at each other for a few seconds. I glanced at the door. I didn't know if they were listening. They probably were. But now I had questions, "Enough about me. I want to know what happened to you. You just vanished from your room." He passed a hand over his jawline, rubbing across the stubble.

"I know you know about the email. GAI sent me multiple emails, asking me to join them. They tried recruiting me directly through Caden. I resisted and apparently, they wanted me enough to transgress to kidnapping. That night I was doing some research when this guy came through my window. Before I could say anything, he had me pinned and injected me with something. Everything went dark and the next thing I knew, I woke up in the lab in Scotland. I was there for almost two years. That's when I met Rick. He told me what he wanted me to do and when I refused, he blackmailed me. He claimed he would send Caden to our house and kill you all. I didn't know if he would, but I couldn't take that chance. I started trying to make the creatures he wanted. I don't want to lie to you Ari, a small part of me was excited to be able to do what I had been researching for so many years, but I would never have chosen to do it that way. Not 'bringing myths to life' as Rick put it. I just wanted to see how it could be used to help us. I started small with Pip. I have to say, that name suits him," he dimpled a grin at me.

"He was one of the very first creatures I made and, it seems, one of the most successful. After that, they just wanted more. They had me experiment with loads of different creatures, but their goal was always Nessie. It took me multiple attempts and when I did get it right, it didn't feel as great as I'd hoped. They took the viable creature and left the one you saw to die. In between all of that, I overheard phone calls with Caden. I knew you were looking for me, but I wasn't going to get my hopes up. I should have known better when it comes to you. You never give up, never did, even when we were little. Since I'd made Nessie, they moved up to Freiburg to start on the Lycan project-"

"Werewolves." I interjected, unable to keep the disgust out of my voice. He looked at me, some unnamed emotion in his eyes; it almost looked like shame.

"I know Ari. It's a step too far, but they kept using you as blackmail. I couldn't refuse anything. They had a camera set up in our house, a live feed and if I tried to say no, they would show it to me. They would tell me what they would do to you and our parents." I could hear in his voice how much it had pained him. How much they had hurt him. Even so, I had to ask the question that had been burning in my throat,

"Why didn't you try to contact us? Surely you could have found a way? You're so smart." He couldn't meet my eyes now and a little bit of me fell, already not wanting to hear his answer. He cleared his throat before answering,

"I tried when I was first kidnapped but every time, they caught me and every time they threatened me. Eventually, it was like I gave up hope. I shouldn't have and I'm so sorry Ari. I can't even imagine how hard it was for you. At least I knew you were alive. I even saw you every so often on the live feed. You grew up so much in three years." Even though there was still some awkwardness between us, I could see more of my brother in the person in front of me now.

"You grew up too Eli. You look different." I smiled ruefully at him. We couldn't change it now, but it would take some getting used to. He patted my hand,

"I'm still your brother." There was a sound outside and his head snapped to the side. Holding a finger to his lips, he crept over to the door, cracking it open. As he did, my phone buzzed. I pulled it out, frowning at the unknown number,

Be careful. He hasn't told you everything – C

I'd thrown Caden's phone away but of course he

got another one. I was more annoyed that he had bothered to remember my number. His text puzzled me. What hadn't Eli told me? Why? Or was this another of Caden's tricks? I hurriedly put my phone away as Eli came back over.

"What was that?" I kept my voice light. I'd just got him back; I didn't want to start doubting him now. He shrugged, holding a finger to his lips again. Going over to Rick's desk, he disappeared underneath. I heard a *click* before he reappeared.

"We need to get out of here. Now you're here, they can't hold that over me. Caden isn't nearby anymore to get to mum and dad. We can escape." I struggled to respond, my mind whirring. That had been the eventual plan, but I hadn't expected it to be right this second,

"What?" He gave me the look he used to give me when I wasn't using common sense. That hadn't changed.

"I just disarmed the bug under Ricks desk so they definitely can't hear us. We only have a few seconds before he comes back in. He would have been listening. But we can leave, we can get out." He took a deep breath as if he couldn't quite believe what he was saying, "We're going to escape Ari, you and me. We're going to go home."

Chapter 15

I was still staring at him when Rick burst back into the room, giving both of us suspicious glances. He looked around the rest of the room, but nothing was out of place.

"I think that's enough catching up for now." He flashed us his smile. It still made my skin crawl. Caden hadn't come back into the room and I was glad. I wouldn't have been able to avoid looking at him and I didn't want Eli to read my face. I didn't care if Eli did kill him. He'd burned that bridge when he threw me into the Loch. I stood up as Eli squared up to Rick.

"Ari stays with me." There was no question in his voice, no room for argument. It was this confidence that made me falter, made me think about Caden's text. Maybe something had changed. Maybe there was something he wasn't telling me.

Not the time Ari. Right now, you've got to figure out how to get both of you out of here. Then you can find out what he's hiding. If he's hiding anything.

Rick glanced at me, his expression dubious. I

could see, now, partly where Eli's confidence had come from; he was indispensable to Rick. They couldn't make the creatures without him so he could probably demand whatever he wanted. I took some comfort in that, knowing that he could have asked for anything he needed over the last three years. Rick's attention went back to Eli and after a few heated seconds, he nodded curtly.

"Very well. But I will be assigning some security...for your own sakes." It might have been my imagination, but it looked like his eyes flickered back to me again. Clearly there was something going on; hopefully I would find out before it came back to bite me in the arse. Rick gestured towards the door; Eli grabbed my elbow and pulled me out of his office so fast I had to take jogging steps to keep up. We walked back through the hallways in silence. I was still trying to figure out how we were going to get out of here, especially if Rick assigned us 'security'. I was mulling it over as Eli stopped, pulling me up short. Looking up I realised we were outside Lab 2. I wasn't sure what I was going to find in here; it was one thing knowing my brother had created all the creatures I'd seen up until this point. It was another thing entirely to watch him do it. He pushed the door open and walked in with a practised ease. I scurried in behind him. The lab looked pretty much the same as the one I'd hid in next door, just with more Eli in it.

He had notebooks scattered on the metal tables and a half-eaten bag of marshmallows propped up by a computer screen. I smiled as I saw them remembering how he'd crammed for his sixth form exams and eaten nothing but marshmallows for days. Apparently, they helped him think. I'd scoffed at the time but looking around at calculations scrawled on whiteboards, maybe they did. I jumped as I realised Eli was watching me, chewing his lip.

"What?" My voice seemed tiny in the white, polished space of the lab. He stopped chewing his lip and shook his head, smiling,

"Nothing. I'm just… nervous, I guess. What do you think?"

Think of what? The experiments? Nothing good.

I chose to avoid the real subject of the question,

"I think you need to clean up in here." I stuck my tongue out at him; there was a flicker of hurt in his eyes but then he grinned at me.

"I happen to like it this way. It's messy organisation." It was strange how easily we fell back into our old routines. I should have been happy, but something was stopping me.

"Just like you." I shot back. Before he could say anything else, there was a pitiful howl from the corner of the room. My head instantly snapped round. I'd noticed the cages when I'd come in, but I hadn't paid much attention to them. Or

I hadn't wanted to. But now my attention was firmly focused on them. I walked over, trying to see into the shadows. As I got closer, the howling stopped. Crouching down, I peered into the cage. Light yellow eyes met mine. Behind me I heard Eli flick on a switch and a lamp above the cage slowly flickered to life. In the lightening gloom I could make out pointed ears and a black nose.

"Is this...did he come from the wolf in the other room?" I asked in a low voice, not taking my eyes off of the animal in front of me. Eli moved next to me, also crouching down,

"Yeah. They brought him in earlier this morning and called me in." He was watching the pup too, but I could see he was calculating something.

"Do you know...do you know what they did?" I didn't hide the tremble. I wanted him to know I wasn't happy; I was dreading his answer. He didn't say anything for a few seconds. "Eli." He pushed his hair back from his face, standing up and turning away. I didn't stand up, but I turned to follow his movements. He leant on a table, head bent down. "Eli, they cut it out of her and left her there. She's *dying.* Do you realise that? I can't even imagine how much pain-" He slammed one hand down on the table, cutting me off. From here I could see that his forearms were shaking, but his face was hidden by his hair.

"I KNOW ARI. I HAVE *LIVED* WITH THIS. I KNOW WHAT THEY DO. THERE'S NOTHING I CAN DO TO CHANGE IT!" His voice snapped across the room, vicious. I turned back to the cage so he couldn't see the hurt in my face. Even though I was trying not to shake, I couldn't resist,

"You could have tried. You clearly have power over Rick. You could have stopped them from being cruel." I didn't keep the judgement from my voice. I never thought Eli was the kind of person to let someone be cruel. Something clattered behind me and I jumped.

"You weren't HERE Ari. You don't understand!" This wasn't my brother. He had never yelled at me like this. I flinched as his footsteps came towards me, but I didn't look at him. The wolf pup seemed to feel the tension, starting a low whine in his throat. I could hear Eli pacing. He'd never been this angry. He wasn't angry or aggressive.

He hasn't told you everything.

I was beginning to believe Caden. As Eli paced the wolf pup struggled forward. I watched it, puzzled until its leg came into full view. I couldn't stop myself from gasping. Eli stopped. His legs were dragging behind him and, rather than looking in proportion with his body, extended far beyond his back. They hung at an odd angle. As I watched him struggle closer, I realised why. His legs, though covered in fur, were human in formation, with a knee joint that bent inwards halfway down. But it didn't look like he could use them at all. He reached the bars, pushing his wet nose through to touch my hand. I stroked his nose through the cage, feeling my heart break as I watched him. I heard ragged breathing behind me. I spun round, pushing myself up. The pup let out a pitiful bark as I moved away. Eli was back leant against the table, his back heaving up and down, breathing in short bursts.

"Eli?" I didn't want to speak any louder than a whisper. I approached cautiously; as I got close to him, I could see that he was sweating, beads rolling down his neck and face. I reached out to put a hand on his back but before I could touch him, he shifted away. I caught a glimpse of his face as he moved. He looked inhuman. Even his eyes were glazed. I moved back a step, waiting until his shoulders stopped heaving. After a couple more moments he looked up at me. His face looked drawn, like he was in pain. "What the hell was that Eli?" I kept most of the tremor out of my voice; hopefully if he heard it, he would think it was anger. He didn't answer me; instead he walked over to a cupboard at the other side of the lab and pulled out a syringe. Grabbing a vial, he filled it up and plunged it into the crook of his arm. As he pressed the plunger down, a wave of relief passed over his face. I was open-mouthed. My mind was racing as he finished pushing the syringe and tossed the needle into a sharps bin. Instead of saying anything, he simply began tidying up the mess I'd mentioned earlier. Frustration welled up in my chest. I wasn't used to this Eli. I knew he'd been through a lot, but I couldn't equate the person in front of me with the brother I used to have. He moved around in silence, the shuffling of papers joining the whining of the pup. I watched him for a few minutes before moving over to a stool and sitting down, crossing my arms. Clearly, I would have to wait until he was ready to talk. My eyes kept drifting back to the pup. I knew they were trying to make a werewolf but a wolf with deformed legs that couldn't even walk was evidently not the way to go. Maybe Eli couldn't figure this one out. The clock on the wall ticked by. After fifteen minutes had passed, Eli sighed and came to a halt on the opposite side of the table to me.

"I'm sorry." He said the words so softly, I almost didn't hear them. I didn't reply, keeping my arms crossed. I was going to need much more than that. "Since being here, I've had attacks of anger. I use a dilution of a mild sedative to calm myself down." At least it wasn't the kind of drugs I was originally thinking. I couldn't forgive him, not entirely, but given where we were and what he had been dealing with for the last three years, I could understand being angry. I softened my face and he relaxed. All it meant was that I was more determined than ever to get us out of here. I moved over to him, casting a glance towards the door. Rick had mentioned security and, even though I hadn't seen them, I was willing to bet they were waiting outside the door, just in case we decided to leave.

"We aren't done with this, but right now, we need to focus on getting out of here. Like you said." Eli nodded and I lowered my voice to the smallest whisper I could manage, "I don't think we can leave this lab. Which means we need to make them think we're still in here... do you have any vents?" He cocked his head to the side, thinking, then nodded. Tugging me over to the far side of the room, he pointed behind a desk. I crouched down, the prison bars of the grate gleaming back at me.

Perfect.

I didn't know where it led but hopefully it was somewhere better than here. We probably had another half an hour of silence before someone checked on us. I stood up again and leant into Eli's ear.

"Any cameras?" He shook his head, "Grab what you need in a bag. Nothing more than you can carry through that vent. You have literally five minutes." He flashed me a grin and hurried over to his notebooks, stopping to grab a small backpack on the way. I went over to the cages, bending down to the wolf pup. He licked my fingers and I wished I could take him with me, but there was no way I could when he couldn't even walk.

"I'm so sorry. But I'm going to make sure the government shuts this whole place down. I promise. I'll stop them from doing anything else to you." He cocked his head to one side and I almost broke down. "I'm so so sorry." He gave my hand another lick. I forced myself to stand up and pull away. Eli hurriedly went back to what he was doing, but I knew he was watching me. Remorse was written across his face. I couldn't meet his eyes, so I grabbed my backpack, settling it in between my shoulder blades. A couple of seconds later Eli appeared next to me, his own straps slung over his shoulders. Shuffling under the desk, I pulled out my 5 pence coin again, thankful that they had used the same screws. I could feel Eli jigging about behind me; it made my own hands shake, the screws rattling as I pulled them out of the vent cover. After an agonising few seconds, I had all four screws out and was pulling the cover aside, placing it flat against the wall, hidden behind a large piece of machinery. The vent was completely dark, and I couldn't feel any breeze. Casting a glance back at the closed lab door, I took a deep breath and clambered inside. Eli was close behind me, pulling the vent cover back over.

I really hope this works.

We crawled through the darkness; it was slow progress. I had to stop every few seconds and move the torch I'd pulled out of my backpack from my mouth to my hand to see if there was any change up ahead. We carried on for a while, eyes slowly adjusting to the darkness. We eventually came to a corner; as soon as we turned it, small beams of light started to filter through. I started to speed up. I could hear Eli shuffling behind me as I moved through the vent. Up ahead I could see an opening and, as we approached, a slight breeze ruffled through. Cautiously, I approached it. Through the grate I could see a large open room.

"Eli." I hissed, "Do you recognise this?" He shuffled up beside me and looked through the grate as well.

"Yeah; it's the delivery entrance. It leads out into the clearing. They don't normally have many people here unless there's a delivery due." That could work. I thought back to the clearing I'd come in through and the hidden doorway.

The camera...

"There's a camera directly outside the doors; it's motion activated." I heard him snort,

"I've got it covered sis, don't worry." I made a face that I knew he couldn't see in the darkness. By this point I had this down to a fine art.

The vent cover was off in a matter of seconds. I squeezed out into the room, moving out of the way so that Eli could clamber in behind me. We both stood up, casting quick glances around the room. As far as I could see, it didn't look like anyone had been in here recently. We got to the doors but before I could open it, Eli put a hand on top of mine.

"Wait a second." He pulled a small device from his pocket, almost identical to the one Caden had used to control the collar. I took an instinctive step back; he shot me a strange look and pressed the button. No ear-splitting screeches. Instead there was a click and a low hum. Eli seemed to be waiting for something. After a few seconds, there was another click. He put the device away and grabbed my wrist,

"We need to move quickly. The remote deactivated the camera for ninety seconds." He pulled open the door and we slipped outside, also sidestepping a thin film that covered the doorway. Instantly, the cool air enveloped me. I took in a deep breath, loving the pine needle scent that accompanied it. Eli shut the door behind us, and we started moving through the undergrowth. I couldn't help but cast glances back over my shoulder to the hidden doorway. The film had settled back over the doorway, obscuring it completely from view but I was expecting it to move at any second as GAI chased after us. It didn't happen. Eli stepped on a twig, the sound of it breaking harsh against the soft silence of the trees. We both froze for a split second, completely on edge but, apart from a soft breeze, nothing stirred. We walked around the edge of the clearing, keeping to the same path I'd used only a few hours before.

This is too easy.

I peeked out through the trees, checking across the clearing, but it was empty. I couldn't shake the feeling that this had been far too easy. Eli was quiet beside me, his eyes flitting across the treeline. I found the start of the trail I'd taken through the forest following Caden and moved ahead, leading Eli around the tree roots. The light was starting to fall, the sun setting in the distance. I didn't really want to be in the forest overnight but there was no way we would get back to Freiburg before nightfall. Playing with the toggle on my jumper, I tried to come up with a plan. I'd seen a small shed near the tower earlier. If we could get into it, we could use that to stay in overnight. I wasn't that comfortable staying so close to the GAI headquarters, but hopefully they wouldn't have any idea which way we'd gone.

"Eli." My voice shattered the silence of the forest and I cringed, hopping over a tree root and turning around so I could face him. "I don't think we can get all the way back to Freiburg before it gets completely dark and the trail I came on earlier definitely cannot be done in the dark. We need to find somewhere to wait out until morning. I think there's a small building in the next clearing. Once we get there I'm going to try and get into it and we can stay there for the night, is that okay?" He nodded, his eyes still flitting. I didn't like the tremors that were running over his skin.

You don't have that far to go until you reach the tower. Then you can deal with Eli. One thing at a time.

I pushed on through the forest. Night was encroaching around us; even the air felt different. What had been a comforting blanket had turned into something a lot more sinister. Gnarled roots stuck out from the ground, primed to trip us up and knotted fingers tangled in my hair as we crept past. I reached back to take Eli's hand, pulling him faster through the trees. I wanted to get out of the crush of trunks and into the clearing, where hopefully the moonlight would chase away some of the shadows. Every time something moved around us, my mind instantly went into overdrive. After what felt like an age, the trees began thinning again; relieved, I pushed forward, breaking through the treeline. The tower leapt out in front of me, reaching up into the night sky. I could see the building off to the far side of the clearing and I all but ran towards it. The door was locked, but it was pretty flimsy.

With a well-placed shove of my shoulder, I had the door open, falling into the room. Eli stepped in after me, shutting the door. I found a light switch on the wall and flicked it on. The room was pretty bare, with just a couple of chairs; it looked like some kind of office. There was only one window at the far side of the building, facing out into the trees. I pushed some boxes in front of the door before turning around. Eli was slumped on the floor, his eyes wide.

"Eli, are you okay?" I crouched down next to him. He didn't seem angry now, just scared. I'd been so used to Eli comforting me that I almost forgot what it was like for it to be the other way around. He nodded but didn't relax. There wasn't much I could do at the moment, not when we were so far away from home. I took off my jumper and balled it up. "Maybe you should try getting some sleep? I'll stay up for a few hours." He nodded again, still staring into the distance, but he let me push him down, resting his head on my jumper. I moved over, turned the light off and sat in one of the chairs, able to see both the door and the window from the faint moonlight. Nothing seemed to be moving outside and after a few minutes Eli's breathing settled into something deep and peaceful. I tried to resist the call of sleep, my eyes heavy in the darkness, but eventually my head lolled to the side as I drifted off.

I woke to Eli shaking my shoulder.

"Ari." He hissed urgently, "Something is outside." I woke up immediately, blinking off the last vestiges of sleep. I could hear the scuffling as well, against the wood of the building.

We shouldn't have stopped.

Feeling around for my backpack, I pulled out the first thing I could to use as a weapon. It turned out to be the torch. The shuffling increased, coming from directly under the door now. I tightened my grip on the torch, waiting for the inevitable break in. Instead, the shuffling stopped and a couple of seconds later a braying howl filled the air.

It's a fox.

I almost rolled my eyes. Eli had relaxed as well. I let my hand drop, the torch falling back into my backpack. We were okay. I squeezed Eli's hand, waiting for him to squeeze back. He didn't. A split second later, he crumpled face first into the floor, hitting the wood with a concerning *thunk.*

"Eli?!" A laugh came from behind me in the darkness and my voice dried up in my throat.

"He can't hear you sweetheart." *Rick.* I tried to scramble up, but strong hands pinned me down against the harsh wood of the chair. There was another movement in front of me. I couldn't tell how many were in here, but I knew I didn't have a chance against even one of them. "You really shouldn't have run away. You know that was a stupid move. Not only have you failed, but you've ruined any cautious truce Eli had. He is now my prisoner. And you my dear, are little more than collateral damage." The person I'd sensed in front of me moved again and I struggled against the hands but they stayed firm. I tried to calm my breathing, but the darkness was amplifying the anxiety I was feeling.

"She could be useful." It was whispered behind me. I knew it was Caden, but I didn't know why he wasn't all for me being killed.

"She's expendable." I shivered at the lack of emotion.

"Not to him." It was delivered with the finality of someone who knew they had won their argument. The hands pinning me down relaxed slightly and someone moved through the darkness again.

"You're lucky Caden has taken it upon himself to act as your spokesperson. But I agree with him. You could be useful. Eli has taken a turn for the worse recently, especially with his episodes and we need something to control him. I can't keep placating him. I need him to move forward with the Lycan Project and I don't have time for him to think he is in charge." There was a tapping sound, like fingers drumming on wood, "So Miss Farrow, where does that leave us? With you in my hands, I think. Caden, take her and Eli back to base. I'll meet you there." He stalked across the floorboard, kicking the boxes out of the way and opening the door. Moonlight streamed in, momentarily illuminating him but he quickly shut the door again. There was a beat of silence, then a rush of movement. Caden was in front of him, his face so close to mine that I could feel his breath on my lips.

"You were an idiot to think you could get away. Haven't you learnt that? We will win."

"And yet you keep saving me. Why is that?" I couldn't help it. I wanted to goad him. He laughed, stepping back.

"There's something about your prize being claimed by someone else that makes a guy do crazy things." I knew he wasn't talking about me, but about killing me.

He's a dick.

Before I could think up a retort, I felt a needle press into my neck and the world fizzled into darkness.

Chapter 16

When I came to, the first thing I noticed was that my wrists were restrained. I could feel the rough fibres of the rope against my skin. Blinking against the heavy fog of my brain, I looked down to see thick lines of rope tying my arms to a chair. The memory of the needle came rushing back in and I struggled against the ropes, trying to find some give in them but it was no use. As I struggled, I realised I could see a lot of my skin through my swimming vision. I was only wearing my bra and underwear.

"Not fun is it?" Caden's voice broke through my struggle, "Waking up to find yourself tied to a chair." He bit the words at me, but I couldn't see where they'd come from. In fact, the only thing that seemed to be illuminated in the room was me. When I didn't respond, he carried on. "I can see it from your side though. It's quite satisfying to watch." He trailed off with a throaty chuckle. There was a shuffling of fabric behind me, the sound of denim scraping across a rough surface, before his face appeared by the side of me. Blearily I turned my head, still woozy from whatever drugs they'd pumped into me. As I did, the world wobbled and I quickly tried to right myself, but all my limbs were tied down, leaving my head spinning.

"Why…couldn't…you…just…give…up…" Each word was difficult, the letters snaking up my throat and hooking themselves on my tongue. Caden let out a snort and crouched in front of me, his grey eyes the only part of him that wasn't wavering in my gaze.

"I thought you'd have realised by now that I don't give up. I'll play the long game. It would have been satisfying to do away with you straight away, especially after all the trouble you've caused me with Rick, but then Rick came up with an even better suggestion. You probably won't agree." I caught a glimpse of his perfect teeth through my dizziness, but I couldn't keep them straight. I knew that whatever they had planned was going to be painful and I knew that I was probably going to die and with my head spinning like a carousel, there was nothing I could even do to think my way out of it. "But first, let's give you a little backstory, shall we? Since we've got a bit of time to kill before the main event."

He stood up and dragged a chair over, the legs scraping against the floor with an ear-splitting screech. I winced against it, but I couldn't cover my ears, no matter how hard my fingers strained against their bonds. He lounged in the chair, one leg hooked over the arm, grinning at me. This was the Caden from the Loch, no doubt in my mind. That's how I knew he was going to kill me; the fervour in his eyes as he looked at me. Whatever help he'd given me, whatever feelings he may have once had for me, had clearly been an act, a way to get what he wanted, his revenge. I closed my eyes for a few seconds, taking a couple of deep breaths. I didn't want to face whatever was coming whilst I felt like I was on a Waltzer at the village fair. When I opened them again, the spinning had lessened, now a gentle wave that crashed over me every few seconds. I could deal with that. Caden was watching me with amusement. We stared at each other for a couple more seconds before he clapped his hands together,

"Right. Let's start the show, shall we?" He paused, as if he was waiting for a response. I spat on the ground in front of him. "Charming. I think the very best place to start is with the real story of your dear brother Eli, not the pile of bullshit he gave you in Rick's office. I mean the kidnapping is true. But when he got here and realised what was going on, he wasn't scared of it. He was excited. He *wanted* to figure out the puzzle. Those other creatures you found in the lab, they weren't requested. He just started to experiment with what he could do." I shook my head, unwilling to believe that Eli would do that. That wasn't my brother. "Shake your head all you like sweetheart, but it's true. Of course, it got worse after he started experimenting on himself."

My stomach dropped like a lead weight.

"Yeah, I can see you knew something was wrong. It wasn't anything crazy, but he started using the different human components that he'd been attempting with the animals, like the growth accelerant, on himself. He made himself stronger and smarter and faster. To begin with, Rick was thrilled, and Eli was given more freedom to experiment. But, as most of the studies had shown, some of these human components came with unknown side effects. Eli's behaviour became erratic; one moment he was the same boy we'd taken from his room in the middle of the night, the next he was in such a fit of rage that he was a danger to anyone around him. I think even Rick, crazy bastard that he is, could see Eli was on a path of self-destruction. But there was no way he was losing his chief scientist. So, he came up with a mixture of drugs that would calm Eli down every time he had an episode and essentially managed to control his outbursts…"

Just like another one of the monsters… No. Eli's not a monster.

"But in Eli's mind, nothing was wrong. He started talking about you, almost constantly. He had overheard one of my reports and was suddenly obsessed. He was convinced you would come for him. Rick couldn't let that happen; he would lose any control he had over Eli if you showed up and yet, somehow you managed it. If I didn't hate you, I would admire you Ari. You've somehow dealt with a lot of shit to get here; it's a shame it would never have worked. I don't even know why Rick decided to bring Eli to you. It was like he thought it would somehow fix Eli. Well..." he fixed me with a look, "It obviously didn't. You were lucky Eli didn't have an episode and hurt you."

I thought back to the lab and Eli's anger. I couldn't focus on everything else Caden had said. I didn't want to believe what he was saying, but I'd seen Eli turn into someone I'd never known in an instant. It made sense. Since I'd seen him again it was like he was *almost* my brother, but there was something keeping him from being the brother I'd lost. Other bits of it made sense as well, like his bullshit reasoning for letting them do horrible things to the animals. He hadn't really seemed remorseful, even when I confronted him. He just seemed to want to cover it up from me. I'd seen him passionate about his projects before, all through school, but I had never imagined it would get to this, to this crazed zeal that removed his humanity. As my mind raced through all the new information, Caden lulled into a charged silence. When I finally met his eyes again, he looked expectant,

"How... can I trust... you're telling me the... truth? You weren't... even here. You... you were off...playing pretend...with me." At least I could string a couple of words together this time. Caden's jaw clenched, expression coated in... disappointment?

"I watched the security footage and read Rick and the other scientists' reports when I got back." He waved a hand in the air, as if it was inconsequential. Then his eyes narrowed, "For some reason, you decided to try and escape. I think you broke something in Eli. He suddenly wanted to be the older brother he used to be to you; it was like he mentally renounced who he has been for the past three years, trying to cover it up from you so you wouldn't think of him differently. I don't understand it. Although I never had siblings, so maybe I never will. But you know Eli wouldn't have been able to stay your brother from three years ago forever, right?" he raised an eyebrow at me and sighed when I didn't reply. "You're not completely stupid, so I know you realise that. How did you think we wouldn't find you? If you'd run back to your parents? I'd love to know what your plans were. Unfortunately, we don't have the time for that. See, our problem now is, whatever you broke in Eli, *we can't fix.* He's refusing to do anything, screaming that he wants to see you. Given how badly that went last time, obviously we aren't going to let you two be in a room alone together. But he'll get to see you. Eli might have been the bargaining chip before, but now it's your turn. In order to get him to co-operate, we need him to understand that there will be consequences and, since the only thing he's focussed on is you, well..." he trailed off, smirking.

The consequences will be me.

I'd known it since he'd started talking. It was all leading up to a grand reveal, that I obviously had a key part in, given that I was tied to a chair. That was never going to be anything good. But the only thing I could take from this, if I was a bargaining chip, I would have to remain alive, at least for now. Caden moved suddenly, swinging his leg down from the arm of the chair and leaning forward, propping his elbows on his knees, hair falling into my face. He had it down now, the ends reaching mid torso.

"Given, my dear, that you are the bargain, it's also to be said that you won't get to see Eli. But..." he stood up and grabbed something from behind me, placing it on a nearby table. I squinted to make it out, "He'll be able to see you." He pressed something and a little red light started blinking,

It's a camera.

There was more movement, some rattling and

scraping and then Caden reappeared, setting something down by his side. He flashed me a grin,

"I think it's time that you and I show Eli what happens when he doesn't cooperate…" the words were uttered directly into the camera, the red light a pin-point flame in the darkness. He leant down next to him and pulled something out, showing it first to the camera and then me. The blade glinted under the harsh lightbulb above me, slithers of light dancing on the sharp edge. I tried to push down the fear. I didn't want Caden to see it. His eyes were storms now, raging, ready to create chaos.

With slow, deliberate movements, he moved the knife towards me, placing it on my cheek. I sucked in a breath that I know he heard from the low chuckle that drifted through the air. The knife was dragged lightly down my face, curving around my jaw and the soft skin of my neck. I could feel my pulse jump out to greet it, my heart hammering as he paused for a second, enjoying it. But he didn't strike; instead he continued to drag the tip of the knife down my chest, feather-light, until he reached the edge of my ribcage. His head turned to look at the camera for a split second before snapping his face back round and slashing the knife down my ribs. White-hot pain lanced through me, the knife leaving behind a line of fire in its wake. I gasped as he moved away; I could see a thin line of my blood clinging to the edge of the knife. I didn't think it was deep; it wasn't meant to be. He needed to cause me pain, to use the nerve-endings and a gradual build up.

I resolved to keep my reactions to a minimum. Eli was no doubt being forced to watch and if I cried out, it would only make it worse. Caden wiped off the knife with a small rag, making sure he did it in full view of the camera. Once it was cleaned, he turned his attention back to me, sliding the knife under my chin to force my head up,

"What should I cut next?" His voice was low, but I knew the camera could pick it up. He licked his bottom lip, moving my head left and right with the blade, pressing just enough for it to hurt but not enough to draw blood. "Your pretty little face? Mmm, I could enjoy that. How about I carve a line from here" he moved the knife, quick as a whip, to the edge of my eyebrow, "to here?" and dragged it down to the corner of my mouth. I pressed my lips together. I wasn't going to answer him. He grinned even wider and looked over his shoulder, "What do you think Eli? How would your poor little sister look with her face slashed up? I don't mind… I'll enjoy it."

Before I even had time to steel myself, the knife was back on my ribs, another gash parallel to the first. I managed to stop my gasp, biting down on my lip. I could feel the blood trickling in hot lines down my torso now. "How long do you think it would take her to bleed out like this Eli? I'll just keep cutting and cutting... how long can your sister last?" *Slash*. Another line. I made a sound at the back of my throat. I heard the knife clatter down onto something and looked up to see Caden pick up a pair of pliers. He gripped my mouth, hard, forcing it open. I twisted my head in his grip, but he just held on tighter, still wearing that grin. He tapped the top of the pliers against my teeth, eliciting a clacking sound. "What if I pulled out her teeth? That would make her scream, I guarantee it. Would you co-operate then Eli? If I..." he gripped one of my canines with the pliers, "Pulled this out?" I closed my eyes, waiting for the pull. He chuckled instead, releasing my tooth and putting the pliers back on the tray.

I'd started shivering. The room was cold anyway and my lack of clothing, combined with the fear of what he was going to do had caused my body to react. I clenched my hands to try and hide the shaking, but he saw.

"Oh look, she's shaking. How much do you love your sister Eli?" I glared at him as my teeth chattered. He blew me a kiss and picked up a larger, longer blade. "I don't think teeth pulling is enough, do you?" Kicking the chair away, he knelt down in front of me and tugged at the bandage on my leg, unwrapping it. As it fell to the floor, he sucked in a breath, "This looks bad Eli. I'm sure it's incredibly painful. What would happen if I did this, I wonder?" I screamed as he drove the knife into the edge of the wound, slashing upwards through the stitches. I tried to stop, but the searing pain beat through me. As he pulled the knife back, I could see it was coated in thick, dried blood, scabs clinging to the edge of the blade. Tears began streaming down my face as I gasped in air around the pain.

Breathe...one...two...it hurts so much...

Caden didn't clean the knife this time. Instead he ran it down my cheek, leaving behind a wet trail. I cringed away from its touch.

The blood is still warm. Oh God. I think I'm gonna throw up.

I took another deep breath, trying to keep down the bile. Caden watched me, amused. There was a clacking and a shuffling; I blinked through the tears to see him move the camera closer. I tried to turn my face away from the lens, but he grabbed my mouth again, forcing me to look at it,

"Show your brother. Show him what he's done to you." I had never hated anyone more than I hated Caden at that exact moment. I was completely weak; I couldn't do anything to get out of this. I dreaded to think what was happening to Eli on the other end of the camera feed. But I wasn't giving up. Snapping my mouth shut,

I kept glaring at Caden. He rolled his eyes and grabbed something from next to my chair, placing it at my feet. A bucket. Some kind of liquid sloshed around inside.

"I don't know if she told you Eli, in your little catch up, but I almost killed Ari once. I threw her in the Loch. She was drowning and she was ready to be eaten by your very own monster. How would she fare, do you think, if I made her think she was drowning again?" He held up a large flannel and my eyes widened as I realised what he was going to do. "Would she beg for mercy? Or would she just give up?" He paused as something buzzed in his ear. I looked closer and realised he had a comms unit in, clearly attached to wherever Eli was.

"Oh Eli, you shouldn't have done that." He murmured and turned back to me, still holding the flannel. "She won't be able to breathe, you know? She'll panic to the point of passing out. Then not even she can stop me; I can do *whatever* I want to her." He held one hand up to his ear as the unit buzzed again and dropped the flannel back into the bucket of water. "That's better." Picking up the smaller knife again, he twirled it around his fingers. "It looks like we're getting somewhere Ari. You should be glad. I wasn't sure your brother was going to give in." I panted, the adrenaline that had surged through my body at the thought of feeling like I was drowning again slowly dissipating. Swallowing a couple of times, so my mouth wasn't quite as dry, I spat at his feet again. He found it hilarious. "Do you want to thank your brother Ari?" I wanted to say something, that was for sure. There was no way I was letting Caden win; even if Eli wasn't who I had lost anymore, there was no way GAI were going to win. I nodded meekly and Caden turned the camera, so it was just on me,

"Eli... don't give them what they want." I saw surprise ripple across Caden's face for a split second, followed by anger, "I don't care what they do to me, don't let them win. Then it would all be for nothing-" I stopped as Caden slapped me, dropping the camera on the table where it fell to it's side.

"You fucking bitch!" I turned my face away as he hit me again, punching my cheekbone. I didn't know if it was his knuckles or my face that cracked. "You're going to regret that." The knife was back. He was right in my face, his nose grazing my cheek. "I'm going to make sure you do, every time you look in the mirror." He pushed the tip of the knife into my skin where he had it earlier, just below my eyebrow. I felt the skin break, the blade piercing through and settling in amongst my blood. The pain from it lasted a split second, blossoming across my temple. Then, ever so carefully, he dragged the tip of the knife down, keeping the same amount of pressure. My skin broke under the encroachment of the knife with agonising slowness; the pain rushed at me in tidal waves, shattering across the left side of my face in an unrelenting tsunami. I couldn't stop the screaming. As he continued to drag the knife down my face, I screeched, until my throat felt like it was raw and bleeding. Blood dripped from the top of the wound into the corner of my eye, painting one half of the world a faded scarlet, a harlequined reality. When he reached the bottom of my jaw, pushing even harder on the knife as it came into contact with bone, he stopped. I was panting, trying to blink the blood from my eye, trying to stop the fast-approaching panic. With a malicious grin he twisted the knife on my jawbone, holding it there for a few seconds before dropping his arm. The stained blade clattered to the floor and I slumped forward against the restraints, my hair falling across my face. Droplets of hot blood hit my pale thigh spreading along the minute lines of my skin like a macabre watercolour. Suddenly there was a camera in my face,

"Doesn't she look pretty Eli? I think she needs a matching one the other side though. What do you think?" I closed my eyes against the camera. I heard him put it down; the next moment he was lifting my head up, my blood staining his palms. "Do you want to see what you look like sweetheart? I can show you." I kept my eyes closed, my head pounding. I was taking long breaths, trying to keep the panic at bay, trying to take myself away from here. There was a chuckle as Caden released my chin, letting my head fall forward. "It's very rude not to answer when someone asks you a question, Ari. I said, would you like to see what you look like?"

You're not here... ignore him... he'll go away eventually...

"Arrrriiiii...look at me." He said it with a singsong but there was an edge to his voice. "Ari." I felt the blade of the knife press against the other side of my face and jerked my head back, my eyes shooting open. He stayed there, holding the blade in the air, admiring his handiwork. "That's better. Look." He held up a small metal tray. My eyes dropped to it and tried not to cry at the version of myself staring back. In the tray my face was distorted, curved and chopped in odd places, but even the fun house mirrors of me couldn't hide the left side of my face. I'd heard it said once that head wounds bled a lot, but I'd never seen one. Now, the left side of my face was a Picasso painting, red blood streaming down my cheek in haphazard lines, interrupted by my mouth. Strands of hair were caught in the torrent and one side of my lips had been stained a burgundy blush. I flicked my tongue out despite myself, the sharp metallic tang sitting on my taste buds. Blood had even mixed with the tears caught at the corner of my eye, running themselves down my face and dropping off the sheer edge of my jaw. That bit looked the worst. Where Caden had twisted the knife was a starburst of broken skin and bleeding tissue. A falling star. I couldn't hold back the sob. Caden lowered the tray as I broke down; I was still shivering, the spasms becoming more and more violent as my thighs turned red. "Do you see what you've done yet Eli?" he whispered.

There was some more clattering, ringing sharp in my ears and he crouched in front of me, a wad of cotton in one hand and a bottle in the other. "Look, I'm not completely heartless. I'll clean the wound for you. I wouldn't want it to get infected." He daubed the cotton with some of the clear liquid and held it up, "By the way, this might hurt a little bit." Without hesitation he pressed the cotton to my face. There was a beat, a pause as the liquid worked its way into the wound, then liquid fire blazed the length of my face. I was screaming again before I even realised it was me. The edge of my vision went starry, tiny specks closing in on my pupil. Caden began to pour straight from the bottle onto my face, causing an inferno. The grey fuzz at the edge of my vision rushed in, my scream fading into the blood splattered air as the pain pushed me over the edge and into the dark.

Chapter 17

The first thing I felt was more pain. I came to with a jolt, desperately gasping for air, my mind scrambling. Then the dull throb hit me. My left eye had lost its rose-tinted spectacle but none of the searing had left me. It was only when I looked around that I realised I was alone. I wasn't in the same room anymore. I'd been moved to a bed, laid down on a blanket. My hands were no longer restrained. I sat up slowly, the spinning in my head cautioning my movements. As I swung my legs around, another throb greeted me.

The stitches,

I remembered Caden ripping them out with the blade. I went to look at my leg, expecting to see an open, gaping wound, but was greeted instead by a loose black fabric. Looking at the rest of my body, I realised I was dressed; not in my clothes, but I was no longer in my underwear.

Did we get rescued? Are we free?

I tried to glance around the room but moving my head set off a sledgehammer in my skull. I winced, lowering myself back onto the bed. Once

I was lying down, the pounding stopped, my head settling itself back into a stationary form. I tried to sort through what had happened, but I had no recollection from after Caden had doused my face in what I assumed was alcohol. The pain had been blinding, I remembered that much. But I didn't know where I was, or how I had got here. Or, alarmingly, who had dressed me. As I felt the material of the top against my breasts, I realised someone had taken my bra off. I was trying to sort through the jumbled mess of my thoughts when the door opened. I tensed but didn't move. I wasn't strong enough to do much more than swat a fly, I had no chance against a person. I didn't recognise the face that appeared above me; she was young, with coffee coloured skin and a mass of crazy curls tied up behind her head. She smiled at me, though it didn't reach her eyes.

"I'm glad you're awake. I was beginning to get a bit worried about you. I need to check your wounds." Her voice was soothing, a gentle caress that I welcomed. But I still didn't know where I was. She made a move to touch my face, but I brought my hand up to stop her. She blinked at my fingers now wrapped around her wrist as if she'd never expected me to move.

"Wh-who are you?" my voice was scratchy, my throat sore. Even my mouth moved with difficulty, the skin stretched and tender. She dropped her hand.

"My name is Illiana. I'm- I've been assigned to treat your wounds." She seemed cagey. Her eyes kept flicking to somewhere I couldn't see.

"Okay." I clearly wasn't going to get more than that about her, "*Where* am I?" She shifted her eyes again and sighed,

"You're in a safe place." That wasn't an answer.

"Where?" I let my voice go pitchy at the end, the inflection rising more than it should. Worry immediately crossed her features, "I need you...to tell me where...or I will start screaming..."

"You're in the GAI Freiburg building." She rushed out, her eyes pleading with me. I shut my mouth from my threatened scream, disappointment settling on my chest. Taking my silence as satisfaction, she moved her hand to my face again but before she could touch skin, I turned my face to the side. I caught her look of frustration.

"More." It wasn't a question this time. I'd really had enough of being lied to. She shook her head and I painfully raised an eyebrow. Casting another glance out of my eyeline, she relented,

"You were moved here after you passed out in order to facilitate your recovery. The Director's orders." I assumed she meant Rick, "You've been unconscious for nearly three days. We were beginning to think you'd sustained a more threatening injury..."

"Oh, I'm sorry, was my torture not threatening enough for you?!" I knew it wasn't her fault, not directly, but I was pissed. She couldn't meet my eyes.

"I have- I have been caring for your... wounds. Unfortunately, we believe they will scar." I snorted,

"I don't think that's seen as unfortunate by some people." Somewhere, in the back of my mind, I was freaking out, but I didn't have time to deal with that right now. She didn't say anything, and I rolled my eyes. "I'm done. Do whatever you need to do." I snapped, closing my eyes. I felt her gently probe the skin on my face. It really fucking hurt. From where she was pressing, I could tell there was swelling, as well as the obvious giant wound from my eyebrow to my jaw. I only had a vague recollection of what it looked like and part of me was wondering if I could go the rest of my life without looking in another mirror. If I lived in the woods I probably could.

She applied something to my face, a cold balm that numbed some of the pain and moved down to my leg, rolling up the fabric. As she peeled away the bandage I hissed, the wound a lot more painful the second time around. She worked silently, applying more balm to my leg and quickly rebandaging the wound. As she continued, I stared at the ceiling, wondering how long it would be before I could get some real answers.

Hopefully, when I did get a chance, the room would considerately stop spinning long enough that I could at least sit up. I'd rather not question someone whilst staring at a badly-painted ceiling.

Luckily, after a few more minutes she left, shutting the door quietly behind her. I closed my eyes, listening to the gentle hum of the machines in the corner. I think I drifted off to sleep for a few minutes, only to be jerked awake by the sound of the door opening again. I sat up, glad that the room didn't spin this time, only to groan as I was greeted by Rick's face. He was leaning against the now closed door, watching me. As my eyes met his, he gave me a tight smile. I didn't return it,

"What do you want, *Director?*" He might not have been present when Caden was torturing me, but I know he had a hand in it. In fact, I was willing to bet the only reason he was here instead of Caden was because I would have immediately tried to kill Caden. I was going to get some information out of Rick first. A muscle in his jaw ticked at my tone but instead of answering me, he stalked forward and sat on the chair in the corner. I swung my legs round, my eyes following him. I might not want to slaughter him just yet but that didn't mean I had any kind of trust in him. For all I knew, he was here to finish the job Caden had started, and failed, twice now. His icy gaze flicked over my face and then down to my ribs, thankfully covered by the clothing and finally settled on my leg. Illiana hadn't done anything to my ribs so I could only assume they were surface wounds. We stared at each other in silence, the low hum the only thing that was breaking the tension. I raised an eyebrow.

"Illiana said you had some questions." Each word was tight, forced between his teeth. There was something in this situation he wasn't happy with. I wasn't thrilled with any of it, so I didn't see how there was anything he could be upset about. Apart from the fact that I was alive. There was no point in bringing that up though. So, I nodded,

"Why am I here? What happened in the last three days? Where is Eli?" Those were the main ones. I had a couple of subsequent questions such as 'Why are you all psychotic?' and 'Would you prefer to be killed quickly or slowly?' but I figured I could save them for after I'd got something useful out of him. He ran his hands down the lapels of his suit, smoothing them out, the deep navy flush against his skin.

"Eli made a deal." Even as he paused, my stomach was already sinking. This couldn't be good. "As you know, he was watching your... interaction with Caden via live feed-" I snorted, interrupting,

"Oh, please, call it what it was. Torture." I didn't

know if this guy had a conscience; I was pretty sure he didn't but if there was even a chance that somewhere in there, there was a guy with actual human emotions, I was going to play on them. I wasn't just going to let him forget. He inclined his head and when I remained silent, continued,

"He was watching Caden torture you." He didn't even flinch as he said it. I did though, the pain blossoming again in my skull. I pushed it away. "To begin with he seemed remarkably unmoved." Ouch. "Until we realised he was verging on an episode of anger like we had never seen. He killed one of the lab technicians and seriously injured another, just through trying to get out of the room. But he wouldn't relent and do what we needed him to do. I told Caden to step up the intensity, which was when he-" he gestured to my leg and I repressed the involuntary shudder as I remembered the knife slicing through the healing wound.

"He was almost ready to give in and was about to agree to carry on with his research into the Lycan Project but then you-" he glared at me as he paused. I returned the favour, "You told him not to give us what we wanted. It was like a switch flipped. He regained his composure, completely calm and refused to continue with the project. He almost- *you* almost cost us everything. None of this would work without Eli's research, you have to understand that! I didn't tell

Caden to attack you again, he did it of his own accord. He has some anger issues of his own."

Pot calling kettle black much?

"When you passed out, and Caden kept going, he finally relented. He told me he wouldn't continue with the experiments, but he would continue his research for application on a different subject." My heart dropped. I drew in a breath, holding it as he continued, "In return for your immediate safety and care for wounds inflicted, as well as subsequent release, Eli agreed to modify his research for use on an adult test subject... him." The room crashed down around me. Injections were one thing, but I knew what he had been working on. I knew what modifying his research meant. Rick didn't seem surprised as he watched my face, and the realisation that was dawning on it. Clearly, he knew I was aware of the research.

"Per our agreement, we have been caring for your wounds and when you are well enough to leave, we will let you go. However, I have some stipulations of my own. You cannot tell anyone about GAI. If anything is leaked to the news, if I have even an inkling that you've told anyone, I will kill Eli there and then. I won't even blink. Furthering this, for the agreement to hold, you must leave here without any argument. If you don't, your safety will immediately be rescinded. Am I clear?" My mind was still reeling from the realisation that Eli was, or maybe already had, turned his research on himself. I nodded, my eyes not really focussed. Rick carried on, "He has spent the past two days preparing our team of scientists and the procedure that they have agreed upon took place this morning. He recorded a video message for you." He placed a tablet on my lap, a video already loaded on the screen. Eli's face beamed out at me, but I could see his smile was slightly strained. It was the same smile he used to flash me across the dinner table when he was stressed about exams. With shaking fingers, I pressed the play button and he immediately came to life,

"Hey Ari... I don't know where to start. I'm really sorry that you got dragged into all of this. I never meant for you to be involved and I'm sorry that I lied to you as well. I know you told me not to give them what they wanted but I couldn't just sit there and watch Caden kill you. You were upset about the animal experimentation, so I'm stopping that. This way, the only person I can hurt is me... anyway. I wanted to tell you how proud I am of you. You've been the most amazing sister I ever could have asked for; you were willing to die for me and I'm willing to do the same to keep you safe. I spent three years thinking I would never see you again, that we would never be able to have a conversation about whatever weird tv show you were watching or go to the

Coffee Cup. I know we won't get to do most of that, but when I walked into Rick's office, and you were there, it felt like the best day of my life. I've never forgotten you or Mum or Dad, not even for a day, but I didn't expect you to keep searching for me. I thought you would have moved on with your life. In a way, I'm sorry you didn't. It might have been better for you if you'd thought I was dead, if you'd been able to grieve and start afresh. But I will be forever grateful that you came to find me; that you literally fought the Loch Ness Monster to get to me. So, this is my way of making sure you're safe now. You can move on. I don't know if I'll make it through the procedure; it's never been done before and I haven't really had enough time to prepare but they were going to keep you here until I did it and I just really want you to be able to get home, to see our parents and your friends. If I make it through, we won't be able to be in contact. GAI feel it's too dangerous, but I won't ever forget you little sis. I'm so so sorry, I hope you forgive me. I love you." He was crying by the end of the video and, as a tear fell onto the glass, I realised I was too.

This was nowhere near the goodbye I needed but at least I had something. My mind sank as I thought of going back home having come so close to saving him, to bringing him with me only to leave empty-handed. I wasn't even sure I could move on with my life. I wiped the tears off of the tablet screen, Eli's face paused in a sad smile, and handed it back to Rick. He took it silently, not meeting my eyes. Maybe he did feel bad after all. But Eli was wrong, in his video. He wasn't just hurting himself; he was tearing me apart. I sniffed, wiping the tears on the back of my hand and blinking up at the lights. If I had to leave, I at least wanted to know if my brother was alive,

"Can-can I see him?" I asked, my voice wavering as more tears built up, ready to fall. Rick looked down at the floor. "What?"

"He hasn't woken up yet. We don't know if he will." He looked sad, but I knew he was thinking about his project, without his lead scientist, not about the person behind the science. I tried to swallow the fear, the desire to break down in gut-wrenching sobs teetering on the edge. "I can show you the footage we have from the lab and, if you want, I can take you there before you leave." I nodded, cautious of the sudden kindness. I could only assume he was anticipating getting rid of me as soon as possible. He pressed a couple of icons on the tablet, bringing up a slightly grainy screenshot before passing it back to me. Before I pressed play, he stood up, the fabric of his suit brushing against the chair upholstery as he did so. "I'll leave you alone to watch that. There are some street clothes over there for you." He pointed to a bag by the door. "When you're ready, come outside and I'll take you out." He paused for a second, mouth open as if he wanted to say something else, but didn't, closing it with a snap of his teeth and stalking back out of the doorway.

I waited until I heard the door click into place before I turned my attention back to the tablet screen. Residual tears were still leaking from my eyes, making trails down my cheeks, some soaking up into the bandage on my face. I'd almost forgotten about my injuries in the midst of Eli's revelation, but they were still there, adding to the growing panic thrumming quietly under the surface. Taking a deep breath, I tapped the tablet screen, the slightly blurry image immediately jumping to life. It showed three people; one was Eli, I could recognise him instantly, but the other two were people I hadn't seen before. They were stood either side of a table, lowering Eli down and strapping his arms to the side of the table. I pressed the fast-forward button, watching the miniature scene in double time. I wasn't sure I could sit through it otherwise. They hurried around the table, moving in different trays and pieces of equipment. A door at the far end opened and another lab coated technician rolled in a table, covered with a lumpy sheet. They moved the table next to Eli and removed the sheet. I closed my eyes for a second as I realised it was the adult wolf from Lab 3. It didn't look like she was alive anymore or at the most, not for much longer. The two people conferred with Eli briefly; the first placed a mask over his face, which I assumed was some kind of knock out gas.

Within a few breaths, Eli had gone very still on the table. I pushed the video into an even faster speed, my stomach churning. The technicians flitted about the room, moving from one table to the other. They seemed to be taking skin from the wolf and attempting to graft it onto Eli which must have been what he meant when he said he needed to change tact. Instead of trying to create an animal, modifying a human to look like a werewolf would have the same effect and would probably be easier to control.

It was when they began to mess about with components other than skin that I had to turn away, only sneaking glances when I felt like I wasn't going to throw up. I paused the recording when I could get a clear picture of Eli's face, leaning in close to try and make it out. What I could see from the blurry image made me feel like I was going to pass out all over again. They'd not only attempted to alter the surface of his appearance, but it seemed they'd tried to change the actual shape of his face as well, a lot like plastic surgery, just on a much bigger scale. Even from the high, blurry angle, I could see they had extended his nose to make it look more like a snout and had attached more cartilage to his ear to elongate it. One side of his face, however, was still human, with Eli's skin and his ear and his hair. It was like a mash-up.

From what I remembered of reality tv on plastic surgery, sometimes procedures had to be done in stages in order to ensure they didn't overload the body. It looked like they were trying to do something like that here. The only thing that puzzled me was the abundance of different injections they seemed to be giving him. I already knew that Eli used a growth accelerant in most of his research, but what else he could have suggested they use, I didn't know. He wasn't at his most sane right now. I skipped ahead to the end of the video, unable to watch the scalpel cut through another part of his body. I started playing the video again when they left the room, leaving Eli covered in bandages on the table. They wheeled what was left of the female wolf out of the room with them. As the main light turned off, the video cut out, leaving me staring at a blurred image of half of Eli's face. I threw the tablet to the side and jumped down from the bed, grabbing the bin from the corner as the vomit that had been building throughout the video finally won out. I was shaking as I threw up, most of my brain refusing to believe that what I had seen was real. The tiny part that had accepted this crazy world was calmly telling me that Eli was probably dead. I leant back from the bin, sweat beading on my forehead.

This isn't happening. THIS ISN'T HAPPENING. It's a dream. You'll wake up any second now.

Unfortunately, when I opened my eyes, I was still confronted with the same room. As I glanced around feverishly, my eyes fell on the bag of clothes. I didn't know what else to do. Dragging myself over there, I pulled out some jeans, a t shirt and a hoodie. Standing on shaking legs, I threw off the slacks and shimmied into the pieces of clothing, the mundane task of buttoning the jeans and zipping up the hoodie momentarily distracting me from this altered reality I seemed to be living in. Every part of me that wasn't on edge was in pain. The skin across my face was sore, irritated by the tears that kept slipping from my eyes. Any pressure I put on my leg sent spikes up and down my entire side. Even my ribs were aching, each breath a little more rattling than the last. Eventually, I was dressed; I clutched onto the wall to keep myself standing and inched to the door that felt a hundred times heavier than it looked.

The hallway was light, daylight streaming in from an overhead skylight covered slightly by fallen leaves. A nondescript man in black was waiting just down the hall. He nodded at me as I edged my way towards him and set off at a brisk pace. I struggled to keep up, but stumbled along, keeping my eyes on his back as he led me through a maze of corridors. Soon, we began to fall into darker hallways, the lino and the metal creeping back in, signalling the start of the labs. I tried to take in my surroundings, but my ears were ringing and most of my energy was taken up trying to keep upright. When we passed through some double doors into a lab however, I did snake my hand out and grab a pair of scalpels from a nearby table, just in case I ended up needing them. I didn't want to be completely defenceless in the middle of the vipers' nest. After another few minutes of walking, we entered an even darker corridor with a long glass window. The man stopped in front of it, waiting for me to catch up. As I neared him, he turned and nodded at someone in the shadows. Rick stepped out.

The hatred that ran through me was intense, almost causing me to stumble to the side. He didn't say anything, just turned to face the glass, so I did too. I recognised it from the recording; directly in front of me was a table with a body on it. His feet were bare, but he was still wearing jeans and I knew if I could see his face, I would see half of Eli. A light flickered on above the table as the two technicians walked in, their faces drawn. They made their way over to Eli, pulling at corners of the bandages to inspect the grafts. As they got to the face, they paused, surprise flickering across their features and they quickly pulled the bandage off, discussing something between them. I looked at Ricks face, not missing the small moment of relief as he watched them smile and nod through the glass. I was less relieved. I looked back to Eli as they hurriedly began jotting something down.

Did his toe just move?

I snuck a sideways glance at Rick, but he was watching the technicians. As I looked again, Eli's right big toe moved, ever so slightly. I couldn't help my small grin. The technician's unwound the bandages from the rest of Eli's torso, a pile of gauze building up on the floor. When they had undone the last bandage, they shared an amazed glance and turned away from the table to study a machine that was attached to his arm. They didn't see his sudden twitch, a full body convulsion that seemed to spasm from his chest.

We did.

Rick tapped on the glass, his eyes wide and they turned to look at him. As he pointed frantically to Eli's body, I saw his toe twitch again. My hand went to the scalpel in my pocket. This wasn't over yet. Both the technicians turned back to Eli as he bolted upright with a furious yell. I let out a small gasp as his eyes met mine through the glass, one a golden yellow, the other the same sea-green. His lips pulled back in a grin, revealing sharp canines. Black fur covered one side of his face, his ear pointed. The technicians began to back away as he leapt at them, their screams muted by the glass. Rick was staring in open-mouthed horror at the scene in front of him, but I was more focussed on him. As I prepared to bring the scalpel out of my pocket, I realised that at this point, I wasn't sure there was a good guy in this story.

Just a brother driven mad and a sister who would do anything to get him back.

INVERNESS INQUIRER

Tourists found dead in Loch Ness. Seventeen still missing.

Eye witness reports claim a tour boat from the company *Nessie Boat Tours* was attacked by the Loch Ness Monster yesterday afternoon.

On Tuesday afternoon, four dead tourists and three members of ship crew were pulled from Loch Ness amid reports that a boat had been attacked by what eyewitnesses are calling the Loch Ness Monster. The four tourists, at this point unidentified, had been out on the morning *Nessie Boat Tour* when there had been a large disturbance under the water. They had not been the only ones in the boat; seventeen other people are still missing, at this point presumed dead. Initial reports from the Captain, who radioed back to the main office, said it looked like some kind of whale that had caused a surge in the current. The office then lost all contact with the boat.

Eye witnesses around the Loch said that the boat seemed to be being thrown about in waves that had apparently come out of nowhere. There was no wind and no forecast storms. Reports then claimed that a large creature had risen out of the water with a 'long, snaking head' and 'whip-like tail'. The creature began bombarding the boat, knocking the side until the passengers started falling into the water. One man, who saw the event from Urqhart Castle, said that as soon as people had fallen in, they had been pulled under by something and the water around the boat had turned red. The bodies that came up onto shore were allegedly missing limbs and had bite marks across various parts of their bodies.

At the moment, the police have restricted access to the Loch, grounding all tour boats and private vessels whilst a full search is conducted into the reasons behind the passengers' deaths. So far there have been no more sightings of the alleged Loch Ness Monster and no photographic evidence has been found, although there were multiple eye witnesses who claimed to catch the entire attack on video. When they were asked to produce these videos, the files had been corrupted. This attack follows a blurry image taken by a hiker of a strange creature in a Loch near the village of Kincraig. The image appears to be of a large creature surfacing in the Loch. It matches the description of the alleged attacker in Loch Ness, with the same snaking head and long tail. However, the body of the creature cannot be seen in the image so scientists are contemplating if this could in fact be a multitude of creatures instead. We will continue to bring you more on this story as it develops over the next few days.

FREIBURG GAZETTE

Strange creature found in Freiburg B&B. Currently at large.

A maid found an otter-like creature locked in a room in a Freiburg B&B yesterday morning.

A maid heard scratching from a room in a local Freiburg B&B when completing cleaning rounds yesterday morning. A *Do Not Disturb* sign had been placed on the door, but when the scratching continued, she unlocked the door to check. Upon entering the room, she was confronted with a small, furry, light grey, otter-like creature. The creature allegedly squeaked rapidly before darting between her legs and disappearing down the corridor. The maid spoke to us and informed us that she had never seen anything like the creature before and that it seemed distressed. In the room, she also found provisions for the creature, along with a large backpack. No identification of the person renting the room was found and, despite a search across the B&B, the creature was not found. A local later revealed that they saw a creature fitting that description racing into the Black Forest not long after the incident was reported at the B&B. As of now, the creature has not been found.

To Be Continued...

Acknowledgements

Under Loch and Key has been years in the making and since I first decided I'd challenge myself to write a book in twenty days, I've had a lot of people help me with it and a lot of people to thank.

First, and always, I want to thank my parents. Mum, for reading it through countless times over the last few years (and hopefully never getting bored of it even if it's not your kind of book). Dad, for our discussions that saved me a lot of Google searching and for going through the book with a fine-toothed comb to check for any last mistakes. I also want to thank both of you for continuing to support me, not just with this book, but with all my writing. Here's to someday buying you that villa!

Barney, thank you for putting up with years of my back and forth, self-doubt and anxiety, for reading each chapter as I wrote it and coming back into the room to ask me to write the next chapter so you could keep reading it and for pushing me to branch out on my own and finally publish it.

Gemma, Emily, Catherine, Mary, Izzy, Tegan, Jess, Adri; thank you all for your support, for late night messages and video calls, for reading Under Loch and Key at its various stages and for listening to me try and figure all of this out (and helping me not give up altogether).

To both Sophie and Kerry from Loughborough University, I think I'll be thanking both of you for the rest of my writing career! Without your advice and teachings through my degree and job, I wouldn't have ever been able to write Under Loch and Key. Thank you for your support with previous work (Case Files of the Supernatural) which only made me more determined to keep producing books and striving towards my dream!

To Tom and Mark for inspiring two of the characters.

To everyone who read Under Loch and Key or who supported me with Case Files, who has ever read any of my work and reviewed or given me feedback or even just support, thank you.

Here's to the next step in my writing journey. I hope you all enjoy the ride.

Printed in Great Britain
by Amazon